GALLAGHER'S HOPE

A Montana Gallagher Novel
Book Two

MK MCCLINTOCK

LARGE PRINT EDITION

Trappers Peak Publishing
Montana

Published in the United States by Cambron Press.
Originally published in trade paperback by
Trappers Peak Publishing in 2012.

LARGE PRINT EDITION

McClintock, MK
Gallagher's Hope; novel/MK McClintock
ISBN-10: 0996507698
ISBN-13: 978-0-9965076-9-1

Cover design by MK McClintock
Deputy with Rifle © Naluphoto | Dreamstime.com

draw you in, but the story and the people keep you there." —*Donna McBroom-Theriot*

"Ms. McClintock's stories are adventurous and full of budding romance that transports you back in to a simpler time where the outside world ceases to exist once you open one of her books."
—*My Life, One Story at a Time*

MONTANA GALLAGHER SERIES
Gallagher's Pride
Gallagher's Hope
Gallagher's Choice
An Angel Called Gallagher
Journey to Hawk's Peak
Wild Montana Winds
The Healer of Briarwood

BRITISH AGENT NOVELS
Alaina Claiborne
Blackwood Crossing
Clayton's Honor

CROOKED CREEK SERIES
"Emma of Crooked Creek"
"Hattie of Crooked Creek"
"Briley of Crooked Creek"
"Clara of Crooked Creek"

WHITCOMB SPRINGS SERIES
"Whitcomb Springs"
"Forsaken Trail"
"Unchained Courage"

SHORT STORY COLLECTIONS
A Home for Christmas

& more to come!

To learn more about MK McClintock and her books,
please visit www.mkmcclintock.com.

1

Rousseau Mansion, New Orleans
October 1883

Nothing existed of the life she had known. Her slender arm wrapped around the little boy's shoulder and pulled him closer to her side. She could feel his slight trembling and wished more than anything that she could take away his sadness. They were alone in the world. They had each other, and she prayed that would be enough for them both.

They stood and listened as the priest gave the final blessing, and two men lowered the caskets into the ground. The few other mourners who had been kind enough to attend the funeral asked her to leave with them, but she needed the closure. She needed her eyes to see what her heart refused to accept. "An unfortunate affair," everyone called the incident, for it wasn't every day that a man murdered his wife and then shot himself. Isabelle wished not to think on the possible reasons why, but she couldn't seem to help herself. She never imagined her family to be anything but happy. Their father's death, however, revealed the truth. No one spoke of it with them, of course, but the lawyer had made the situation quite clear.

They were penniless.

Isabelle thought back to the days before college, when she kept the family's books. *Did I miss the signs?* She remembered her father's stories and struggles about commerce during the war and knew how difficult it had been for him. They enjoyed great prosperity after they left Philadelphia for New Orleans five years after the War Between the States ended. His struggles paid off, and wise investments in land and timber after the war ensured the Rousseau's wealth. Her mother did not seem to care about the hard work it took her husband to make it through the war, but she enjoyed spending his hard-earned money. She thought of little more than to host party after party, ball after ball.

Isabelle recalled their last ball—her mother lay unmoving on the ballroom floor. Dr. Simmons assured them of a full recovery.

Her mother's episodes began four months later. She argued with her husband over the most mundane details of their lives. She treated the servants and children deplorably. Isabelle's father placed his wife under the care of a doctor, and after a month of treatments, she returned to her family, once again herself. No one knew what caused the illness.

Isabelle's father gave her the opportunity to attend college—she wanted to be a teacher. When she returned from school, she had planned to take a position at Landers Preparatory School for Girls rather than keep the family books. Therefore, she didn't know the truth of their dire finances. The only truth

Isabelle knew now stood solemnly next to her. She would give up everything for him, but right now she needed to find a way to support him properly.

Isabelle managed to set aside enough funds from her modest teacher's salary to last a few months, but they couldn't stay in New Orleans. She wouldn't do that to Andrew. She refused to let him grow up in a city where whispers and gossip could reach his ears.

Gently and with great love, she guided her brother away from the church cemetery to the waiting buggy. They'd be without a buggy after today, for the bank wanted all of the property, down to the last piece of furniture and candlestick in her home, to pay off her father's recent and massive debts. The lawyer kindly informed them that they may stay at the mansion until the end of the week.

Isabelle helped her brother into the waiting buggy and sat down beside him, pulling him close and covering them both with the light, woolen, travel blanket. He'd been silent in the three days since their parents' death, and she worried for him fiercely. She swore to herself to find a way to give him a better existence and to help chase away his haunting memories.

Andrew fell asleep with his head of golden hair resting against the crook of her shoulder, as the smart-looking black curricle made its way through the streets to the home they no longer owned. Without waking her brother, Isabelle pulled out the small advertisement she had found the week before in the paper. She didn't know at the time that what should have been an adventurous idea would now be a necessity. It was a chance at a new beginning, and she longed to grasp it, if for no other reason than to keep her brother safe. With resolve, she placed the notice back in her voluminous skirt pocket and laid her head back against the buggy. Sleep and appetite had eluded her the past few days, but at least for these precious moments, she closed her eyes and dreamed of what could be.

Her life now followed a path she never imagined, but a more traditional path was no longer an option. Her lack of desire for marriage or to carry on in society had vexed her mother for many years. Most women and acquaintances of her age married and dutifully began families of their own. They frequented the city's best tea rooms and spent their evenings at parties, while their children stayed at home with nannies. That might have been her had she made other choices. Isabelle preferred not to socialize, but she was always encouraged to attend the balls and parties, much to Isabelle's dismay. She knew her mother's only purpose had been to ensure her daughter's place in society and secure a good marriage with a man of wealth and influence. Her tall stature, long, golden hair, and soft-gray eyes made her popular among society's young gentlemen. Isabelle recalled the last time a young man courted her—an experience she had no desire to entertain a second time.

Isabelle studied the mansion one last time. The driver loaded the luggage onto the buggy for the ride to the train station, and the heavy air of the Garden District weighed heavy on her skin.

She had imagined such a different future.

No matter how her father had left them in the end, he had given them good a good home. He didn't arrange a marriage for her as many other fathers in their social circle had done.

Isabelle gazed out the window of the train as it slowly carried her and Andrew into a wilderness that excited her as much as frightened her.

During the war, Isabelle had heard stories of men and boys heading west to avoid joining the fight. Their family had been lucky in that regard. With her father old enough to have been left alone and her brother not yet born, their family had remained intact. When her father moved the family to New Orleans, society welcomed them, regardless of where they had lived during the war. Their French heritage and wealth had certainly helped.

That acceptance mattered little now. She left behind no one who meant anything to her. When it became known that she and her brother had been left penniless, many of those she called friends stopped visiting after they'd paid their initial respects. One young man offered marriage. She declined and immediately sent a telegram to Briarwood, Montana Territory, accepting the position as a schoolteacher.

Isabelle scanned the changing landscape. The last three days offered views of dense trees and farmland but nothing to excite her about what lay ahead. Before they left, she had spent hours reading accounts about massive mountains so high a person could never climb them and land so vast that people lived lifetimes on it and never saw everything.

She glanced down at her brother, who rested quietly in the seat next to hers, his head against her arm. Isabelle brought her gaze back to the landscape and welcomed a small rush of pleasure at what she saw in the distance. The grand mountains loomed over the landscape, and pine trees became more plentiful the closer they came to those majestic peaks. Her heart raced as excitement overpowered the fear, and for just a short time, she allowed herself the pleasure of imagining something better.

2

Briarwood, Montana
October 1883

Isabelle allowed the portly man with a graying mustache to help her down from the stagecoach. He'd been traveling in their same direction ever since St. Louis and though kind, he told Isabelle more about himself than she wanted to know. Even so, when he let go of her hand and tipped his hat in a farewell gesture, a small sense of loss crept into Isabelle's heart. He had spoken to her more on the journey than her family's so-called friends had after the funeral. Shaking the maudlin thoughts from her mind, she held Andrew's hand as he stepped off the stage. One of the stage drivers unloaded their baggage and then accepted a pouch from an older man who waited nearby. The man turned toward them, and Isabelle saw kind, brown eyes in a wrinkled face.

"You waitin' for someone, ma'am?"

"No, sir, we're not." She glanced around, uncertain about what to do next. Andrew squeezed her hand, and she looked down at his tired eyes. The last stretch had been long and tiring for them both. "Is there a place to eat nearby?"

"Well, sure. Tilly's Café is just over yonder." He pointed toward the telegraph office. "Walk that way and you'll see it."

"Thank you, sir." Isabelle paused, never having been in a situation to carry her own bags. She released Andrew's hand and lifted one bag into each hand, then studied the large trunk.

"Uh, ma'am?" The man stepped forward. "I'm Loren Baker, proprietor of the general store." He pointed to the building behind them. "You can leave those here for a spell. I promise to keep an eye out."

"That's kind of you, Mr. Baker, but . . ." Isabelle glanced down at Andrew's tired eyes. "If you're sure it's no trouble."

"No, ma'am, no trouble at all." His warm smile helped put Isabelle at ease. "Might you tell me your name, ma'am?"

"Miss Isabelle Rousseau. I'm the new schoolteacher."

"Well, I'll be. Miss Rousseau." Mr. Baker smiled. "We've been expecting you. A lot of folks around here will be mighty pleased you've come."

"That's kind, Mr. Baker. Thank you." She'd taken another step and realized kindness was not missing from the world.

"Now, you go on and get yourselves a good hot meal at Tilly's, and you just tell her who you are and that I sent you over." Mr. Baker looked as though he might shoo them away, so with Andrew's hand in hers, Isabelle walked in the direction Mr. Baker had pointed.

Isabelle's eyes took in everything around her,

from the dusty streets to the men in odd clothes. The few women she noticed stared at her, and Isabelle did her best to ignore the curious glances. She knew they looked out of place in this wilderness. Time in New Orleans had not prepared them for frontier living.

Tilly welcomed them to town and ushered them to a table that had a lovely view of the meadow. "Now, who do we have here?" Tilly smiled brightly at them both, her warm manner as comforting as the storekeeper's.

"I'm Isabelle Rousseau, and this is Andrew."

"Well I'll be, child, I'd recognize that accent anywhere!" Tilly slapped her hand on a thigh and grinned. "Are you all from New Orleans?"

Isabelle preferred to keep her past private but wouldn't lie to the woman. "We are."

"Too many years since I've been home." Tilly tucked a white towel into her apron. "Now, you just go on and tell me all about yourselves."

Gabriel slipped his brother's telegram into the pocket of his brown duster and smiled. Ethan said he'd finally be coming home next week and bringing along a couple of surprises. Gabriel had received Ethan's letter about marrying Brenna, but he found himself a little curious as to what the other surprise could be. He was just happy that his big brother finally made peace with the fact that he'd fallen in love. Ethan and Brenna had an unusual beginning, but Gabriel supposed that was to be expected when a woman from Scotland accepted help from a Montana rancher. Their determination brought them together, and their stubbornness had kept them apart. Luckily, Ethan had come to his senses and followed Brenna to Scotland.

With a light heart and long, efficient steps, Gabriel stepped away from the telegraph office and into the dirt street. He still needed to pick up the supplies on Mabel's list and a few things for Eliza. With list in hand, Gabriel headed for the general store after a quick detour at the livery.

"Hello, Loren." Gabriel sauntered into the store, as comfortable there as he was at home.

"Anything new off the stage today?" Gabriel set his list down on the wood counter and narrowed his deep-blue eyes at the other man. "What has you smiling so big?"

"New schoolteacher finally came."

"How about that." Gabriel glanced outside the store windows to the schoolhouse. "It's been too long since we've had a proper teacher for the kids."

"Ain't that the truth?" Loren rubbed his chin. "You ought to head on over to Tilly's for a look. Sent her over just a short bit ago for a meal. Introduce yourself."

"I don't have any kids going to school, Loren."

"You're the most prominent family here. I'm thinkin' it wouldn't hurt to make her feel welcome."

Curious, Gabriel considered the storekeeper. *What is he up to?* "I guess I'm going to meet the new teacher."

"You do that, and I'll take care of this here list of supplies for you." Loren's enthusiasm might have worried Gabriel if he thought the man was capable of manipulation. "Your wagon out front?"

Gabriel nodded.

"I'll just have one of the boys help me load it up, then."

What the hell just happened here? Gabriel set his hat on his thick brown hair and made his way to Tilly's Café. When he rounded the corner of the telegraph office, he stepped up to the boardwalk in front of the small restaurant. His eyes scanned over the few patrons sampling Tilly's amazing food. He found the woman at one of the tables next to the window.

He took a moment to admire the beautiful woman with her golden hair partially hidden under a dark-blue hat. The morning sunlight shined directly on her face and revealed features as clear as a painting: smooth, alabaster skin; a small, pink smile; and light-colored almond-shaped eyes.

His eyes darted to the boy sitting next to her, and one look told him they were related, for the youngster had the same golden hair. Gabriel wondered about the boy's relationship to her. Both woman and child were smartly dressed. She wore a deep-blue dress of fine wool and a long, black cape that fastened just below her chin while the child wore a tailored, gray suit that he appeared to be comfortable in. As they ate, the woman glanced up from her plate of Tilly's hotcakes and met his eyes.

Loren Baker isn't as old a fool as people think.

Isabelle noticed the tall stranger staring at them through the window. She held little trust for men, though she'd have to admit to herself at some point that she needed to start trusting someone if they planned to survive out here. Most of the men she'd seen appeared far too filthy and of all the things to worry over, she hoped that she and Andrew would find a place nearby for daily washings.

The man continued to stare, and she found herself smoothing down the invisible wrinkles in her overcoat. He donned the same odd clothes she began to see a few days after they left the city.

Work clothes were common on field workers at the plantations back home, but these looked different, from the wide-brimmed hats many of them sported, to the long coats on their backs and the odd boots on their feet. Some donned chaps and spurs, but this man wore neither. However, he did wear a cloth tied around his neck. Isabelle couldn't see much more of him since he stood in the shade of the building, but she did wish he would stop staring. As though he heard her thoughts and simply didn't care, the man moved away from the window and into the café.

Gabriel wanted to do more than just meet the new schoolteacher—he wanted to know her. Uncertain as to whether her cold expression stemmed from fear or annoyance, Gabriel decided to risk being told to mind his own business. He stepped into the café, and walked to the table closest to the window, tipping the brim of his black hat.

"Hello, ma'am. Loren Baker over at the

general store told me you're the new schoolteacher." He removed his hat and offered his hand. "The name's Gabriel Gallagher."

Her voice sounded courteous but wary when she finally spoke, and her sweet accent charmed him. "Isabelle Rousseau, Mr. Gallagher. Will you have children attending school?"

"No, no children. I just wanted to welcome to you to Briarwood, though if you don't mind my saying, I noticed some luggage out in front of the store. Are those yours?"

Isabelle wanted to be left alone, but she glanced down at Andrew's curious eyes and remembered she needed to make an effort. "Those are, yes. Mr. Baker kindly offered to watch them while we took breakfast."

Gabriel smiled at Tilly when she came over to clear away the empty plates.

"See you've met the new schoolteacher." Tilly continued to smile while she gathered the cups. "Folks sure are glad she's come." Tilly patted Isabelle's shoulder with her free hand and walked briskly away, carrying the dishes.

"You'll find this is a friendly town." Gabriel turned the focus back to the conversation they were having before Tilly came over. "My wagon is over at the store right now. I'd be pleased to offer you a ride to your destination."

Isabelle's eyes discreetly scanned Gabriel. From the thick, dark-brown hair showing from beneath his hat and the startling blue eyes, to the long legs and broad shoulders beneath his coat, Isabelle took it all in. She looked at her brother once more and believed she had no other choice than to accept help from someone. "I need to find the church."

"The church, ma'am?" He gave her a questioning gaze.

"Yes, I'm looking for Reverend Phillips."

"Oh, well the church is the right place though not much for accommodations." Gabriel fixed his gaze on the small boy at the woman's side. He couldn't have been more than five years old.

"And who are you, young man?"

The kindness in his voice kept Isabelle from snapping out at him for speaking to her brother.

"This is Andrew." Isabelle stood up from the table, motioning for the young boy to follow, and took his hand.

"It's a pleasure to meet you both. Why don't we head on back to the store, and I'll load your trunks into my wagon? I can give you a ride over to the church. I'm sure the reverend is still there with it being so early."

"Wait there now, Gabriel!" Tilly shouted to them from her place at the stove. She picked up a basket covered in cloth, hurried toward them, and handed the basket to Isabelle. "You take this, child. Just so you aren't worrying about supplies your first day here."

Isabelle glanced down at the basket in her hands and then back up at Tilly. "That's very kind of you, but—"

"No arguing now." Tilly pushed the basket into her arms and grinned. "Welcome to Briarwood."

Isabelle stared after Tilly and then lifted confused eyes to Gabriel.

"I told you it's a friendly town." He held open

the door for them and motioned toward the street. They walked companionably, though he sensed Isabelle's wariness, and kept a good space between them. He glanced up at the sound of muted voices mingled with deep laughter coming from the saloon and hoped the reverend's arrangements included a safe place to stay.

When they reached the store, Gabriel asked her to wait a moment while he loaded their trunks into the back of the wagon already filled with supplies. Usually, one of the men from Hawk's Peak would have made the supply run, but Gabriel had ranch business to tend to in town. Gabriel had been annoyed at the inconvenience when the army supplier moved their meeting from the ranch to town, but now he found himself silently thanking the officer.

Mr. Baker stepped outside. "Well now, how did you enjoy your breakfast at Tilly's? She treat you right?"

"She was lovely, Mr. Baker. Thank you for the recommendation." Her voice sounded stiff and unfriendly, even to her. She made an effort to relax.

"I see you're in good hands, too." Mr. Baker pointed to Gabriel. "Now don't let me keep you. I've a store to tend to." The storekeeper disappeared, and Isabelle prepared herself to take the next step.

Gabriel helped them to the seat, placed the boy between them, and set the two blond horses in motion for the short ride to the church. Gabriel had a feeling that she didn't want to talk, which didn't bother him. He wasn't much of a social person himself unless he enjoyed a game of cards with the boys at the ranch or spent time with his family. But he did want to be social with the new teacher.

Gabriel halted the handsome team in front of the white structure just as Reverend Phillips pulled open the front door. The reverend stood tall and slender with graying hair and large brown eyes. Gabriel met him on a few occasions, and he'd taken an instant liking to the cheerful man.

"Good morning, Gabriel. It's a fine day when you show up in front of the church."

Gabriel gave a small smile for the reverend. "Now don't go getting any ideas, Reverend. I'm just delivering a couple of newcomers looking for you."

The reverend stepped up to the wagon and beamed at the woman and child. "You must be Miss Rousseau."

"Yes, Reverend. I do apologize for arriving early."

"Oh, no need to apologize." He waved a hand as though the matter wasn't worth the concern.

Gabriel jumped down from the wagon and deftly lowered the boy, who waited by his side until he placed Isabelle next to him. His hands lingered a moment longer than necessary on her trim waist, and his eyes sought hers.

Reluctantly he released her, and she stepped away, once again lifting the boy's hand into her own.

"I am so pleased you've come, Miss Rousseau. I began to wonder if we'd ever find a teacher and then your telegram came and our prayers were answered."

Gabriel's eyebrow shot up, but he said nothing. The reverend turned, catching Gabriel's attention.

"Gabriel, since their items are already loaded in your wagon, would you mind taking them over to the school?"

Gabriel nodded. "Not at all, but wouldn't we just have to move them again?"

"We'll be staying at the school for now, Mr. Gallagher." Isabelle's clipped tone surprised him. Gabriel took a better look at her now, and though her eyes indicated strength, she obviously hadn't been taking care of herself. She looked far too tired and in need of a few large meals.

"I'd be happy to take your things over, Miss Rousseau, but if it's permanent accommodations you're seeking, there's a vacant cottage in a nice spot. It's about half a mile down the road behind the schoolhouse. The rent is reasonable," he added when he saw her hesitate.

If it had been only her, Gabriel thought she might have refused on the spot, but he saw her eyes drift to her brother who huddled close to her side. Whether or not she fought her pride, he couldn't tell, but he smiled at her answer.

"Very well, Mr. Gallagher. We'll look at the cottage."

"That's wonderful." The reverend clapped his hands with excitement and urged them all back into the wagon. "I can show you the school tomorrow, and you can spend today getting settled."

Isabelle thanked the reverend, and Gabriel, once again, lifted them up like feathers into the wagon. She remembered a time when she'd been stronger and fuller, and cursed the past few weeks. They weren't without the money for food, and Andrew always ate his fill, but her lack of appetite prevented her from eating more than a few morsels at each meal. She knew her frame suffered for it and was grateful that the folds of her cloak hid the looseness of her dress.

The short ride to the cottage passed in quiet

much like the ride to the church, but Isabelle couldn't stop the slight gasp that escaped her lips when they came upon the small dwelling, so beautiful and unexpected in this wild and remote world. Made entirely of stone with a large white porch in front, the small cottage nestled between groves of stately pine and apple trees now spent of fruit. On either side of the whitewashed door set two large windows with empty white boxes beneath. The garden appeared well-tended with the flowers recently cut back in preparation for the coming winter.

Without a word, Gabriel stepped down from the wagon and lifted both of his passengers out. Her reaction to the cottage pleased him, as it held dear memories for his family. It had been his mother's escape from the ranch, and she and his father often found themselves tucked away here. The cottage didn't get much use unless one of the Gallaghers stayed overnight in town, but they hired a woman from town to clean it once a week. He knew the money went to help feed her three boys, so he didn't mind paying the unnecessary expense. They all helped to keep the place up, but the inside remained much as it had before their parents died. No one used it but family—until now.

Isabelle stepped away from Gabriel and faced the cottage. It took her a moment to gain her composure before she turned back to look at him. "Do you know what the owners are asking in rent?"

Gabriel shrugged. Curiosity drove him mad and his was insatiable. With the expensive attire the pair clothed themselves in, he wondered how money was an issue.

"A dollar a month is reasonable in my estimations."

"One dollar? That can't be. Even a place like this would go for at least ten times that in New Orleans."

"Ah, that explains the accent."

She shot him a defensive look, but he returned it with a smile.

"I mean that with the kindest respect. I happen to like the accent myself. In fact my new sister-in-law is from Scotland, and every time she speaks, it sounds like a song."

Isabelle smiled, and though slight, Gabriel took that as a good sign and returned the gesture. He pulled a small gold key out of his pants pocket and handed it to her. Each sibling kept a key when they went into town in case their trip became an overnight stay. Gabriel hadn't slept in the cottage in over a year.

She stared a moment at the key. "You already had a key?"

"I help keep an eye on the place." Gabriel set the key in her outstretched palm. "Go ahead inside; I'll just bring your trunks in."

With an absent nod, Isabelle and her brother walked to the front porch, and she turned the key in the door. It opened without a creak, and she stepped into the cozy front room. She jumped, a hand pressed to her chest, when Gabriel spoke up behind her.

"It would have just been cleaned a few days ago, so it's not too dusty and all of the linens should be fresh." He scooted around her and set the trunks next to a large high-back chair in the front room.

"This is lovely and so much more than I expected." She momentarily dropped her guard, and Gabriel accredited that to the weariness he noticed earlier.

"To whom do I give the rent each month?"

"I can go ahead and take care of that for you."

Isabelle didn't relent. "I'd like to meet the owners and thank them. It's a kind person who would rent their lovely home to a stranger."

"You're not a stranger any more. You're the new teacher and a part of this town, and the folks who built this place would be happy to have you here."

Before he gave her a chance to ask any more questions, he listed off some information. "You've already met Tilly, and the general store should carry everything you need, but if you can't find something, Loren—Mr. Baker—can order it for you. The weather's going to get a little cold here soon, and we're expecting a good long winter. I imagine there will be some days you'll have to close the school. The snow will get a little deep to walk in, and we've got an extra wagon and horse at the ranch you could borrow until you get your own. I'll bring it by tomorrow."

Gabriel looked at the other two occupants of the room. Even the boy looked at him as though he'd lost his mind. Gabriel simply smiled, tipped his hat, and left the cottage.

He was gone before Isabelle could respond, though he didn't sound as though he was giving her much of a choice. She turned to her brother and gave him a soft smile. Her heart nearly leaped out of her chest when he spoke his first words in over a month.

"That man sure did talk a lot, Ibby."

3

Isabelle wept.

She wept out of joy and love for her brother. Isabelle worried for so long that he wouldn't speak to her or to anyone else.

She told her brother how much she loved him while she fed him a dinner of cold meats and bread from the basket Tilly gave her. Together they read the story of *Robinson Crusoe* from a small collection of books she refused to leave behind. Once she tucked Andrew safely into bed in one of the two small bedrooms, cozy beneath the fresh white linens and heavy quilts, Isabelle sat down next to him.

"Why did you stop speaking for so long, Andrew?"

Andrew lowered his eyes for a moment, seeming to concentrate on his hands. He looked up at his sister with big blue eyes. "I'm sorry, Ibby."

"I'm not upset with you." She smoothed back his hair. "I just missed hearing your voice."

"I was sad when Mama and Papa went away."

Isabelle reached over and hugged her brother. "I was sad, too."

"You won't ever leave me will you, Ibby?" Andrew held onto his sister.

Isabelle's tears threatened to fall. "I promise I won't ever leave you."

Isabelle walked through the front room, the small parlor, the kitchen, and finally the other bedroom. There hadn't been time before now to look at everything in the cottage. Her trunks still waited on the floor where Gabriel set them, and they beckoned to her. Isabelle knew that once she unpacked those precious books and the stylish gowns that currently fit too large and made her feel out of place here, she would be admitting her need and desire to stay.

Briarwood seemed like a good town and a good place to make a new start. She had to believe that. They needed a new start. It may not be grand like New Orleans—this cottage could fit into the parlor of their mansion—but this breathtaking land could feel like home. Her first glimpse of the majestic mountains from the train had stunned her with their beauty. The towns had begun to be farther and fewer between with people slowly being replaced by cattle and herds of wild game she'd never before seen. When they transferred from the train to the stage, the force of the beauty around her had become more apparent. She had wondered if they could make it in this wild land, a world so different from the one in which she'd been raised. But the crisp fresh air that had surrounded her when she stepped off the train had given her just enough fortification to get into the stagecoach.

Isabelle moved over to the side of the bed and sat down. She ran her hand across the beautiful hand-stitched quilt and up the post of the bed. The tears came unbidden again, and she lacked the strength to stop their descent.

This time the tears were for her. After her parents' death, not once did she shed a tear. But she couldn't stop them and knew why. This place was a safe haven, and she could succumb without worry. The tears fell as she lay down on the quilt and let sleep whisk her into peaceful darkness.

The following morning Isabelle woke before dawn, feeling refreshed. She chose to forget the sadness and embrace their new life. Andrew was her greatest hope and she reminded herself, her greatest responsibility.

She woke him an hour after she dressed, breakfast already on the table.

"Good morning, Ibby." He yawned then bestowed her with a big smile.

Love for her brother swelled up within Isabelle, and she bent to kiss his brow. "And a good morning to you, Andrew. I hope you're hungry."

"Where did you get the food? Did you go to the store without me?" He sounded disappointed by the possibility, and she hid her smile.

"Of course not. This is the last bit of what Tilly, the nice lady from the café, gave to us. We will go to the store after I speak with Reverend Phillips at the school." She set a plate of eggs and thick bread in front of her brother and went back to the stove to fix one for her.

Isabelle set the plate down at the table and took a seat. It was time she worked on getting her figure back—she dreaded the chore of taking in all of those dresses. For the second time in a month, Isabelle finished the food on her plate and watched happily as Andrew enjoyed his.

"Are you going to be my teacher too, Ibby, or am I still too little?"

"You're never too young to learn. I will be your teacher, and there will be lots of other children for you to make friends with." Isabelle took the plates to the washbasin and told her brother to go and clean himself up for the trip to town. He wasn't moving quickly enough for her, but when she turned around to tell him again, she paused. His head was slightly bent, and he looked close to tears.

"I don't think they'll like me." Andrew spoke barely above a whisper, and he wouldn't look up at her. With a confidence she didn't quite feel, Isabelle sat down next to her brother at the small, polished, pine table and lifted his chin with her slender hand.

"Why don't you think they'll like you?"

"They didn't like me at home. They looked at me funny. I don't like New Orleans. I never want to go back, all right?"

His lower lip quivered, and for a moment Isabelle realized she almost forgot how very young her brother was—only five years old but already such a brave boy.

"We never have to go back, I promise."

"Can we stay here? I like it here and that Mr. Gallagher was nice." Andrew wiped his nose on his sleeve and apologized to his sister since he wasn't supposed to do that.

"Yes, I think we can stay here, and yes, Mr. Gallagher is a nice man. Now why don't you go and clean up so we can meet with Reverend Phillips?"

She watched him leave the table, but her thoughts turned back to the man who helped them the day before. Isabelle hadn't given Gabriel Gallagher much thought since he left them at the cottage the previous morning. She'd been far too tired and full of unspent emotions to take care of herself properly, and she wondered if he noticed. She was determined to gain some of her weight back, and with that goal in mind, she mentally made a list of the supplies she needed to purchase at the general store.

Isabelle didn't have much left in the way of funds, for it took a fair amount to get this far, but they had enough to see them through the first few months in Briarwood. Not once did she feel a moment's guilt for taking her mother's jewels from the box on the dresser. The collectors took their time and hadn't packed everything before Isabelle and her brother left New Orleans, and she needed whatever she could carry. Isabelle managed to sell a few pieces when they stopped in St. Louis, but the few she had left would have to be safely tucked away. Isabelle doubted that the area demanded such finery.

An hour later they stood outside of the small schoolhouse as the reverend walked up to meet them.

"It is a beautiful day, isn't it?" His beaming smile became contagious.

"It certainly is that, Reverend Phillips."

"I just want to say again how pleased we are you've come. We fretted even being able to open the school back up for the winter term." The reverend opened the door to the schoolhouse and motioned them in ahead of him.

"As you can see, it's not overly large or what you're used to, I'm sure, but it is room enough for the students we have, and of course we do keep it well stocked."

Isabelle ran her hand over the top of one of the small desks and walked slowly to the front of the room. There stood two large blackboards behind the teacher's desk and what appeared to be a new wood stove in the corner. Four square windows proudly looked out to the mountains on either side of the small structure, letting more than enough light in for working. It was a lovely room and though not as elaborate as the school she used to teach in, it certainly inspired her.

"This is perfect, Reverend. Thank you for this opportunity."

Andrew came up next to her and stuck his hand in hers. Though he found his voice again, it appeared he chose to remain quiet around strangers.

"Oh, we're the lucky ones, Miss Rousseau. With your experience and education, the children of this town have the opportunity to learn more than we ever hoped." The reverend's bright brown eyes darted happily from Isabelle to Andrew, and he clapped his hands together, though Isabelle couldn't understand why. He appeared to be a man of great energy.

"Have you settled into the cottage?"

"Oh yes, it's wonderful, though I meant to get the names of the owners so I might thank them."

The reverend gave her a blank look for a moment. "Well that cottage belongs to the Gallaghers. Surely Gabriel told you."

Isabelle shook her head in response and the reverend continued. "Their folks built it when their children started getting older, or so I've been told. They passed on some years back, so Gabriel, Ethan, and their sister Eliza tend to the place now."

"Well, I will be sure to thank the Gallaghers next time I see them." Isabelle did wonder why Mr. Gallagher avoided telling her the truth. It sounded like charity, but she was stuck. To turn it away now would be cowardly and more so, she couldn't do that to Andrew.

Reverend Phillips nodded as though agreeing to something, and Isabelle just assumed that the man found it difficult to go long without moving.

"Well, I think that's about all I can show you. Classes start in two days if you're ready."

Isabelle wondered if she looked as nervous as she felt. "I'm ready."

"Wonderful. I'll have Mr. Simmons put the notice in the paper, and you can expect around ten or twelve children to show up. Sometimes it's more, sometimes less." The reverend shrugged as if to say it's just the way of things. "Some folks will keep their older children home, helping to prepare for the coming winter, but most of them find their way to school at least a few days a week."

Isabelle wondered why they even bothered to have a teacher and then scolded herself. Every child deserved the chance at an education. She thanked the reverend for his time. "I'll be here Monday morning next, bright and early."

Isabelle looked down at her brother and smiled. "So what do you think?"

The little boy found a smile of his own, and it warmed Isabelle's heart. "He's a funny man."

"Andrew, you shouldn't speak that way of your elders." Then realizing her rebuke sounded ridiculous when she herself smiled, she stifled a quiet laugh of her own. "I suppose he did seem a little funny, and I thank you for showing him the proper respect in his presence. But I meant, what do you think of this place?"

"I like it, Ibby. I like all of the big fields, and there are lots of places to play outside instead of the small park where we used to live."

Where we used to live. Isabelle squeezed his small hand. "I like it too, Andrew, I like it too." With a soft sigh and a smile, she walked with her brother outside the schoolhouse and gazed at her surroundings. A person could certainly make a new beginning for themselves in a peaceful place like Briarwood. Isabelle wondered if she would get used to the quiet, though the night before had been one of the best night's sleep in recent memory.

"What do you say we go on over to the general store, and perhaps we can get some pie over at the café?"

With eager enthusiasm, Andrew nodded his head, and they made their through the meadow to the main street of the small town.

The dirt road beneath Isabelle's feet was a new experience. She'd been to the countryside before, but within towns she'd lived, the roads were paved. The sound of her city boots meeting the wooden planks as she ascended the steps of the general store brought a smile to her face. A world so different from everything familiar she'd ever known, and yet those differences gave her hope.

Isabelle paused inside the wooden doors of the store and took in the small space. Nothing like the emporiums she used to patron, the store appeared to carry everything a person might need, or at least everything the storekeeper thought a person needed. Glancing around, Isabelle thought it wasn't such a horrible thing they had limited funds because there was nothing extravagant to purchase. Shelves along the back wall contained books on one side, lamps and household goods in the middle, and food staples on the other side. Her gaze flickered to a corner where she saw a selection of both men's and women's clothing, though in short supply. Baskets, blankets, and sundries were set out on a table near the clothing and more food staples filled shelves on another wall. At least the town had their priorities in order. The store appeared to have a storeroom behind the counter, but a canvas curtain hid the room from view. She mentally adjusted the list she made when Mr. Baker stepped out from behind the curtain.

"Well, hello there." As before, his generous smile put her at ease. "Glad to see you two back here. Are you settling in?"

"We are, thank you, Mr. Baker. We've just come for a few things." Isabelle glanced around the store. "Though I'm not certain if you have everything."

"We've got what you need and if we don't, I'm thinking you won't be needing it. Heard tell you rented the Gallagher's cottage."

News moved quickly among the society set in New Orleans, but not this fast. "Yes, we have."

"Well, you'll need some supplies." She swore that's what she already said. Mr. Baker seemed excited about the idea, though Isabelle couldn't tell if it was because she moved into the cottage or because she was a new customer.

"Just some food items." Isabelle listed off what she hoped would tide them over for a couple of weeks. "I didn't notice a butcher. Is there one in town?"

"Nope." Mr. Baker shook his head, but his smile remained. "Just me. Most folks hunt their own meat or raise animals for such purposes. My sister's husband just slaughtered a cow yesterday. I've got some good cuts."

Isabelle pictured the slaughtering of the animal she planned to purchase. She didn't know anyone who had slaughtered an animal before, but this was her life now, and she was certain to encounter many new experiences.

"I'll take a side of whatever meat cut you have, Mr. Baker, and some eggs, too, please."

Mr. Baker smiled and went about collecting the items on her list. She watched as he carried a bag of flour and a bag sugar to the counter and realized she'd have to make two trips. Andrew tugged on her hand and she lowered herself to hear him, but he didn't say anything. Her eyes found where he pointed, and she smiled.

"We'd also like two pieces of the licorice, please."

Loren kindly agreed to hold her supplies at the store while she and Andrew enjoyed some pie at the café. He suggested she talk to Otis Lincoln, the blacksmith, about borrowing a wagon to move the supplies. Isabelle didn't feel right about asking for such a favor but nodded and decided to make the two trips. They left the supplies at the general store and walked hand in hand across the dirt road to Tilly's Café. Tilly looked just as pleased to see Isabelle as she'd been the day before, and Isabelle smiled at the woman's kindness. Like the reverend, Tilly moved as though there weren't enough hours in the day to accomplish everything, and Isabelle wondered if it was just them or if the fresh mountain air stimulated everyone.

Andrew glanced up at Ibby. "Does she have the pie?"

Isabelle didn't mean to laugh, but she couldn't stop herself.

Neither could Tilly who answered, "Of course I have pie! Do you like cherry?" Tilly smiled down at Andrew, and he shyly returned one of his own and nodded.

Tilly chuckled and waved her towel to a nearby table. "Well, you just sit on down there, and I'll bring you a big slice of cherry pie."

Gabriel took the final box of supplies from the young boy who currently helped out at the livery and watched as the pair of them walked into the café, holding hands and smiling. The sight warmed his heart in places he didn't know could be warmed. Gabriel never understood what his brother meant by an instant bond with Brenna Cameron. He thought perhaps he understood now. Something about this pair tugged at him and brought his protective instincts to the surface, but there was something else about them that didn't seem right. The expensive clothes and the smooth cultured accent didn't fit with a woman and her brother in the middle of nowhere all alone with few funds.

Gabriel had seen the proud look in her bright eyes when she had mentioned staying in the schoolhouse temporarily. Whatever had happened to them, it must have been recent.

Content for now to let her know he was a friend, Gabriel walked into the café and over to their table. "Hello, Miss Rousseau, Andrew." Gabriel tipped his hat but didn't move to sit down. He'd been right about her upbringing because she automatically offered him a seat, as though she played hostess in a fancy parlor.

"Much obliged, ma'am."

Gabriel smiled when Tilly walked over and asked if he wanted some lunch. Gabriel noticed that his table partners were just starting on some fresh cherry pie. "I believe I'll have a slice of the heaven these two are enjoying and some coffee." He gave Tilly a broad grin, which she responded to with a blush and a swat of her towel to Gabriel's shoulder.

Gabriel's antics amused Isabelle since she had just learned from Tilly that she was in her fifties and happily married to the same man for over thirty-five years. During the exchange, Isabelle allowed herself a quick perusal of Gabriel Gallagher, beginning and ending with his startling blue eyes. It took Isabelle a moment to realize that Gabriel said something to her and she turned, flushed a little, and shifted her focus away from his admirable features.

"My apologies, Mr. Gallagher."

Gabriel grinned privately and repeated his question.

"Oh, the cottage is wonderful. Reverend Phillips kindly informed me that I have you to thank for it."

Gabriel was unapologetic. "Does that bother you?" he asked as Tilly set a slice of cherry pie and a steaming cup of coffee in front of him. The aromas of both made him silently thank the talented chef who first created pie.

"It shouldn't bother me, so I won't let it."

Gabriel thought that was an odd way to put it and turned his attention to the boy.

"What about you, Andrew? How do you like our town?"

Isabelle was amazed that her brother showed no shyness around this stranger, but he had been kind, giving Andrew no reason not to trust him.

"I like it." Pie interfered with the boy's speech, but Gabriel caught the meaning.

"Don't speak with your mouth full, Andrew."

The boy apologized and continued speaking. "I've never seen so many horses in one place. Does everyone have a horse, Mr. Gallagher?"

"Well you may call me Gabriel, and yes, I suppose just about everyone in these parts has a horse or two."

Andrew appeared to be considering something Gabriel said. "Why can I call you Gabriel, but Ibby has to call you Mr. Gallagher?"

"Quiet, Andrew."

"Well your sister is more than welcome to call me Gabriel if she chooses." Gabriel left it at that and consumed the last two bites of his pie.

Andrew finished his off and followed it with a big swallow of milk, then turned to his sister. "Ibby, do you think I could ride a horse?"

Isabelle saw the excitement and pleading in

her brother's eyes and wanted to tell him yes, but they could hardly afford a horse. She was about to explain to him when Gabriel spoke up.

"Tell you what, Andrew. If it's acceptable to your sister, you can come out to the ranch sometime and ride one of our horses."

Andrew's eyes opened so wide, Isabelle nearly laughed. He begged her with the best manners a five-year-old could summon when faced with such an offer. Grateful for the offer and seeing no reason to turn it down, she nodded in agreement.

"When Mr. Gallagher says it's convenient."

"Oh, any time is fine. In fact I happen to have time this afternoon if you'd both like to come out. I know Mabel would love to meet you."

"Mabel?"

Gabriel grinned. "My one and only love if she'd ever say yes."

Isabelle's back stiffened, and her eyes drew closer.

Gabriel chuckled. "Mabel's our housekeeper, though she's more of a mother to me and my siblings."

Isabelle's face became warm and she cleared her throat, grateful that Gabriel turned his attention back to Andrew.

"Can we go now, Gabriel?" Andrew's pleading eyes drew a smile from Gabriel.

"Ask your sister."

"Ibby, can we go now?"

Isabelle looked from the boy to the man, and her own heart lurched in her breast. They shared a few similarities between them. Both possessed aristocratic-like features, expressive eyes, and a full mouth. She'd never seen her brother at such ease with a man before, not even their father, and she wasn't sure what to make of it. The pleading pathetic looks they both wore drew a genuine laugh from her.

"Oh, very well, we may go now, but we can't stay too long." She directed her statement to Andrew but looked directly at Gabriel.

He raised his hands in defense. "I promise I'll have you back here the moment you tell me to."

With a nod of agreement, she reached for her

change purse, but Gabriel beat her to it.

He shrugged when she looked at him. "I never learned how to let a woman pay for a meal if I sat at the same table."

It was all he'd offer, and Isabelle decided to graciously accept with a soft thank you.

"Oh, I almost forgot. The storekeeper is holding our supplies for us."

"We can pick those up and drop them off at the cottage on our way out of town."

Isabelle raised her brow up at that. "Exactly how far out of town do you live?"

"About an hour." He shrugged, figuring that the distance wouldn't make her back out. He already learned that she would do almost anything for her brother.

"I concede."

"Very wise." That comment only got him a hard stare. He smiled back.

Gabriel made quick work of loading her two baskets of supplies into the back of a wagon already filled with large bags of oats and helped them into the seat. When they pulled up in front of the cottage a few minutes later, Isabelle noticed a small wagon off to the far side of the cottage by a corral and small enclosed shed that she hadn't noticed before. A lovely blond horse nickered at the fence of the corral.

Gabriel nodded toward the corral. "The horse and wagon, remember? I had one of the hands drive it in earlier."

Not knowing exactly what to say, Isabelle absently placed her hands on Gabriel's shoulders, and he hoisted her down from the wagon.

She stared at the horse and wagon while he collected her baskets from the back of his wagon. "I can't accept them."

"You don't have to. I'm loaning them to you. Though come to think of it, I'll probably need to give you a lesson in hitching a wagon, but that can wait until tomorrow." With a flourish he followed her into the cottage and set the baskets down on the kitchen table. He took a quick look to see what needed to go into the icebox. He put away the meat and eggs and scooted her back outside.

Isabelle didn't care for being manipulated and nearly said so. However, when she stepped outside, she saw her brother sitting in the wagon with the biggest smile she'd ever seen. Every difficult or uncomfortable decision she'd made since their arrival had been for the best.

Gabriel deftly helped her back into the wagon and set the team in motion on the road going out of town.

"Weren't you in town yesterday for supplies?" She motioned to the boxes in the back of the wagon.

"Yes."

He wasn't in the habit of explaining himself but chose to make an exception. "I didn't have enough room for everything and rather than hire an extra wagon for the night, I decided to come back into town today." Gabriel left out that he could have sent one of the hands into town, but he wanted a chance to see Isabelle again.

Isabelle had no response and was content to let Gabriel and Andrew talk for the duration of the ride. Gabriel explained a little about the area and the different trees and plants that Andrew asked about. He wanted to know about the eagle they saw soaring above them and the name of the small animal he saw crawling into a hole in the ground. When her brother asked Gabriel if he'd ever seen Indians, Gabriel laughed and told him he'd only seen them twice and they'd been fairly friendly. Andrew's disappointment in this didn't stop the questions. It wasn't until a group of wood and stone structures came into view that her brother quieted down.

His eyes opened wide with amazement, and he turned to look up at Gabriel in awe. "Is this all yours?"

"Yes, but there's also Ethan, my older brother, and Eliza, our younger sister."

Isabelle looked at him in surprise, and Gabriel wasn't sure what to make of that.

"It's just a ranch, Miss Rousseau. We work just as hard as anyone else wanting to carve a life on the frontier."

Once they reached the house and he secured

the wagon, Gabriel helped them both down, but Andrew looked as though he wanted to bound for the corrals. An ornery mustang was being worked, and Andrew watched in glee as the wild animal bucked the rider into the air, but he managed to fall back into the saddle.

"Don't worry, Andrew, we'll get to that. For now, I'd like you to meet Mabel." Gabriel guided them up the wide front porch and opened the door to let them in. Isabelle took in her surroundings while a familiar recognition washed over her. For all of his rugged ways and comfortably worn clothes, Gabriel Gallagher belonged to a wealthy family. A family much like hers had been at one time, except here there appeared to be no pretenses. Gabriel didn't wear his wealth as a badge of honor but rather as a man who felt comfortable with his accomplishments.

A shout came in from the kitchen followed by a tall, black woman chasing a sleek, black cat through the hall with a rolling pin. She stopped immediately upon seeing them and used her free hand to smooth down her white apron.

"Well saint's alive, Gabriel. Don't you boys ever bring women home the proper way?"

Isabelle thought the comment rude, and made even more so when the older woman studied her the way someone might when buying something at an auction. But the woman held out a strong hand and offered Isabelle a kinder outreach of friendship than she ever expected. "I'm Mabel. Welcome to Hawk's Peak."

4

Montana offered one surprise after another. First Tilly and now Mabel, who didn't behave like any housekeeper Isabelle had ever known. The woman her parents employed for more than fifteen years never offered a kind word to Isabelle or later, to Andrew. Her mother must have liked her because the woman moved with them from Philadelphia to New Orleans, but she'd been barely more than a stranger after all those years. Isabelle didn't even remember the woman's first name. She had always been Mrs. Potter.

Mabel bustled about like a whirlwind, and Isabelle watched as the older woman fussed over Andrew and promised him warm cookies. She handed out orders to Gabriel about supper, and Isabelle stood amazed that the big, tall man just nodded and kept saying, "Yes, Mabel."

When they finally made it back outside, Isabelle turned to Gabriel. "Are you certain she's a housekeeper?"

"She just likes us to think she is, but we all know the truth. My mother adored that woman, and she's family." Gabriel turned to look down at his side where Andrew tugged on the edge of his coat.

"Horse!" Andrew pointed out to the corral where one of the ranch hands removed the saddle from a mare and began brushing her down.

Gabriel draped an arm companionably on the boy's shoulder. "Simple pleasures, Andrew. That's what our time here is all about." Andrew didn't seem to understand what that meant. "Come on, let's get you on the back of a horse."

Gabriel led Isabelle and Andrew to the corral opposite the one where one of the ranch hands worked a mustang. "That's Ben over there riding that ornery mustang." Gabriel indicated the man currently being flung around on the horse. "He's one of our best roughriders."

"Can I ride like that?"

Gabriel chuckled. "Perhaps someday, but let's start with something easier." Gabriel led them to the fence where another ranch hand was cooling down a mare. "Carl, did that mare get a hard ride or could she handle this big guy here?" Gabriel lifted Andrew up and braced him so he sat on the fence. "I'd like you to meet Miss Isabelle Rousseau and her brother, Andrew. Miss Rousseau is Briarwood's new schoolteacher."

"Pleased to meet you, ma'am." Carl smiled at Andrew and tipped his hat at Isabelle. Carl was a lanky cowboy with thinning brown hair and light brown eyes. He'd been a loyal ranch hand with Gallaghers for almost five years.

"Oh, I reckon she'll handle it." Carl patted the mare's neck. "She's just had a bit of exercise, but I'm thinkin' she'd like to take you for a couple of rounds."

Andrew nearly jumped off the fence and would have landed in the dirt below without Gabriel holding him. Gabriel said to Carl, "Could you grab one of Eliza's old saddles for Andrew? It should do well enough for him."

"Sure thing." Carl dropped the brush into a bucket and disappeared into the barn.

"She's lovely." Isabelle reached her hand out. The mare surprised and pleased her by stepping forward. "Are you certain she's gentle enough?"

"She's about as gentle as they come. And here's your saddle, Andrew." Gabriel let Carl put Eliza's old saddle on the mare, and when she was ready for her rider, Gabriel lifted Andrew onto her back. "Thanks, Carl. Fits him nicely."

"Just about does." Carl picked up the bucket and gave the mare another friendly pat. "Well now, I need to get some of the other horses exercised." He looked up at Andrew. "You listen to Gabe here, Andrew. He's about the best there is with horses." Carl smiled, tipped his hat at Isabelle, and sauntered off into the barn.

Isabelle looked up at Gabriel. "You must be

quite the horseman, though he implied there was someone better with horses than you."

"Well, most folks will say it's me, but to be honest, there just isn't anyone better with the four-legged creatures than my sister, Eliza."

"Your sister isn't here?"

"Unfortunately, no, but you'll meet her soon." Gabriel adjusted the stirrups, tied the end of the reins in a loose knot in case Andrew let go, and cautioned him to hold on tight. He made certain Andrew was as secure as he could make him and took great pleasure in Gabriel's joy.

"Now, keep a tight hold of the reins, but don't pull on her head unless you want to turn her or stop. Got that?"

Andrew nodded his head eagerly while he sat atop Hawk's Peak's smallest and most gentle mare.

"Now, take her for a little turn around the corral." Gabriel gave the mare a soft pat on the rump and moved to stand near Isabelle at the railing while remaining inside the corral to keep a close eye on Andrew.

"His smile is about as big as Montana."

"He hasn't smiled like this in a long time." Isabelle watched her brother's ease with the large animal. "You don't move slowly into anything, do you?"

"I've always believed that the only way to learn something is to do it." Gabriel glanced at her and gave her a half smile. "He'll be fine, Isabelle."

Startled, because it was the first time he used her Christian name, Isabelle took a moment to respond. "I'm not too worried about that, though I did learn at a more leisurely pace. In fact, I wasn't even allowed in the saddle until I correctly named each piece of equipment and learned how to bridle and saddle the horse properly."

Gabriel's eyebrow rose but with some curiosity this time. "You ride?"

"Oh, yes. I rode my first horse when I stood barely taller than Andrew, though with a different saddle, and I was never allowed outside of the park."

Gabriel noticed the smile that shifted to a slight scowl when she mentioned the park. It was just another mysterious piece of the Isabelle Rousseau puzzle. Her gaze fixed on her brother, and though Gabriel conversed with her the entire time, she noticed he always knew what Andrew did.

"You'll like Eliza, my baby sister. She's about your age. I hoped to introduce you to her, but Mabel said she disappeared somewhere this morning and that she'd be gone for an entire day."

Actually, Mabel told him that Eliza told her not to wait up because she might be home late, but she didn't give an explanation. Gabriel knew they didn't have business off the ranch except for the meeting with the army representative. Eliza disappearing without an explanation might have worried Gabriel if he thought she'd really do anything foolish. He turned his attention back to Isabelle when he realized she'd spoken.

"You speak as though you care for your sister very much."

"My family's my everything."

"I know what you mean." They both looked over at Andrew.

The boy beamed. Gabriel took a small bit of pride in knowing he helped Andrew find something to be happy about.

"You're a natural, Andrew." Smiling, Gabriel walked up to horse and rider.

"I want to do it again!" He smiled a toothy grin.

"I remember feeling the same way when I rode my first horse." Gabriel chuckled and lifted Andrew down from the back of the mare.

"I bet nothing will ever be as good as riding horses, huh?"

Gabriel grinned devilishly. "Oh, I can think of something that just might be better."

Andrew's eyes opened wide. "Really?"

Isabelle's face turned red when she caught onto what Gabriel meant.

Gabriel's grin left his face, and he did his best to give Andrew a serious expression. "I'll tell you all about it in another ten years."

Before the boy asked anything else, Gabriel put a hand lightly over his mouth and led him over to his sister. He glanced briefly up at the sky. "It's going to be dark in a few hours, but Mabel will skin my hide if I take you away before she can feed you. What do say?"

Andrew nodded his head up and down rapidly until Isabelle gave in—again.

"Excellent. I have some things to attend to but should be along directly. Just go ahead and make yourselves at home. Mabel will take care of you."

Two hours later, when everyone was fed, happy, and tired, Gabriel helped Isabelle into the wagon and lifted a half-asleep Andrew up to her. Gabriel followed and set the horses in motion for the ride back to town.

Gabriel looked down at the young boy with his head down on his sister's lap, and he experienced the same tug at his heart that he'd noticed ever since he caught a first glimpse of them at the café. Isabelle smoothed the hair back from Andrew's face, and Gabriel saw great love in her eyes. He pulled a wool blanket out from under the bench and spread it over the sleeping form.

"Thank you," Isabelle said softly and glanced up at him.

"He's tuckered out tonight."

She nodded. "He hasn't expended this much energy in a long time." A few moments of silence passed as the first hint of stars twinkled above them. "Thank you for today. It meant a lot to Andrew." She paused for just a fraction of a moment. "And it meant a lot to me."

Gabriel's eyes met hers, and he guided the horses on instinct alone. "You're welcome, Isabelle."

His whisper-soft words caressed her skin, and she pulled her cloak closer to her body. She wasn't accustomed to the cold temperatures of this northern land, but she loved the cold crispness of the air as it moved around her. She would remember this as the day Andrew found happiness again and that was a debt she could never repay.

Little more than an hour later, Gabriel pulled

the wagon to a soft stop in front of the cottage and helped Isabelle down. He told her to unlatch the door while he lifted Andrew, still wrapped in the wool blanket, and carried him inside. He immediately went to the smaller of the two bedrooms and set Andrew down on the edge of the bed. The boy wasn't any help as Gabriel gently removed his shoes and clothes. Isabelle stood at the doorway, and when Gabriel asked her about the boy's nightclothes, she finally moved to the small bureau and pulled a nightshirt from the top drawer. Without asking, Gabriel took the shirt, settled it over the boy's head, and tucked him nimbly under the covers. Isabelle moved around him to place a light kiss on her brother's brow, then followed Gabriel from the small bedroom.

Isabelle closed the door quietly behind them and turned to Gabriel. "You look as though you've done that before."

Gabriel shrugged. "Actually Andrew's the first kid I've ever tucked into bed."

"You're a natural," she murmured and moved

around him to the kitchen.

Gabriel saw her pull out a small envelope, like the ones they use at the telegraph office, and place it on the table.

"Would you like some tea or coffee before you leave? I must admit that I'm not overly tired, but you do have a bit of drive back home, don't you?" She stood there with the kettle in her hand and was about to light the wood in the stove, but waited.

"I'd enjoy a cup of coffee, thank you." He took a seat when she motioned toward the table and tapped the top of the envelope.

"You get a telegram already?"

Isabelle glanced at the telegram. No one knew where they went to other than her parents' lawyer. She retrieved some sugared biscuits from one of her market baskets that she still needed to unpack and set a plate of them in front of Gabriel. Isabelle pulled out the other chair at the table and picked up the envelope.

"It seems so. I found it on the door step."

"Do you have family somewhere? A fiancé or

someone?" Gabriel tried to sound nonchalant when he picked up a biscuit, but she merely shook her head.

"No, there's no one." She quietly read the telegram. "The only person who knows where we are . . . is my father's lawyer. Oh no, it can't be."

Isabelle's eyes scanned the telegram once more as Gabriel knelt in front of her. Her face paled, causing him immediate concern.

"Isabelle, what's wrong?" His hands gripped her thighs softly though neither noticed. "Isabelle?"

"They want to take him from me."

"Who?" Instead of answering, Isabelle handed him the telegram.

Gabriel scanned the short missive and glanced back at her. She still looked ghostly pale. "Can they do this, Isabelle? Did you know about this aunt that your father gave custody of Andrew to?"

She shook her head as the tears started to flow. "I never met her. We never met any relatives of

Papa. We heard of a sister in France, but she never left home."

"It appears she has."

Isabelle slammed her fist down on the table and remembering her sleeping brother, glanced quickly toward the bedroom door. Gabriel regained his chair, drawing her attention back to him

"He's fine, Isabelle, safe and sound." His voice was just the soothing balm she needed to hear.

"Why? Why would Papa give her custody of Andrew in his will?"

"You didn't know about it? The custody, I mean."

She nodded solemnly. "Yes, but Papa's lawyer said that since she wasn't in the country, Andrew could stay with me until she came to fetch him, but it would have taken over a month for her to get word of their deaths. I didn't worry about it because I never imagined she'd actually leave France. I never thought I'd have to go to such measures just to keep Andrew with me."

Gabriel knew she didn't realize all that she said

aloud and as much as he wanted to know about her past and her reasons for coming west, there was a more important issue at hand.

"What measures, Isabelle?"

Isabelle shook her head vehemently.

"Isabelle?" His strong, tanned hands found her smaller, pale ones, and he held them tightly, doing his best to give her some of his strength.

"Papa's will stated that I would be able to retain sole guardianship if I married."

"Marry me." The words came out before Gabriel realized that he didn't want to stop them.

Isabelle tensed and pulled her hands from his grasp.

"How dare you joke about such a thing." She stood and moved toward the stove where the coffee was ready. Mechanically, she lifted two cups down from a shelf and filled them. She had noticed that Gabriel drank his coffee strong and black at the ranch. She set it down on the table, but he stood and forced her to face him.

"I'm quite serious, Isabelle." She tried pulling

away from him again, but he held her shoulders firmly.

"Gabriel, I can't."

It was the first time she used his given name, and he liked the sound of it coming from her lips. "Not even for Andrew?"

Her head automatically turned to the bedroom door where her brother lay sleeping, not a care in the world. Her eyes turned back to Gabriel, her tears on the brink of slipping.

"Yes, I could do anything for him." Gabriel heard defeat creep into her soft words.

Gabriel lifted her chin to look into her light-gray eyes, and his thumb brushed away a tear that escaped. "I know this isn't what you want, but I want to help you and I hope that you will let me. I will make you a promise, Isabelle. I won't demand anything from you. Your life can go on just as it is. Stay here in the cottage, teach school, and live as you choose, but Andrew would be able to stay with you always."

His selflessness overwhelmed her, but she couldn't stop the guilt from rising. "What about you? I decided not to marry and so a marriage of convenience won't hurt me, but what about you? You wouldn't be free to marry someone else."

His tender smile was an unfamiliar but most welcome gift. "There isn't anyone else I have a mind to marry, so don't go fretting your pretty head over that. Agreed?"

It took her a few moments, but Isabelle finally nodded. She was amazed what she had agreed to do when faced with such a desperate choice. It wasn't supposed to happen this way.

"Is that a yes?"

She glanced once more to the bedroom door and with firm resolve, nodded again. "That's a yes."

Gabriel placed a soft kiss on her brow, and it took all of his strength to step away.

"We can have the reverend take care of the ceremony tomorrow at the church if that's agreeable with you."

"That's fine," she whispered, though her mind ran wild at that point.

"When did that telegram say you had to bring Andrew back?"

Isabelle picked up the piece of paper again and reread the words that irrevocably changed her course. "Immediately, and if I don't, my aunt will come here." She crumbled the paper in her hand. "I may as well tell you now, Gabriel. We're virtually penniless. I'm sure you already figured that out, but it wasn't always the case. My family was once one of the wealthiest in New Orleans, but after my parents' death . . . I never met my aunt, but my mother said that the relationship between her and my father was distant and strained. Why should she care so much about gaining custody of Andrew?"

Gabriel took her hands once more into his own and kissed them lightly. "That's a good question, but let's take care of one thing at a time." He watched her push an errant curl behind her ear. She'd gone without a hat or bonnet today, and he wondered if her hair felt as silky as it looked. "I've given you my word, and you never have to worry that I won't keep it, but let me protect you and Andrew. That's all I ask out of this." His soft voice crept inside of Isabelle's heart and without her realizing it, a seed of hope had been planted.

Finding her first smile since she read the telegram, Isabelle let out a soft sigh. "I sometimes wonder if you're even real, Mr. Gallagher."

He smiled in reply. "Oh I'm real, Isabelle. I promise you that."

5

She was married.

Isabelle found it difficult to believe that she actually married after she vowed never to marry following her last disastrous courtship. Her only concern had been Andrew, but it turned out that she couldn't even do that on her own. She moved the polished silver band with a single diamond in the center around her finger, wondering how Gabriel managed to procure it in such a short time. She'd been surprised when he pulled it out of his jacket pocket at the appropriate time and placed it gently on her finger.

His clothes also surprised her. She saw the evidence of his wealth at the ranch, but she had only seen him in comfortably-worn work pants and casual shirts. The dark wool pants weren't too out of place, but the black frock coat, trimmed to fit him perfectly, was not something she expected to see on him. It looked as though he attempted to tame his thick hair, but it curled around his ears and neck. Isabelle might have thought he needed a hair trim, but in this case, he looked wonderful. She smiled when she looked down and saw he still donned his usual black boots. Gabriel Gallagher was indeed an incredibly handsome man, and his ruggedness made him all the more appealing in Isabelle's eyes. She had grown weary of the dandies and society men who crowded the streets and ballrooms of New Orleans. Gabriel was what she imagined her mother had meant when she had spoken of real men.

Andrew had been confused as to what was happening, especially when Isabelle explained that they would be staying in the cottage and not at the ranch.

"But, I will take you out as often as you want to ride the horses."

"Really?" Andrew's spirits soared considerably, and he looked at his sister. "Can I?"

Defeated yet again, Isabelle nodded. "Yes, but we can't interfere with Gabriel's work."

"You won't. Now, about that pie." Gabriel escorted them over to Tilly's Café after being assured that the reverend wouldn't reveal the knowledge of their marriage to anyone in town. He'd rather have celebrated with a nice, large, family meal back at the ranch where afterward he and Isabelle could spend the night together in his room. But Gabriel made a promise, and he'd never broken a promise.

He was pleased with his decision. Gabriel wanted nothing more than to keep Isabelle and Andrew forever, and the realization surprised him. He wasn't sure how he was going to get Isabelle to agree to a real marriage rather than a marriage of convenience. For now, Gabriel would be content knowing that he had been able to keep Isabelle and Andrew together.

In the form of a quiet celebration, they ate a

hearty meal at Tilly's, who kept remarking on how nice everyone looked that day. Isabelle shifted uncomfortably and Andrew smiled through a bite of apple pie.

Gabriel spared Isabelle any further discomfort and glanced up at Tilly. "Just a little welcome and good luck lunch for the new teacher."

"Well, I must say that we are all pleased you've come, Isabelle. It's been the talk of the town since before you arrived." With another smile and a pinch to Andrew's cheek, Tilly left them to finish their dessert.

"I don't like deceiving people," Isabelle said quietly, once Tilly moved away from their table.

Gabriel wanted to take her hand in his own. Instead, he left his hand on the table. "People will know when it's time." He watched a look like uncertainty pass over her lovely face. "Do you regret the choice?" Gabriel wasn't sure if he wanted to hear her response and was bothered more than he should have been when she hesitated in answering.

"I don't regret the choice. Please don't think

that for a moment." Careful to keep her voice close to a whisper, Isabelle smiled when Andrew glanced up at her strangely, and she gently told him to finish his pie. "It wasn't a choice I ever planned on making, and now that it's been made, I worry about the consequences."

"As far as I'm concerned, right now there aren't any consequences." This time Gabriel did take her hand in his. "More good will come out of this than bad, I promise you."

Their family could use some extra "good" these days. That morning, Mabel found a note in Eliza's room. The older woman had been worried when the youngest Gallagher failed to come down for breakfast at her usually early hour and went up to see if she was all right. Eliza's bed had never been slept in, and she had left a note next to her bed along with a telegram about some horse. The note offered no explanation as to why she left for Kentucky, but she promised to wire as soon as she arrived. Gabriel's first instinct had been to chase after his sister, but he couldn't leave the ranch without a

Gallagher in residence.

In addition to a runaway sister, he expected Ethan and Brenna any day now. Ethan had been in Scotland far too long, and Gabriel had come to the realization that Hawk's Peak needed all three of them to get through the tough seasons.

The Gallaghers had certainly led exciting and sometimes tragic lives, what with their parents' deaths and Brenna's kidnapping by her grandfather, Nathan Hunter. But never did he imagine that he would be adding marriage to the list. Hunter had occupied most of the family's thoughts and time over the years, and Gabriel believed the war between the two families wouldn't end soon, as much as they could all hope otherwise. It had been a blessing that Brenna didn't know her grandfather until she arrived in Montana and even more of a blessing when she saw the man for who he really was. But as long as Hunter lived and walked upon the ground of the territory, the Gallaghers wouldn't know peace.

Gabriel's thoughts drifted to Isabelle, now his

wife, and for a moment, he imagined something better. He imagined what it would be like to have a marriage like the one his parents had nurtured. Gabriel had admired them deeply but never believed their choices were for him. He was content with his life on the ranch and never noticed a need for something more. With all the turmoil at the ranch, he worried about what the future would hold for him and Isabelle.

Isabelle pulled her hand away from Gabriel's when it looked like Tilly was headed back to their table. Isabelle had enjoyed getting to know Tilly the day before and made a mental note to return soon for another long visit. She could have friends and a home here—if she allowed herself that gift. When Tilly approached them again, they praised her pie and promised to return soon.

Tilly waved them off with a smile and went back to bustling around her guests.

Once back at the cottage, Andrew raced over to pet their newest resident, a brown gelding with a big white mark up and down his face.

Isabelle waited until her brother was out of earshot before addressing Gabriel. "I'm not sure what you expect now."

"When I give my word, I keep it. Nothing will ever happen that you don't want to happen."

She had the good grace to blush. "I didn't mean to offend you. I'm just . . . new at this."

He laughed and kissed her brow. "I am too, but you have nothing to worry about. I'm going to go and wire your father's lawyer and let him know you've married and that Andrew is staying with you. Don't worry; I'll sign it from you," he added, when she was about to protest.

"I can never repay you for this. I still don't fully understand why you did it."

He allowed himself a few seconds to enjoy the sight of her and realized he didn't have a good answer. "You don't have to repay me anything. I know we barely know each other, but I would do anything to keep Andrew safe—both of you safe. I'll be by tomorrow to show you how to hitch the wagon."

Gabriel said his good-byes to Andrew,

climbed up to the seat of the wagon, and headed to the telegraph office. He'd never spent so much time on the seat of a buckboard, and he sorely missed the saddle. Then again, the wagon wasn't so bad when Isabelle sat next to him.

Gabriel made quick work of the telegram and stopped off at the blacksmith's to pick up a couple of tools being repaired.

"Been seeing you in town a lot lately, Gabriel."

"More to do than usual."

"Can't be easy on you and Eliza with Ethan gone. He ever coming back?"

Gabriel smiled. "In fact he is, and soon." Gabriel opted not to mention that Eliza left, and he didn't know when she'd return. "Do you have those tools Ben dropped by last week?"

"I sure do." Otis lifted the items from pegs on the wall and handed them to Gabriel. "Like you bought them yesterday."

"Appreciate it, Otis. What do I owe you?"

Otis waved him away. "I still owe you. I'm grateful to you and Ben for helping me here last week. Would have lost all my stock, and everyone else's, if you two hadn't brought them back."

"Did you ever find out how the fence came down?"

Otis shook his head and picked up his blacksmith's hammer. "Cut clean through. Don't know anyone around these parts who'd do that."

Gabriel did, but Nathan Hunter and his men generally left the townsfolk alone. It was the Gallaghers they continued to fight.

"You take care of yourself, Otis, and thanks again for getting these done."

"Anytime."

Once his business in town was completed, Gabriel headed back to the ranch. He normally enjoyed the drive out to the Peak but that day the quiet offered no comfort.

The following morning, Gabriel rode up to the cottage, grateful to be back on his horse. He managed to make the trip into town in almost half the amount of time, which proved fortunate, because he was needed at the ranch, and his extra visits to town couldn't go on indefinitely.

Andrew hung over the edge of the small corral, petting the horse, and gave Gabriel a big grin before he dropped to the ground and ran over to him. In a natural response, Gabriel lifted Andrew into his arms and swung him in the air. Andrew let out a long peal of young laughter as he was thrown over the strong shoulder like a half-filled sack of grain.

Isabelle heard the commotion outside and stepped onto the porch in time to see her brother slung over Gabriel's shoulder. She still struggled with the fact that she married the man and guilt for tying him to a family he didn't want. Their smiles were contagious, and she stepped down to join them.

"Good morning, Gabriel."

Isabelle stood at the edge of the porch above the steps looking like the most beautiful teacher he'd ever seen. He may have enjoyed his younger years of school a little more if there'd been a teacher like Isabelle Rousseau.

"Good morning, Isabelle." Gabriel lowered Andrew back to the ground and helped straighten his clothes. "Ready for your first day?"

She nodded. "Yes, though it's not my first teaching post, which certainly helps."

"Oh, how long have you been teaching?" His question stemmed from genuine curiosity, as he still didn't know much about the woman he married.

"Two years. I taught for a short time before my parents' death."

Gabriel walked over to her and gave her a sheepish grin. "I really should have asked you this before, but exactly how old are you?"

Isabelle couldn't stop the smile. "Are you worried I'm too young?"

"No, I figured you about twenty-two or so."

"Close, twenty-four."

"Ah, well, you're close to Brenna's age. I imagine you'll get along well together."

"Who's Brenna?"

"She's Ethan's wife and we're expecting them

home any day now. They've been over in Scotland."

"Will they mind?"

Gabriel paused and sent a questioning look her way. "Mind what?"

"That you married and to a stranger, no less."

"Not at all." Gabriel effectively dropped the subject and moved over to the corral where the gelding eagerly waited for attention.

Gabriel put his hand on the animal's head, rubbing his ears. The horse wasn't used to standing around for days at a time. He pulled the animal out with a lead rope and grabbed the harness from the back of the wagon. Isabelle told Andrew to go inside and get cleaned up for school, and she prepared herself for her first lesson on how to hitch a horse to a wagon.

Isabelle learned quickly and was stronger than she looked. After two restarts, she managed to harness the horse and hitch him to the wagon.

Isabelle stood back and studied her work with a big grin on her face. "I think I could get the hang of this."

Gabriel chuckled. "Seems you're suited for this land. I expected the harness might be too much for you. You're a lot stronger than I first thought."

Isabelle shrugged her shoulders. "I'm not usually so skinny." Her reply was curt, and Gabriel let the subject go.

Andrew ran out of the cottage looking clean, if not a little rumpled, from his earlier tussle with Gabriel.

"Well, have you ever driven a horse?" Gabriel thought that no matter how quick of a learner she was, teaching to drive would take much longer. She surprised him again.

"I've driven a buggy, so I imagine it's not so different."

"It's the same idea. Where'd you learn to drive?"

Her shoulders lifted into another shrug though he wasn't sure she realized it. "Back home." What she left out was that during their last week at the mansion, all of the servants picked up and left to find other employment. If she hadn't learned how to drive, her shoes would have worn through the soles, and she could ill afford the luxury of new ones. It was humiliating enough to confide her financial circumstances to Gabriel, but he didn't need to know the embarrassing particulars.

Gabriel knew that there was a lot more to the story than she revealed. Few young women in the city ever learned how to drive, most especially those with servants. From the condition of her soft hands and skin, it appeared as though she'd once enjoyed that comfort. She did say her family had been wealthy.

"Well, let's see what you can do. You want to go for a ride, Andrew?" Andrew nodded eagerly, and Gabriel helped him into the smaller wagon, this time allowing him to do a bit of the climbing. The youngster proved to be quite nimble, and Gabriel stopped worrying that Andrew would be injured climbing in and out of the buckboard.

Once they were all on the high seat, Gabriel handed the leather reins over to Isabelle with a grin. "Lead on, my lady."

Isabelle laughed and slowly turned the horse ever so slightly to maneuver away from the corral, and with easy grace, guided the animal toward the schoolhouse. Gabriel couldn't help but be impressed with her skills on the short drive, and he no longer worried about her being able to handle the horse and buckboard on her own. She'd already proven herself capable.

"You've hidden talents, Isabelle. It makes me wonder what else you could possibly do that you are hiding from me."

He meant his words to be as a bit of a jest, but for reasons unbeknownst to her, Isabelle found herself blushing. "I assure you, sir, that I am an open book."

Gabriel gave her a look that plainly said, "I don't believe that for a minute."

Isabelle merely shrugged and pulled the wagon to a stop in front of the schoolhouse.

"It's a bit early, still. Perhaps I'll take us back and leave the horse and wagon at the cottage. It's a short walk to the schoolhouse, and Andrew and I could do with the exercise."

Gabriel thought that she needed food more than exercise, but he nodded, knowing it wasn't his place to say anything—yet.

Isabelle pulled the wagon around and drove back to the cottage. She even allowed Andrew to hold onto the reins with her. He was positively delighted to be included in such a grown-up lesson.

A short time later, Gabriel watched as Isabelle made quick work of unhitching the wagon and removing the harness. He took the burden from her with a pleased smile and placed the leather trappings in the shed. He always preferred to take care of such things for women, but after so many years of living with a woman like his sister, Gabriel and Ethan both learned quickly that though a woman appreciated a man's strength, some didn't want to be made to feel helpless— like Isabelle. She would need that strength to survive in the wild lands of the west.

When the horse was safely inside the corral, Gabriel carefully instructed her on how to measure out the oats.

"I think you'll do fine here in Montana."

"I don't have much of a choice." Isabelle brushed her hands off on her long skirts.

Gabriel swore he'd learn the rest of her story, but he had no intention of scaring her off trying. "Would you join us for supper at the ranch tonight?"

Isabelle didn't know what to make of this man she now called her husband. Other than the ring on her finger, she didn't feel married. Completely changing the subject, Isabelle posed a question of her own. "How did you happen upon a ring on such short notice?"

Bewildered and amused, but not forgetting that she had yet to answer his question, Gabriel answered hers. "It belonged to my mother. For some reason everyone always thought that I'd be the one to marry first, so Ethan and Eliza decided that I should keep it to give to my wife."

Isabelle spun the ring once on her finger, the band warm against her skin. "Gabriel, such an heirloom should be saved for the woman you truly take to wife, not for our arrangement."

Gabriel took her soft hand in his own and thumbed the ring. "I did give it to my wife and that is all you need to concern yourself with." He dropped her hand and moved to mount his horse.

Andrew, unaware of what took place between the adults, walked over to stand a few feet from Gabriel and his horse. "Does your horse have a name, Gabriel?"

Gabriel soothed his frustrated brow and smiled at the boy. "I never did get around to naming him. Would you like to name him?"

Once again, his gray eyes sparkled, and the boy nodded.

"Well, you think of some names and the next time you come out to the ranch, you can let me know which one you chose."

"All right!"

Gabriel turned his horse around but before he said his good-byes, Isabelle's soft voice stopped him. He turned and looked at her.

"Will you be in town today, Gabriel?"

He nodded, wondering why she'd asked. "I'll be working at the ranch most of the day, but I have some business in town with an army supplier again late this afternoon to finalize their purchase."

"You do business with the army?"

Gabriel nodded. "There are still a few army forts up here, and the soldiers need beef. There are a few ranches closer to the forts, but they can't supply in the high quantity that we can, so the army generally comes to us first."

"What happens when the army leaves these parts?"

"Do you know something I don't?" Gabriel asked and winked at her. "It may cut into business a bit, but the army leaving would mean peace for the natives up here."

"You asked me about today. Did you need help with anything?"

"No, it's not that. I fear today will be a long day for Andrew and me at the school as it will be our first day, and therefore too late for us to ride out to the ranch for supper. But if you're still around this evening, would you join us instead?"

Gabriel's smile softened his expression, and he nodded. "I'd like that. I should be done with my business here around four o'clock. That's a little early, but perhaps I could give Andrew another riding lesson."

"He'd like that." A moment later Gabriel rode out of town, leaving a soft trail of dust behind him. Isabelle looked down at her brother, who didn't cling quite as tenaciously to her as he used to, and gave him a little sigh with her smile.

"Are you ready for our first day?"

The boy nodded. "Do I get to learn with the other kids?"

"You do, but there probably won't be other children your age. Is that all right?"

He nodded again. "I can read and draw pictures though, right?"

Isabelle laughed. "Yes, you may do both, but you'll have to continue the lessons we started back home, understood?"

"Yes, Ibby."

"Good." With a deep fortifying breath,

Isabelle lifted her soft leather teacher's bag, a gift from her father, in one hand and took Andrew's hand in the other.

Isabelle soon realized that teaching out here in the wilderness differed greatly from the refined boarding schools in the east. She knew that the grades would be vastly varied and made adjustments for that. She also counted on not having quite as many supplies as she was used to but had also prepared for that.

What she hadn't prepared for was to have to throw out most of her carefully selected lesson plans. For the first few moments, she worked to ease the embarrassment that most of the children weren't much more advanced than her five-year-old brother, and he was two years younger than the youngest student in the class. Thankfully, the children could all read and write and a few of them had obviously been prepared well by a parent. The rest of the students, however, had deplorable grammar and barely knew the basics of arithmetic and English. Isabelle realized that she'd have to rethink her lessons and hold off for a time on the various geography, modern studies, history, and science courses she wanted to implement right away.

The two children who'd been well tutored by someone in their upbringing were sisters. At the ages of thirteen and eleven, they were both advanced enough to assist her. Isabelle immediately called upon the elder of the two, who gave her name as Darcie, to be her assistant. She separated the class into groups according to their current level of skills. Andrew eagerly joined the ranks of the youngest students, who accepted him despite the few years difference between them.

Darcie proved to be very useful and when she confessed that she, too, wanted to go to college and be a teacher, Isabelle promised that if she helped with the other children, Isabelle would tutor her once a week in order to better prepare her. The young girl set out to prove her worth, which Isabelle happily admitted she did with skill and enthusiasm.

By the end of the day, three distinct groups in

the classroom had been formed. The youngest group of students knew how to read and decipher readily enough but still needed to learn some of the basics of proper English. The second group consisted of those children aged ten to twelve who weren't in much better shape than the younger children, but because of age, Isabelle formed a separate group. The oldest group, which also consisted of Darcie's eleven-year-old sister, Ruth, were advanced enough with their reading and writing that Isabelle believed they could handle some of her other lesson plans. Isabelle supposed that even a healthy, growing town out here in the wilderness found it difficult to keep a teacher staffed at the school.

At three o'clock, Isabelle dismissed the children, giving them each a small pad of paper and pencil to take home with them. She reminded herself to ask the reverend where the supplies came from on such short notice. It was the children's task to write one page describing their town. Although an easy assignment, it would also help Isabelle to better determine the skills of her new students.

With happy smiles and an eagerness to learn, the children left the schoolhouse, scurrying off to play or head home.

Andrew walked up silently to the teacher's desk and waited patiently for his sister to finish writing in her book. When she finally looked up, he gave her a big smile.

"I like school."

Isabelle let out a slow breath, grateful that the first day went so well. She admitted to a small amount of nervousness, but when the students first arrived at nine o'clock in the morning, they eased her worry and welcomed her as their new teacher. From then on, they followed her firm, but kind direction.

"I like school too, Andrew. Though I almost forgot how young you are, my brother."

"I'm not so young," he countered with a furrowed brow.

Isabelle laughed and tweaked his nose. "I meant only that I forgot because of how grown up you behaved today."

Andrew beamed up at his sister.

"What do you say we go to the café for a piece of pie and walk around town a little so that you can better write your assignment?"

"Do I have to do it too?" His petulant pleading sounded sincere, but Isabelle smiled and tweaked his nose again.

"Of course, just like you always did. I know you're younger than the other children that go to school, but you are blessed with a quick mind."

The walk into town was pleasant and the air around them only mildly cold. Isabelle and Andrew enjoyed slices of cherry pie and cold milk at Tilly's Café. Afterward, they walked up and down the boardwalks of the wide dirt streets and even stopped at the livery so that Andrew could watch, from a safe distance, how the blacksmith shod a horse. The young boy found such delight in the process and asked Isabelle if he could write about that instead.

"You can write about anything you see in town so long as you do the assignment."

Sometime later, after their exploration of the town, they walked up to the cottage just as Gabriel dismounted from his tall, sable gelding. Andrew ran to him so that Gabriel could lift him in the air and swing him around again.

Gabriel didn't disappoint the boy and even settled him atop his shoulders afterward. Isabelle, once again, noticed a tightening around her heart that she couldn't deny brought her joy.

"So, how was the first day of school?" Gabriel bounced Andrew up and down a little as the boy answered for his sister.

"Great. Ibby's the best teacher ever. I got to sit with the bigger kids, and they didn't even tease me. I have to write about the town like the other kids even though Ibby's my sister." The boy sounded just a little put out by that, but Isabelle merely shrugged at her brother as though to say he wouldn't be receiving any special attention because he was the teacher's brother.

"Sounds like you had a fun day." Gabriel turned to Isabelle. "And what about the teacher? How did her day go?"

Isabelle did her best to stop the heat from rising to her cheeks caused by the look Gabriel gave her. It was more than just a friendly look from someone asking about her day.

"Better than I expected, though there were a few surprises."

"Oh, not anything bad I hope."

She shook her head. "No, not exactly. Gabriel, when did this town last have a teacher? Reverend Phillips mentioned some time had passed, but those students seem to have been without proper schooling for far too long."

"Four years, I believe, or close to it."

"Four years! Did no one volunteer?"

"My mother did when the school first opened, but she wasn't here that often, and Eliza even came in on occasion when she could get away from her horses, but no one else ever stepped forward."

"And no one ever applied for the position?"

Gabriel understood her disbelief. Having come from a well-educated family, she may not understand the way things are done out here, but she'd soon learn about the hard work required by the farmers and ranchers in the area. In their minds, livelihood came before education. Not everyone was fortunate to have a mother educated enough to teach her children or to have been shipped off to school like he and his siblings.

"Not until you. Don't think too poorly of the people around here, though. Most everyone has a fairly decent understanding of the basics, but they also don't have the time to tend to their fields, animals, and home, let alone add on the burden of teaching. Besides, most of their children probably read and write as well as their parents."

Isabelle did understand to an extent. She didn't know of the existence these people sweated and fought for, or the challenges they faced merely to survive, and therefore could not pass judgment on them for neglecting the education of their children. She wanted to be the person to make a difference in their lives. Isabelle promised the children she'd stay, and she meant to keep that promise. She watched as Gabriel swung Andrew down from the perch on his broad shoulders and tickled his stomach, setting the young boy into giggles and laughter. The sight and sound warmed Isabelle's heart.

"Would you gentlemen care for refreshment before supper?"

Gabriel gave her a dazzling smile and shook Andrew playfully. "What do you say, Andrew? Do want your snack or ride the horse?"

The little boy thought for a moment before he said, "Both!"

Gabriel chuckled. "How about a snack, and then we'll ride the horse?"

Andrew nodded, and they followed Isabelle inside the cottage where she set out cheese and bread.

When they had their fill, Gabriel looked at Andrew. "Are you ready for another quick lesson?"

"Yes!"

"Behave yourself, Andrew."

"I promise, Ibby." Andrew slipped his hand

into Gabriel's, and they left the cottage.

Isabelle began preparing their supper of fried chicken—the chicken she had purchased already butchered from the general store—whipped potatoes seasoned with the few herbs she managed to purchase, fresh peas, and thick, white biscuits she quickly baked. She heard the sounds of laughter outside and took a quick glance out the front window to see her brother perched securely in front of Gabriel on his tall steed. Smiling to herself, Isabelle went back to her cooking and sang a soft melody her nanny used to sing to her.

Andrew's enjoyment in the ride with Gabriel was apparent, and though the older man stayed on the horse with him, he let Andrew control the reins. Gabriel promised that he could ride by himself, once again, but only out at the ranch. As well behaved as his thoroughbred could be, he was still too much horse for such a little boy.

Since Gabriel wanted to learn as much as he could about his new wife, he started asking Andrew a few casual questions. "How do you like living here?"

The boy smiled and bobbed his head. "I like it a lot, better than New Orleans. That's where Mama and Papa are." The boy's smile vanished from his voice, and Gabriel glanced at his face to make sure he was all right. His face grew pensive, but tears didn't appear to be forthcoming.

"Your Mom and Dad are gone, aren't they?"

He nodded again, this time slowly. "Ibby took care of me, though, and the people took our house away and all of our friends who lived with us went away, too. Ibby thinks I don't know, but I do."

Gabriel felt a little guilty grilling a five-year-old boy for information, but he seemed to have a need to speak of it, and Gabriel willingly listened.

"What happened when the people took your house? Is that when you came here?"

"Uh-huh. We rode a train and a stagecoach. I didn't talk, though."

The boy sounded so guilty over that admission that Gabriel pulled back lightly on the reins and asked, "Why didn't you talk?"

Andrew shrugged slightly. "I don't know. Maybe I was scared." He looked up at Gabriel with big, worried eyes. "You won't tell Ibby that I was scared, will you?"

"No need to worry about that. I won't tell." Gabriel let the conversation move along onto another subject when Andrew informed him that he picked a name for Gabriel's horse.

"Oh, what is it?"

"Zeus."

"That's a fine name."

"Ibby read me a story about it once. I can't remember what it was called, though." Gabriel told Andrew the story of the powerful Greek god who lived up high in his heavenly kingdom. The man and boy both enjoyed the story so much that they didn't notice when Isabelle came out onto the front porch to call them in for dinner. When Gabriel finally saw her, he dismounted and pulled Andrew down from Zeus. The boy ran over to tell his sister about the horse's new name.

"You've chosen well, Andrew. Zeus is a fitting name for such a noble animal."

He beamed up at her and didn't even sulk when she bade him to go inside and clean himself up for supper.

Gabriel removed the saddle from his horse and let him free in the corral, giving him a nice portion of oats. He followed Isabelle back into the cottage and made use of the washbasin she filled for that purpose. Once she inspected their hands and allowed them at her table, she served the meal.

"You cook a fine meal. Where'd you learn?"

"Out of necessity. When I accepted my first teaching post, I wanted to be able to look after myself if the need ever arose. I can't manage much more than this, but cooking calms me."

"Well, you have a gift for it. If you ever want to learn more, I'm sure Mabel would be happy to teach you."

Isabelle could think of no reason why she shouldn't, and Mabel set her at ease. Working with the other woman would be a joy, and she was determined to learn how to live on the frontier. She couldn't be certain the day would come again when she would have servants of her own.

"If you don't think Mabel would mind, then I'll speak with her."

"You do that. I'll mention it to her tonight." Gabriel watched the sun begin to set in the sky. "I hate to leave, but I have to get back to the ranch. There's an errant mountain lion on the loose that we've yet to catch. I'd rather not risk racing Zeus back in the black of night."

"Are you sure it's safe to travel back tonight?"

Gabriel gave her that raised brow of his and smiled. "Are you suggesting that I stay here, Isabelle?"

A light but steady blush crept up into her face, and she diverted her eyes so that his own would not see how much the idea pleased her.

"I just meant that perhaps it might be safer for you to stay in town at the boardinghouse."

"Pity."

Though he sounded serious, Isabelle saw a

teasing glint in his eyes. Even so, she thought he did sound a bit disappointed.

"No worries, though. I'll be back before the worst of nightfall descends, and the moon is bright enough. A few men are going out in search of the lion tomorrow, so hopefully that will put an end to its attacks."

With a pleasant farewell to Andrew, who busily worked on his writing assignment, which he had forgotten about, Gabriel walked out onto the front porch with Isabelle. He still wanted to try for a real marriage with her, though he wasn't sure how to go about convincing her of the same. His attraction for her continued to grow as did his tender feelings toward her and the boy. He even hoped that she might be attracted to him.

Gabriel surprised Isabelle by gently lifting her chin and brushing his lips across hers in a soft teasing motion that sent a shiver through her body. He pulled back and softly whispered, "Good night," saddled Zeus, and rode off into the night.

6

The following day at the telegraph office, Gabriel was surprised to find two telegrams waiting for him. The first one came from the lawyer. The aunt demanded proof of marriage before she gave up her rights of custody. Annoyed with this woman he had never met, Gabriel tucked that one away to show to Isabelle after school. The other was from a Ramsey Tremaine in Kentucky. The only Ramsey he knew of was Brenna's brother, Ramsey Hunter, though he couldn't understand why Ramsey would use another name. Since the outside of the telegram only had the addressee and the name of the sender, Gabriel tucked that one, unopened, into his pocket and rode over to the general store. He needed to place an order for a large amount of lumber. He and his siblings had discussed enlarging the bunkhouse before Brenna entered their lives, but Gabriel didn't want to put if off any longer, especially with winter around the corner.

He usually put Ben in charge of things at the ranch whenever he was away. Gabriel realized he'd taken for granted that there would always be three Gallaghers to run things, but Ben worked nearly as well as the three of them. A few years older than Ethan, Ben—tall and built like a bull—had been at the ranch longer than any other worker. Gabriel knew he could always count on him to run things the way he or Ethan would. As much as he trusted Ben and the other men, though, Gabriel wanted to be back at the ranch tomorrow when they brought the rest of the herd down from the higher pastures.

With his order at the store placed, Gabriel rode over to the school. A quick glance at the sky told him that the students would probably be to lunch right now, and he wanted to speak with

Isabelle for a moment.

Isabelle lifted the gold fob from the waist of her skirt and checked the time on the small watch.

"All right children, time for lunch." Isabelle watched as they eagerly picked up their lunches and filed outside. Despite the cool weather, they told her they preferred to eat outdoors until the snow came. One child, a young boy of seven years who Isabelle worried over since she first met him, sat alone at his desk. Andrew waited for her at the door, and his small eyes darted back and forth from her to the boy. With one last look, Andrew followed the others outside.

With great care, Isabelle knelt beside the boy's desk. "Did you forget your lunch again, Mason?"

The young boy lifted his head from the desk. His solemn brown eyes brought an ache to her heart. He nodded, but Isabelle knew it wasn't forgetfulness. From the sunken cheeks, to the dark circles, she recognized the signs of hunger and sleeplessness.

"Would you like to join me and Andrew today?"

Isabelle waited nearly two minutes before Mason nodded again. She knew how proud some children could be, but she saw too many orphans in the city to allow even one of her students to go hungry.

"Come then, let's go and join the others." She held out her hand and gathered the small basket of food before walking outside.

Andrew waited and welcomed Mason at their makeshift table on the school steps. Most of the children had finished and left their baskets and cloth bags near the stairs while they played. Isabelle ate a few of the vegetable slices she packed but left the rest of the meal to the boys.

Her attention was drawn away from her brother and Mason to the excited children in the meadow. They waved, called out hellos, and resumed their play. Gabriel secured the horse and approached. Isabelle stood, and she realized how pleased she was to see him.

He offered them each a smile. "It's a mighty

MK MCCLINTOCK

fine day to be outdoors."

"It's rather cold."

"You won't think so after your first winter here." Gabriel ruffled the hair on Andrew's head. "Would you mind if I spoke with your sister alone for a few minutes?

Andrew shook his head. "Let's go play, Mason."

"Finish your lunch first, then you can play with the others." Isabelle was determined to see that Mason his fill. She could tell that something bothered Gabriel, and motioned him back toward his horse.

When they walked out of earshot, Gabriel pulled the telegram out of his pocket and handed it to her. Her worry was plain to see as her eyes darted back and forth over the missive.

"Proof? Such as a copy of the marriage certificate?" Her eyes flitted upward and over to her brother. Gabriel placed his hands on her shoulders and turned her to face him.

"It's going to be fine, Isabelle. I'll admit, this woman is determined, but we'll simply have the reverend draw up a copy of the certificate, and we'll send it to your father's lawyer."

"And if that doesn't work? What if she comes here? We don't have a real marriage, and she'll see right through it. A judge would grant her custody when she tells them I only married to keep Andrew."

Gabriel refused to let the hopelessness he heard consume her. "Do you think your aunt would just show up like that?" Gabriel already had a plan in mind, but he wanted to ease into it.

"I honestly don't know. She could be on her way here now. As I said, I've never met her, but mother never had kind words to say about her sister-in-law."

"If she comes here, we'll have to make our marriage believable." He knew he probably shocked her, and her next words were proof of that.

"I know I agreed to marry you, and I can never repay you for your kindness, but you promised . . . you said you wouldn't . . ."

In an effort to dispel her fears, Gabriel cradled her cheek in his hand and forced her to look at his eyes. "I'm not going to break that promise, Isabelle, and that's not what I meant. I just think that until we get this situation cleared up with your aunt, you and Andrew should come to live at the ranch. There are plenty of bedrooms, so you don't have to worry on the account."

He waited for the questions.

"I do see the wisdom in this, but I have my concerns."

"Which are?"

"What about the school? Your ranch is nearly an hour's drive from here."

"I'll drive you and pick you up."

"How could you possibly have time for that with a ranch to run? What about your family? What are you going to tell them?"

"The truth. I assure you, they'll understand. As far as the ranch is concerned, I'll find a way to make it work. I'll have the ranch hands take turns driving you, if necessary. I'll figure out a way." He wasn't going to let the idea go.

"That seems like far too much trouble. What about you?"

"What about me?"

"It won't be a secret any longer. People will know that we're married and that would force a commitment from . . . from us both, and I just don't think that is fair to you."

Gabriel didn't even try to hide his irritation now. With all of the women he enjoyed over the years, he never once stayed around one long enough to feel anything more than a baser satisfaction. This woman, however, got under his skin, into his head, and deep into his heart, but he was still irritated.

"I made the commitment when I married you. Now it may seem strange to you since we've known each other a few days, but I actually want to be married to you." He didn't really plan to say that last part, but since he had, there was no turning back.

"Why?"

"Why what?"

"Why do you want to be married to me?" Her

voice came as a whisper, but the noise around them grew. Gabriel became aware of their surroundings before she did and glanced over toward Andrew. The boy now stood and stared at them with a tilted head as though trying to figure out what was going on between them.

"Now's not the time to go into that. Why don't you and Andrew come and stay at the ranch for tonight? See how you feel about it, and we'll discuss this further."

Isabelle also became aware of the children and stepped away from Gabriel.

His hands dropped down to his sides.

"We'll try it, but only until the matter is settled with my aunt. Once she goes back to France, you'll be free of us. Agreed?"

Gabriel didn't answer her question and Isabelle narrowed her eyes at him. Instead, he tipped his hat and smiled. "I'll have your wagon hitched up and pick you up at three o'clock. You can gather what you need, and we'll head out early."

"Wait, Gabriel, there is something else." She

laid a gentle hand on his arm, as though to pull him farther away from the children.

"Do you know the Walker family?"

Gabriel glanced over at the school steps. "Mason Walker's folks?"

She nodded.

"Not well. Met the man once, the boy and mother a couple of times at the store, but they keep to themselves. Has something happened?"

"It's his son. He doesn't bring a lunch to school, and he looks as though he's missed some meals and doesn't sleep enough."

Gabriel leaned toward her. "That's your lunch he's eating."

"Yes, but one meal a day is not going to help that boy. I don't know how things are done out here, but before I . . . we lost everything, I volunteered a few days a week at an orphan home. I know what starvation looks like."

"I'm sorry to say that I don't know everyone too well these days. The Mason's haven't been here long, but if anyone knows about them, it would be Loren. People around here are proud, and they won't take charity, but I'll see what I can do. You see to it that the boy has enough at lunch each day. I'll tell Loren that you'll add the food to the ranch account."

"Gabriel, I can manage enough."

"No arguments. For the boy's sake, do this."

Isabelle searched the meadow for her brother and Mason. Though older than Andrew, Mason Walker wasn't much bigger.

"Yes, of course."

"I'll return at the end of school." Gabriel squeezed her hand and waved to Andrew before leaving.

Andrew ran over the dormant grass to his sister. "Is he coming back?"

"After school."

"Do we get to go back to the ranch?"

"We do, but you must behave yourself there. We're guests while we're in Gabriel's home."

"But I get to see the horses again, right?"

Isabelle laughed, and knew Gabriel would see to it. "Yes, you do. Now it's time for afternoon lessons." She rang the bell hanging from a post on the porch of the school and watched as the students raced back inside. It took her a few moments to clear her head and set her mind to the history lesson she was about to give her students. Mason looked up at her with wide eyes and more alert than he'd been all day.

Gabriel was as good as his word. Just after three o'clock, Isabelle and Andrew walked hand in hand up to the cottage. Gabriel had the wagon hitched and his horse tied to the back. He smiled as they walked up, and Andrew raced to Gabriel and jumped in his arms so he could be swung around in the air. It ended with the customary tickle to the stomach and the onset of laughter from her brother.

Isabelle didn't believe it necessary to argue over the way Gabriel smoothly maneuvered her into agreeing. "I'll just be a few moments. Andrew, please come and help pack up your things for the night."

The boy quickly obeyed and was ready to be on his way to the ranch and the horses Gabriel promised he could name.

Gabriel didn't think Isabelle was thrilled about going to the ranch, and he hadn't figured out how he was going to answer her earlier question of why he married her. In the beginning, it had been to help her protect Andrew, and to keep brother and sister together. However, in just the extremely short time since he'd met her, it had already grown into something more. He was still undeniably attracted to her and being married without the benefits of that marriage proved to be difficult. He loved Andrew already, for the child had a way to tug at every corner of his heart with his innocence. Gabriel realized now that some of the love already flowed over to Isabelle. He couldn't quite explain it, but this possessiveness toward her was a new experience, and he really did want the world to know they were married.

A little more than an hour later, they were safely at Hawk's Peak.

Mabel ushered them inside. "Come, child. We'll get you both settled in, and you can keep me company while I fix supper. I sure would like to hear about New Orleans."

Isabelle and Andrew followed Mabel up the stairs. "Have you been there?"

"Lordy, no, but I got a cousin who lived there before the war."

Isabelle didn't know how to respond to that because there was the possibility that Mabel's cousin had been a slave before the war ended."

"Where is your cousin now?"

Mabel showed them into the guest room. "He didn't make it out, but he sure did like New Orleans." Mabel smoothed down the top quilt on the bed. "Miss Brenna stayed in here when she first came to the Peak. It's a lucky room."

Isabelle wasn't sure what made the room lucky, but she wasn't surprised to find it tastefully decorated and welcoming. The mansion her family once owned in New Orleans had been grand but more flamboyant, and Isabelle found that she preferred this quiet, dignified show of wealth. With Isabelle's permission, Mabel whisked Andrew away to one of the other guest rooms. Andrew was excited to be treated with such importance, and he didn't protest when Mabel showed him to his room. He looked at his sister upon exiting her room and said in the best imitation of an adult that he could. "Isabelle, I will see you at supper."

She thoughtfully refrained from laughing until he walked done the hall. The quiet house settled around Isabelle when she made her way downstairs. Andrew waited at the bottom of the stairs and bowed grandly to her with a broad sweep of his short arm, the lessons their mother insisted upon not forgotten. She noticed, though, that he looked to the side and whispered something. Her eyes darted over, but she didn't see anyone. Once at the bottom, she took her brother's outstretched arm and bowed right back. "You're very courtly tonight, Andrew."

"I'm not Andrew tonight, I'm Squire Andrew."

Mirth danced in her eyes. "A squire, are you?"

"Uh-huh, Gabriel said so. I wanted to be a knight, but he said I had to be a squire before I could be a knight."

She enjoyed her brother's antics and joined in their laughter. "Gabriel is quite right, Squire Andrew. Will you be my escort?"

Gabriel watched from around the corner and winked when Andrew executed a near-perfect bow, letting him know he was doing fine. He waited until they'd gone into the living room and walked in a moment later.

"I see you've found yourself a suitable escort, milady," Gabriel said, his smile infectious.

"I have, milord. Goodness, what stories have you been telling him?"

"I'd think that a teacher would approve of the additional reading." Gabriel had asked Andrew to help him out tonight with his little bit of play acting, and he was delighted that despite her earlier resistance, the light entertainment worked to bring a smile back to her eyes.

"Oh, I do indeed approve, though I've never seen Andrew quite so taken with a role before."

"I'm not Andrew. I'm a squire, Ibby. Gabriel said I could be."

Gabriel moved around the table and stood

behind Isabelle's chair.

"And what do squires do?"

Andrew thought about that seriously for a moment and smiled. "Oh, we have to pull out chairs for ladies, huh?"

"Right you are."

Andrew struggled, only a little, as Gabriel helped guide the chair away from the table as Isabelle took her seat.

"Thank you, kind squire." Isabelle leaned over and bestowed her brother with a kiss to his cheek.

"You have to kiss Gabriel, too, since he helped and you're married."

The tray Mabel carried into the dining room rattled, and she stopped mid-stride to avoid dropping the contents. All eyes turned to her and her slackened jaw. Isabelle turned red, and Gabriel wouldn't look Mabel in the eyes.

"If you think you're going to get off without telling me what's going on Gabriel Gallagher, think again." Mabel set the silver tray on the long, heavy, oak table, held her arms akimbo and stared at the two adults in the room.

It was, however, the youngest of the group who willingly did the telling. "Gabriel married Ibby at the church. He gets to be my big brother now, and he's going to show me how to ride horses just like him." The boy genuinely thought that he'd done well by explaining what transpired between the two adults. He took his own seat and innocently waited for the meal to begin.

"I'm waiting." Mabel didn't move.

Gabriel knew he was in a tough situation, as he had hoped to speak with Isabelle before they told his family what happened. He didn't want her embarrassed any more than she already was, but it seemed he didn't have much of a choice if they ever wanted to eat again.

"We did marry, Mabel."

"It's not what you might think, though," Isabelle hurriedly added.

"And what might I be thinking?"

Mabel's face remained unreadable.

"I promise you that I in no way mean any ill

will toward Gabriel. He helped me out with a little situation, but it isn't permanent, I do assure you." Isabelle prayed that her fervent speech was enough to placate the housekeeper.

"Well, why not?"

"What do you mean?"

"Why is it not permanent?"

"Oh, well . . . Gabriel?"

He really should have helped her along with this, but he did want it to be permanent and said as much.

Isabelle shot him a seething look. "You're not helping."

"Ibby, why are you mad at Gabriel?" Andrew stared at her from his own padded chair stacked with books that Gabriel had added for an extra lift.

"I'm not mad at Gabriel, I'm just going mad," she mumbled to herself, but three sets of ears heard her. Gabriel leaned over and whispered in her ear. "I should warn you, Mabel hears *everything*. At least when she's in the same room."

"I heard that."

"See."

"Gabriel, please." Isabelle was fully exasperated now and fought against showing it in a stranger's home.

"Listen, Isabelle, why don't we enjoy this fine meal that Mabel went to a lot of work to prepare, and we'll speak of this in private afterward." He shot Mabel a look that not-too-subtly told her he wasn't going to say anything else. The elder kept her silence for now.

Isabelle was grateful when the meal ended, and Mabel dragged Andrew away for a bath, which surprisingly he only quibbled at for a moment until Mabel bribed him with a cookie. Isabelle preferred not to use that method with Andrew, but tonight she felt too weary to say anything about it.

"Do you know where the library is?"

Isabelle glanced up to see Gabriel standing next to her chair. She nodded.

"Will you meet me in there for our talk? I have to take care of something out at the bunkhouse.

It shouldn't take long."

"That's fine."

"Wait, Gabriel." Isabelle motioned him into the hall. "I know you haven't had much time, but did you learn anything about Mason Walker's father?"

Gabriel glanced over his shoulder and into the kitchen, but they were well out of hearing distance. "That's one thing I wanted to tell you. Walker was at the blacksmith's when I stopped by. He didn't take kindly to my mention of Mason's situation, but I got the feeling things are tough for them right now."

"Is there any way to help?"

"Didn't need to. Otis Lincoln, he's the blacksmith, offered Walker some work. That's what he was doing there. I spoke with Otis and he'd been out to the Walker farm a few times."

"Then Mason will be all right?"

Gabriel nodded. "We have some building to do on the ranch in a few months, and we can always use another good man to help out. Between Otis and work here, the Walkers should do all right until spring when they can plant their first crops."

Isabelle stood up on her toes, leaned into Gabriel, and brushed her lips to his cheek. "Thank you."

Her eyes glistened, and Gabriel gave into the moment. His fingers swept over hers, gliding up her arms. He caressed her neck above the fabric of her dress and trailed the lines of her face. Their bodies inched together, and he watched her eyes flutter close. Lifting her chin, he stared at her soft lips and lowered his face. Their breath mingled, then a loud clatter and clang from behind broke the spell. Mabel shouted at the pot, and Gabriel watched Isabelle's lips turn up into a smile.

"I'll be back in soon."

She nodded. Gabriel left without another word. Isabelle entered the library in half a daze and walked the length of the room a few times to calm her racing heart, but her smile remained. It was her favorite room in the sprawling stone house. Anyone who loved the written word as she did would have to agree. Isabelle wasn't able to bring along all of their precious books from her family's library, and faint memories flashed to her as she ran her hands along the spines of the hardbound volumes. She found a comfortable settee on which to sit and wait. Ten minutes later, she wondered what could be taking Gabriel so long and found a book of Walt Whitman's sultry and romantic poetry to help pass the time.

Gabriel knew he was taking too long to return to Isabelle, but when he went out to speak with Henry about the supplies he ordered for the addition to the bunkhouse, he needed to work out a few other issues as well. One of the fences in the high pasture had been busted down, and though Henry didn't know by what, he was sure the act was deliberate. He told him that they repaired the fence but were unable to find any sign of what or who did it. Gabriel told him to have one of the hands ride that part of the range over the next week to see if anything else happened. One of the new young men they hired for a trial period was slow to learn and as Henry said, just plain lazy. A few more concerns were voiced and handled, and by the time Gabriel returned to the house, over an hour had passed.

When he went into the library to find Isabelle, he found an angel. Her head rested against the back of the settee, and she had tucked her legs up beneath her skirts on the seat. A book lay open on her lap, but it was obvious she hadn't read far before sleep took over. Gabriel walked quietly into the room, allowing the heavy rugs beneath him to muffle his footfalls. She looked so peaceful, and Gabriel didn't want to disturb her. He wanted only to take her in his arms and hold her tightly against him and never let go.

Gently he leaned down and lifted her into his arms. She appeared to be an extremely sound sleeper for she didn't move as he adjusted her arms around his neck to keep her head up on his shoulder. Her long form fit perfectly in his strong arms, and he carried her from the room and up the staircase. From the quietness upstairs, Gabriel guessed that Mabel had already put Andrew to bed for them. She had such a way with children, so it wasn't a surprise to Gabriel that she'd been able to win over the young boy. The cookie probably helped.

Gabriel carried Isabelle into the guest room and laid her on the large four-poster bed with its sweet-smelling sheets and plump, warm quilts. He removed her shoes, taking a few moments to figure out the small buttons and set them aside. He unbuttoned the top three buttons of her dress and then stopped, realizing that removal of her clothes would only lead to the breaking of a promise. He pulled the downy quilt up to her chin and stared down at her.

Before he thought better of it, Gabriel scooted her slightly over to the center of the large bed. He removed his shoes and jacket, unbuttoned the top half of his white shirt and lay down next to her. In her sleep, Isabelle moved closer to the warmth of his body. A very short time later, Gabriel fell asleep holding in his arms the woman he loved.

7

Isabelle may have been born in France, but she arrived with her parents in New Orleans when she was only a young girl of six. She remembered glimpses of her life back in France, and then Pennsylvania, but the memories were distant and often flitted in and out of her dreams. She realized after a while that the memories came only at times of fear when she would have wished for something else. The troubling dreams haunted her for many nights after her parents' death and even a few times since she and Andrew rode into Briarwood, Montana, on that weathered, red stagecoach. Last night though, nothing haunted her. The old memories, good and bad, had somehow been kept at bay. It wasn't until she groggily rubbed the sleep from her eyes that she knew why.

Her dress was still on and mostly buttoned save for a few at the top, and someone had removed her shoes. She felt warm under the beautiful quilt, but it took only a moment to realize it wasn't just the quilt warming her body. Isabelle had never moved so quickly, and she nearly rolled herself onto the heavy Persian rug below. The quick movements roused Gabriel from sleep, and it took considerably less time for him to grasp the situation.

"You promised, Gabriel, you promised!"

Gabriel wasn't a light sleeper. In fact, it often took a great deal to wake him from a pleasant slumber, and last night had been a peaceful sleep. He enjoyed waking with Isabelle in the room. What he didn't enjoy was being yelled at before he'd even drunk his first cup of coffee. Mabel would most likely be back from her early-morning egg gathering in the barn, and he almost tasted the coffee he knew she'd have brewing. Isabelle's words, though, did enough to bring him about.

"Blazes, Isabelle, it's too early for yelling, and I didn't break my promise." Gabriel moved around the side of the bed until he located his boots and slipped them on. Anger and irritation quickly overshadowed his happy memories of holding her in his arms the night before.

"What do you call waking up next to me, Gabriel?"

"If you'll take a good look at yourself, and me for that matter, you'll see we're both fully dressed. More's the pity." He mumbled the last part but obviously not softly enough.

Isabelle's eyes slanted, and she stopped her tirade long enough to cast her gaze across the room. Gabriel hoped she was calming herself and realizing that he spoke the truth.

"What are you doing in this room? I don't recall walking myself up those stairs last night."

With a deep sigh, Gabriel took a few steps closer but stopped and held up his hands when she took a few steps back.

"You were asleep when I finally got to the

library, which I do apologize for. I didn't want to wake you, so I carried you up here, took off your damn shoes and may the devil take me, I lay down on the same bed with you."

"Why?"

He expected some other response. He wasn't sure what but something other than the innocent look that quickly crept into her eyes. She didn't have a clue and that was just as frustrating as wanting her.

"Because I wanted to and because you're my wife, Isabelle."

"But . . ."

"I know, you don't see it as a real marriage, but since it is legal and binding, you really shouldn't see anything wrong with *sleeping* on the same bed." He put great emphasis on the fact that they'd only slept. She now looked embarrassed and flustered and so beautiful in the soft morning light coming through the window.

"You shouldn't have done it." She spoke softly, but Gabriel heard each word and they didn't please him.

"I'm truly sorry you feel that way." He ran a stiff hand through his dark hair, mussing it more than sleeping did. "It's early still, but we can all have breakfast, and then I'll drive you in for school."

She didn't respond with anything more than a curt nod, and he left the room feeling like a fool. *Though to be fair, it's my own damn fault.* He went down the stairs praying for a fresh cup of coffee and stopped.

His brother never did have the best timing. "Thought I heard a wagon approach. We didn't expect you until next week."

"We managed an earlier train," Ethan said.

Gabriel placed a light kiss on Brenna's cheek and embraced Ethan. "Damn glad to have you back home, Ethan." He glanced at Brenna. "Sorry." Gabriel grinned at them both. "Glad to see the two of you finally came to your senses. I thought I heard Mabel down here with you."

"She's gone into the back of the house. In fact, we have a surprise for you, but first, is Eliza with the cattle?"

Gabriel looked a little disgruntled. "No, because she's not here, and you want to know why? I'll tell you why." He pulled a crumbled letter from his pocket and shoved it at Ethan's chest. With a perplexed look, Ethan smoothed the paper and read while Brenna leaned over to look.

She reacted immediately. "You actually let her go alone?"

"You traveled alone from Scotland," Ethan reminded her.

"I did at that, but I like to believe that if my brother had been there, he most certainly wouldn't have allowed it."

"Now it's not as though Liza gave me much of a choice." Gabriel attempted to defend himself. "She left that letter with a note of her own saying that she wouldn't be away long. She left before dawn. I'm beginning to feel like I'm the only Gallagher at the ranch these days."

"This doesn't say who she planned to meet," Ethan said.

"I'm well aware of that. I went to the telegraph

office to see what I could find out and who sent it, but the damn man won't say anything. Something about a telegraph operator's ridiculous oath."

"Bullshit." Ethan swore and sheepishly looked down at his wife's amused expression. "Sorry." He leaned down and kissed her wrinkled brow. "But it must be the Tremaines if she went to Kentucky."

"The Tremaine's?"

"Oh dear." Brenna leaned back to look up at Ethan. "You didn't tell them in your letter?"

Ethan shook his head. "Not about that. We have a lot to catch up on."

Gabriel took another folded paper from his shirt pocket. "This one also came yesterday." He handed the missive to Brenna.

Ethan saw the expression on her face and took it from her, then glanced up at Gabriel who just stood there watching them. Obviously he hadn't read it.

"Ethan, it's really him, isn't it?" Brenna sounded almost in awe.

"Really who?" Gabriel peered over the top of Ethan's hand for a look at the telegram. Ethan saved him the trouble and handed it over.

"You've found Ramsey?"

"It seems so, but this appears to be written by a Nathaniel Tremaine. Didn't you write to his sister?"

"His sister? These are the Tremaines you think Eliza went to see?" Gabriel tried to keep up with a conversation he knew nothing about. Brenna nodded and looked down again at the note. It was signed Nathaniel Tremaine.

"Yes, but how could she have known about them when we only learned before coming home?"

Ethan brought his wife closer to him and lifted her face up with his finger.

"You want to go out there, don't you?"

She nodded absently, and Ethan offered to go to Kentucky himself.

"No, I couldn't bear to be away from you. Couldn't I go with you?"

"I could go."

Ethan and Brenna both turned to Gabriel after he made this offer.

Brenna shook her head. "No, you shouldn't have to leave either. I really don't know what to do. A strange feeling I have about this. These people seem to know Ramsey, and this man writes back instead of his sister, if it was his sister. None of this makes sense."

"No, it doesn't."

Ethan finally relented. "All right. We'll send a telegraph back to this Nathaniel Tremaine. If Eliza did go there, we can hope she'll get the message. As for Ramsey, let's see what your detective can find out about the Tremaines before we make any decisions."

He waited until Brenna gave him her agreement. "All right?"

"Agreed."

"One us of should go after Eliza."

"I mean it, Ethan. I'll go now that I have a place to look."

Ethan considered that. "I don't like the thought of her traveling out there alone, but I don't think chasing her is the answer, and she wouldn't thank either of us for it. We'll have to trust her, and if we don't receive a response from the telegram, we'll ignore what I said and bring her home."

"Ah, Ethan, funny that you should mention detectives," Gabriel said, "but I hired one last month."

"Why did you need a detective?"

"To track down Nathan Hunter." Gabriel stole a quick glance at Brenna.

"Why would you be looking for my grandfather?"

"Some of our boys have noticed activity over at the Double Bar the past few months. No sign of Hunter yet, but it just didn't sit right." Gabriel glanced back and forth between the two but received no response. "Liza said something strange a few days before she left. It didn't make sense and still doesn't, but I felt we should at least cover our bases."

"What did Eliza say?" Ethan asked.

"Something about healing old wounds. Like I

said, I don't know what she meant, but it's nothing to worry about." Gabriel gave his attention to Brenna. "Being his granddaughter, you had the right to know what I did. I would have asked first but . . ."

Brenna placed her hand on Gabriel's arm and smiled up at him warmly. She always wanted a brother. "I trust you to do what you feel is necessary. And Gabriel? Thank you."

Gabriel smiled at his new sister and was about to say something else when Ethan interrupted.

"We'll talk more about this later. Now if you'll excuse us."

Ethan and Brenna stood at the base of the staircase and watched as a tall pretty woman with gray eyes stormed down the stairs. Her clothes appeared a bit wrinkled, though of excellent quality, and her golden hair seemed to have been hastily plaited. She held her head high and gave the two strangers a curt nod before leaving the house. She ignored Gabriel who turned bright red, his face looking about as it did when they arrived.

"Gabriel? Who was that woman and why did she look so angry?" Brenna stared after the woman.

"My wife. Sort of."

"Your wife?" Both Ethan and Brenna yelled in unison. They looked to the now empty doorway and back to Gabriel, who looked genuinely guilty.

"What do you mean 'sort of'?"

It was Ethan who had asked that, but Brenna cleared her throat trying to hide her amazement and said, "Well, she's beautiful Gabriel. Congratulations."

Ethan wasn't as pleased as his wife. "You said nothing happened while I was away, just business as usual."

"Yeah, well I may have left out a few things."

"A few things?"

"A lot of things. I'll explain everything, and there's a lot to explain, but you'll love her, I know you will. Her brother, too."

Brenna gasped. "Her brother lives here, too?"

"Well no, they live in the cottage. Actually,

they do live here now, but it's not what you think."

Ethan grinned. "You may want to go after her."

Gabriel raced for the door and left the couple staring after him.

"Isabelle, please just wait a moment." She heard Gabriel's voice and attempted to calm herself. Isabelle turned and faced him when she heard the pleading sincerity in his voice. A quick glance on the horizon told her that most everyone was up before the sun made a full appearance. *Didn't people sleep around this place?*

"I noticed that you had company, and I didn't want to interrupt."

"It's not company, it's my brother and his wife. Isabelle, please don't leave angry. I promise you that nothing happened last night."

"I know." Her quiet admission caught him off guard.

"Well, then why the blazes did you yell at me?"

Since he had every right to his frustration, and

she to hers, Isabelle didn't take offense. "At first I was just so shocked to find you next to me in bed. The shock turned to embarrassment, though I don't know why I should have been now that I think on it."

Understanding now, Gabriel pulled her into his arms and that she didn't pull away from him pleased him more than she could know. "That's not all there is to it."

"No it isn't. I sensed that I was safe last night, Gabriel. Very safe, or at least a part of me did. When I realized that, it frightened me because I knew it couldn't last." She didn't pull away, but Gabriel did lean back slightly so that he could nudge her chin up.

His soothing voice caused shivers to course though her body. "It doesn't have to end, Isabelle. It doesn't ever have to end."

Isabelle closed her eyes and leaned back into his chest, her head safely tucked against his shoulder and their arms around each other's waists. She didn't want to hope, to dream that what he said was true. There were more fears she didn't want to share. Her parents, whom she knew loved each other dearly, failed in their love. If a love as strong as theirs could meet such a devastating end, what hope was there for a marriage of her own? Isabelle feared the risk of losing what she loved most in the world. She pulled gently back from him and gave him a soft smile.

"I'm all right, though I believe I unduly embarrassed myself in front of your brother and sister-in-law." Her cheeks flushed a little, remembering her rude behavior a few moments before.

"Don't worry. They thought nothing of it." He ignored her quiet snort with a smile. "I assure you that Ethan and Brenna have stories of their own. What do you say? I'd really like to introduce you."

Isabelle eyed him narrowly. "As what?"

He still stood on shaky ground as far as the subject of their marriage was concerned. Not to mention he already told them. "That's up to you."

He didn't fool her. "They know, don't they?"

"Well, they needed some kind of explanation when you stormed down the staircase, and I wasn't going to lie."

Isabelle looked back up to the house and let out a deep sigh. "Andrew is probably eating everything in Mabel's kitchen."

"I promise it won't hurt, Isabelle."

Reluctantly, Isabelle linked her hand with Gabriel's, and he pulled her along to meet his family.

"Ah, here's the happy couple." The remark earned Ethan a jab in the ribs from his wife, and he wisely shut up.

Gabriel looked at him as though asking for a little sympathy, but it was the embarrassment and defiance Ethan saw in Isabelle that made him apologize, in his own way.

"Mabel explained the situation to us." Ethan stood and walked over to greet Isabelle. His wife, however, sat, and Gabriel noticed she held a baby. He ignored Ethan's statement.

"Well, I'll be. Is this your other surprise?"

Gabriel practically dragged Isabelle over to Brenna and then let go of her hand to demand the sleeping child. With a laugh, Brenna untangled the baby's fingers from her fire-red hair and handed Jacob gently into the arms of her new brother-in-law.

Isabelle enjoyed seeing the smile that lit up Gabriel's face. She'd never seen a man so taken with a baby and that little dream in the back of her mind moved to the forefront, enticing and teasing her.

Ethan thought the look telling, and he decided to wait and see if Mabel happened to be right. Mabel swore on her departed mother's grave that the pair of them were in love and just as stupid as Ethan and Brenna had been.

Gabriel finally came back to them but wouldn't give the baby back. "I have to tell you, Ethan, you've brought back the best present ever, next to a new sister, of course."

"Well aren't you the dear-hearted one." Brenna's lyrical Scottish brogue brought a smile to Isabelle even though Gabriel already mentioned she came from that country.

Isabelle envied Brenna's curvy frame, and she remembered when she'd been able to fill her gowns out as nicely.

Gabriel once again grabbed their attention when he sat down and motioned Isabelle to join him. When the baby started fussing a bit, Brenna moved forward to take him from his reluctant uncle.

"So Mabel enlightened you, huh?" Gabriel took Isabelle's hand. "Well, just to do this right, Isabelle Rousseau Gallagher, I'd like you to meet my brother Ethan and his beautiful better half, Brenna."

"You could charm the cold Scottish winds into a new direction, Gabriel Gallagher."

He laughed at Brenna's apt remark, but his eyes settled on his brother who stroked his wife's back.

"Mabel did tell us," Ethan said, "though there wasn't much she could say except something about you helping Isabelle by marrying her. Do you mind telling us how this came about?"

Ethan wasn't unkind, Isabelle believed, but this affected his family, and he had a right to know.

Gabriel turned to Isabelle. "It's your story, up to you."

She nodded and faced her new brother-in-law, a relation she never dared to hope for. "I suppose I should start with telling you that both of my parents passed on over a month ago in New Orleans where I lived most of my years." She knew some of what she said would be new information for Gabriel, but she preferred to tell them all at once. "We had no one else there, and our financial circumstances changed overnight. You see, I have a young brother, Andrew."

Ethan nodded. "We've met him. Delightful boy. Henry's giving him a full tour of the property. Not to worry, he's safe," he added, when he saw the concern cross her face.

"Well, Andrew wasn't well and neither of us wanted to stay in the city. Shortly before the day of their deaths, I had seen an advertisement for a teaching position here in Briarwood. I hadn't seriously considering coming out here alone, but things changed. When I realized our limited options, we left New Orleans and came up north.

"My father's will gave custody of Andrew to an aunt we've never met living in France. My father's lawyer saw no reason for us to worry over that since she lived so far away and was not likely to ever come. Well, apparently she did come and demanded that Andrew be returned to her."

Ethan interrupted her. "So how does marriage help?"

"My father put a clause in his will stating that if I married, I could retain custody of Andrew."

"An odd clause to be sure," Brenna added with a frown.

"I thought the same thing, but I remember it very clearly because I hoped not to have to take such measures. That all changed when my father's lawyer wrote of my aunt's demand of returning Andrew."

"And your aunt, she's let this go now?" Ethan asked.

Isabelle shook her head. "Not yet. She's

demanding proof of the marriage."

"I'll have Reverend Phillips make up a duplicate of the marriage decree to send to the lawyer." Gabriel offered Isabelle an encouraging smile and held her hand closely within his own.

Isabelle jumped from the chaise.

"Goodness, Gabriel, I have to get to the schoolhouse. It will take an hour to get there and at this rate, I'll be late."

Gabriel stood. "It's not a problem. I'll hitch up the wagon and take you back in right now. It won't be quite a rush with Ethan back. Let me go and round up Andrew and I'll be right back." He turned to his brother. "There are a few things I'd like to speak with you about when I get back."

Ethan nodded, and Gabriel left the room. "Ladies, if you'll excuse me, I need a few words with Mabel." The women nodded and Ethan took his leave.

Brenna motioned for Isabelle to take her husband's abandoned space on the settee. "I know you have to be on your way, but I hope that you'll come back tonight. I realize that your circumstances are unusual, but I'd very much like the opportunity to get to know you." The outstretched hand of friendship was unexpected and so sincere that Isabelle found herself humbled and instantly liking Brenna Gallagher.

"Gabriel feels that until the custody situation is taken care of that I should stay here at the ranch."

"Where have you been staying, if not at the ranch?"

"At the Gallagher's cottage just a little ways down the road from the schoolhouse."

"I've heard of the cottage, but I've not had the pleasure of seeing it."

It was Isabelle's turn to look confused, and Brenna couldn't hold the light laugh. "I've been in Scotland most of the year. Ethan and I didn't exactly have a normal courtship."

Gabriel had mentioned something to Isabelle about Ethan and Brenna having stories of their own to tell. He came back in to tell Isabelle that both Andrew and the wagon were ready to go.

Brenna laid a gentle hand on Isabelle's arm. "Will we see you tonight?"

Isabelle glanced briefly at Gabriel, then back to his sister-in-law. "Yes, tonight."

8

By the time Gabriel let them off at the schoolhouse, Isabelle was grateful that she brought along everything she needed, for just ten minutes later the students began arriving. The day turned out to be an enjoyable one for Isabelle, and she once again gave a silent thank you to have found this position. Isabelle fervently prayed that the copy of the marriage certificate Gabriel was having drawn up today would settle her aunt's ire and let the matter rest.

The end of the school day came too quickly for Isabelle and her students. It was with a small personal pride for her that the students appeared reluctant to leave. They had more than just the eager desire to learn. Since the moment she first met the children, she bonded with her students in friendship and found that even a child's perspective on something could teach her a thing or two.

Gabriel patiently waited outside of the schoolhouse, standing casually next to the wagon. Isabelle suffered a measure of guilt because he drove all the way back into town to pick them up, but Gabriel looked at ease. As something they both enjoyed, Gabriel and Andrew performed their ritual flight in the air and with a gentle landing, Gabriel set the boy on his feet with a grin.

"All is well, I hope?"

"Very well, thank you." Isabelle set her wide-brimmed wool hat on top of her golden hair without bothering to tie the ribbons. Despite the cool October air, the sun beat down, blinding her eyes.

Gabriel watched as Andrew climbed into the wagon and turned his attention to Isabelle. "I sent off the copy of our marriage certificate to the lawyer. Hopefully that will end any questions your aunt has about custody."

Isabelle nodded in agreement. "I can't understand why when she's never shown the slightest interest in even meeting us."

"Well, there's nothing we can do now. Let's go home and enjoy Mabel's delicious cooking. I promised Andrew another riding lesson. That is, of course, if you agree?"

"Of course."

Gabriel handed Isabelle up to the wagon seat and settled himself next to Andrew so that the boy sat safely between them.

Once back at Hawk's Peak, they unloaded from the wagon and Isabelle laid a gentle hand on Gabriel's arm asking for a moment of his time. But Ethan walked up, pulling along a beautiful and grand black stallion.

Ethan tipped his hat to the new arrivals. "Good to see you again, Isabelle. Brenna's been looking forward to your return this evening. I think she's excited to have another woman her age around here."

"You're not enough for her, big brother?"

Gabriel asked with a grin, which earned him a light punch to the shoulder.

"I'm plenty enough," he returned with a grin of his own and turned to the young boy staring admiringly up at his stallion.

"You want to take a ride with me, Andrew?"

The little boy nodded eagerly. "Leopold's one of my favorite horses, even though I didn't get to name him."

Ethan looked questioningly down at the boy and then at his brother.

Gabriel laughed. "I told Andrew he could name all of the horses here. He was disappointed when I told him that you and Eliza already named yours."

Ethan turned back to Andrew. "How about that ride on Leopold, and perhaps you'll convince me to change his name."

With an eager nod from Andrew, Ethan settled on the stallion's back and Gabriel handed the boy up to him.

As they rode off, Isabelle looked on worriedly. "You can trust Ethan."

"Oh, I do. It's just, that is a large stallion. Is he not a little wild?"

"Yes and no. Yes when Ethan wants him to be and no for the same reasons. He'd never put a child up there on the animal alone, but with Ethan behind him, Leo there is as safe as a docile mare." Gabriel gave his full attention to his wife. "You wanted to talk about something?"

Isabelle wrapped her shawl more closely at the sudden and unexpected wind that crept up.

"I wanted to speak with you about this arrangement."

Gabriel didn't want to hear what he thought she was going to say and asked warily, "What arrangement?"

"Gabriel, I'm grateful for everything, truly. You've helped us in ways that I can never repay. You shouldn't have to drive the wagon into town twice a day like this. It's a great deal of time out of your day, not to mention your work." She lifted her hand in a wide arc indicating the ranch.

"I happen to enjoy driving you and Andrew

into town. Besides, we agreed that until the custody issue was settled, you should stay out here to avoid unwanted questions concerning our marriage."

She looked up at him, and Gabriel saw something that he previously only hoped for, at least he thought he saw it. He was just about to voice his thoughts and ask her, when a rider came barreling up on the back of a Pinto. The rider looked like he just ran as fast as the animal. He also wore a worried expression, one that bothered Gabriel.

"What's going on, Henry?"

"It's Hunter. He's back."

Ethan rode up with Andrew just in time to hear that. Gabriel quickly moved around the stallion to gather Andrew into his arms. Ethan nearly yelled, "What the hell do you mean he's back? He was supposed to have been run out of this territory or jailed, and he sure isn't with the marshal."

Henry took a deep breath and told them what he knew. Both brothers grew angrier with each word.

"Colton and me rode to the north range and we found some boy on this side of the fence. We caught up to him right quick when he tried riding away, but I didn't recognize him."

"Where is he?" asked Ethan.

"Colton's ridin' in with him. The kid took a spill from his saddle, so they're comin' in a little slow. Anyway, he said a man from the other ranch paid him to come over here and report back what he saw. The kid said he didn't know nothing else. I almost believe him, and I reckon he's too young and stupid to lie about it."

Ethan and Gabriel glanced at each other only once, and Ethan turned and rode out with Henry.

Gabriel turned to Isabelle. "I can't explain right now, but I will as soon as I get back. Please take Andrew inside and tell Brenna that Ethan and I have gone to the north range." He kissed her quickly on the mouth, drawing a startled gasp from her lips. Gabriel ran on strong legs to the stable and just a few minutes later, Isabelle and Andrew watched as Gabriel raced after his brother. Isabelle led a worried Andrew to the front porch just as Brenna stepped outside.

"What's all the commotion out here? I was putting Jacob down or I'd have been out earlier." Brenna noticed that Isabelle peered over her shoulder, but when her eyes darted over the land, she saw nothing but a bit of dust in the air.

"Gabriel and Ethan went to the north range, whatever that means."

"It's almost time for supper. Did they say why?" Brenna motioned them into the comforts of the sitting room and told Andrew he could go and get some fresh oatmeal cookies from Mabel.

With an eager smile, the boy disappeared from the room. Isabelle removed her bonnet and shawl and took a seat on the settee across from Brenna.

"One of your men, Henry I believe, rode up and said something about finding a boy on the north range. It sounded as though he'd been trespassing, but they also said something about someone named Hunter."

Brenna dropped the tea cup she meant to hand to Isabelle, and the hot beverage splashed on the tea service when the cup shattered. Brenna immediately began mopping up the mess with a white linen cloth. Isabelle put a gentle hand on the other woman's arm.

"What's wrong, Brenna?"

Brenna finished mopping up the mess calmly and glanced at the doorway to make sure that Mabel or Andrew hadn't heard. She turned her attention back to Isabelle and let out a deep, staggered breath. "I apologize for that."

"Don't worry yourself over it. Tell me why you've turned three shades whiter."

"Nathan Hunter is my grandfather."

Isabelle looked perplexed. "Is that not a good thing?"

Brenna shook her head. "No, it's not. He's the reason I first came to Montana. I met Ethan and Gabriel when I arrived and found out right away that Nathan Hunter was not a well-liked man. Because of him, I have a twin brother I've never met, a grandmother who lives too far away to suit me, and the memory of an unpleasant kidnapping and the near death of my husband."

Brenna wiped away the single tear that dropped to her pale cheek, but with a glance at Isabelle, a restorative soft laugh escaped from her throat. Isabelle looked positively confused. "Perhaps I should start from the beginning."

Twenty minutes later, Isabelle didn't feel quite so badly about her unusual situation with Gabriel. "I never would have imagined your courtship to be anything other than perfect. Your love for each other is quite evident. But what about your grandfather? Do you believe that he will come after you again?"

Brenna shook her head. "I'm not sure, though I wouldn't be surprised. He was already angry enough with the family before I came along, and I'm certain that his ire has doubled. He's been gone from here for almost a year, so I don't understand why he's back now."

The thundering of horses riding up to the house drew the attention of both women. Immediately they stood and stepped to the edge of the porch. Ethan, Gabriel, Henry, another man, and what appeared to be a boy, dismounted at the corral. The boy's hands were tied behind his back, and Henry slowly helped him down.

Ethan turned to see his wife outside and quickly walked over to her, kissing her soundly. "Where are Mabel and the children?"

"Jacob is napping, and Andrew went in for cookies." Brenna looked worriedly at the boy and then to her husband's eyes. "What's wrong?"

Gabriel walked up and placed an arm around Isabelle's waist, pulling her close. Isabelle understood his anger and was amazed at the restraint he showed. Anger over what, she didn't know, but his strong body nearly trembled with it.

Gabriel answered Brenna's question before Ethan had the chance. "Kyle Watkins," Gabriel said, indicating the young man who Henry led to the barn. "He was a lookout for Hunter. Apparently the old man is back and pretty set on revenge." He looked down at Isabelle. "Until he's caught it's not safe for you to be wandering around here."

Brenna spoke up before Isabelle responded. "I won't be held prisoner because of my own grandfather, Ethan."

Ethan felt her frustration in the grip she had on his hand, and he pulled her into his arms.

"Listen, love, I want you to go into town with Isabelle and Andrew. Take Jacob. You can stay at the cottage until this is over for good."

Brenna immediately started shaking her head and pulled away. "I won't be run off because of him either. This is our home, and Jacob and I aren't going anywhere."

Ethan debated arguing with her, but he saw her rigid stance and the bright determination in her eyes and knew it was useless. Reluctantly he nodded. "Fine, but until this over, you do not leave the house unless I'm with you. Understood?"

Brenna wanted to protest, but the worry in her husband's eyes made her agree. "I promise."

Only partially satisfied, Ethan turned to Isabelle. "I don't suppose we can get you and Andrew to stay out of harm's way either?" He directed the question to Isabelle, but Gabriel answered.

"They stay here."

Isabelle protested. "You'll only worry about us when you aren't around, Gabriel. At least at the cottage we're close to town."

Gabriel pulled her closer. "I'll only worry more if I can't get to you in case of trouble. Don't argue with me about this, please."

"We'll talk about this later," she murmured, but Gabriel didn't comment on that.

Instead he said, "Look, it's been a long day and we're not going to get any more answers tonight. A couple of the boys are keeping watch between our property and the Double Bar so we'll know of trouble before it hits. Let's have our supper and get some sleep."

Gabriel pulled Ethan aside after supper. "We have a problem, big brother."

"The other rider, the one Kyle told us about."
Gabriel nodded.

"I know, Gabe, but he's already back at the
Double Bar. We can't do anything about him
tonight. Tomorrow we'll pay a visit to Hunter
and hopefully end this."

"Tomorrow won't be soon enough for me."

9

"What happened to the boy?"
"They found him and took him back to the ranch."

"That probably means they know I'm here. Are they all there?"

The man shook his head.

"Only the brothers and your granddaughter. I saw another woman with a kid. I haven't seen the sister for a spell now."

"A kid you say? How old?"

"I reckon he ain't that old. Stood up only a few feet."

The wicked gleam in the older man's eyes caused the younger to back away. He'd been employed by the rancher for only two weeks and if not for the money and a bunk, he'd have left the day he met Hunter.

"Since the boys didn't manage to hold onto a mere girl the last time, I'll be taking care of things this time around."

"What are you planning, Mr. Hunter?"

"Taking someone's woman is one thing, taking a child is another, and it's sure to bring those boys out in the open so that I can end this once and for all."

The younger man looked nervous. "You sure you want to snatch that other lady's kid? From the looks of it, the lady belongs to the other brother."

Hunter shrugged. "It matters not who the woman belongs to. If the brat is there, then they'll both come. You can be sure of that."

"I don't know about this, Mr. Hunter."

Hunter grabbed the other man and jerked on the front of his shirt. "You work for me. Now you can finish the job or you can go back into town face down in the back of a wagon. It's up to you."

Gabriel had sent one of the men into town to give a message asking the reverend to fill in for Isabelle at the school. He explained the situation and asked the reverend to be discreet. The reverend sent a reply guaranteeing not to say anything and that she would still have the post once the trouble ended. He also told them to let him know if he might be of any other help.

"It's kind of the reverend to fill in, though I need to offer Darcie an explanation."

"Who's Darcie?"

"She's one of the students, though more like my assistant. I promised to tutor her after school."

"You can't tell her why, but we'll think of something, and when this is all over, I'll drive her out here if I have to for that tutoring."

"Gabriel, are all of you certain you don't want help from people in town?"

"The hands at Hawk's Peak are better equipped and suited to handle Hunter. Too many men could be detrimental, and we don't need to be risking anyone else."

"What about the marshal? Surely the law could help."

Both brothers looked at each other, and Brenna lowered her emerald-green eyes to hide her own expression.

"Marshal Wallis and his deputies failed to solve the problem the first time around," said Ethan. "We'll handle it this time."

Ethan didn't say anything more on the subject and retired from the room. Brenna glanced from the door and her retreating husband back to Isabelle. "Perhaps we should explain, Isabelle."

"It's all right, Brenna," Gabriel told his sister-in-law. "I'll take care of it. You go ahead and check in on that nephew of mine."

Brenna nodded to Gabriel and glanced worriedly at Isabelle before leaving the room.

Isabelle's eyes remained focused on Gabriel. "What do you need to explain?"

"We won't be involving the law until we have to," Gabriel told her. "Ethan blames Hunter's escaping the first time on Marshal Wallis's ineptitude. I happen to agree with him. The cattle killings and mischief are nothing compared to what happened to a good friend of Eliza. She was raped and later died from what Hunter's men did to her." Gabriel rubbed a hand over his dark hair. "The marshal and his deputies were always two steps behind Hunter. That same incompetence likely got the marshal killed not too long ago."

"Can you do this? Isabelle asked. "Can you, your brother, and the men here really do what you're saying on your own?"

Gabriel walked over, slowly ran his hands up her arms, and gently cradled her face in his hands. "We don't have a choice because losing everything we've fought for—allowing Hunter to win—is not a choice any of us are willing to make. If it takes years, then so be it, but Hunter won't win."

Isabelle lifted her hands and set them on Gabriel's strong arms. She gazed into his eyes and knew he needed her understanding. "Then Andrew and I should settle in for a long stay."

She watched the relief fill Gabriel's eyes and prayed they knew what they were doing.

Restless without Gabriel close to her, Isabelle tried to fall asleep alone. One night in his arms and now she couldn't stop tossing and turning in the large four-poster bed. She momentarily thought to check on Andrew, but after supper he'd been so tired that he probably slept peacefully—something she couldn't seem to manage.

What worried Isabelle at this point wasn't just that she was a prisoner inside the house or that her unfamiliar aunt wanted to take Andrew. The more time she spent around Gabriel as his wife, even if by name only, the more she realized she wanted to remain his wife, and in more than just name. Her affection for Gabriel, now deeply embedded within her heart, crept upon her softly.

He threw odd questions her way, asking her if she wanted more than a temporary arrangement, but she brushed those aside, not imagining he might be serious. She wanted it, though. Marriage had never been something at the forefront of her thoughts, but now she very much wanted to be a part of Gabriel's future, a part of his family's future.

Isabelle regretted missing school, but she now understood the importance of staying at the ranch. If Gabriel spent his time driving her in and out of town, then that left one less man at the ranch.

She lay in the large, quiet house staring at the ceiling after giving up on sleep. She pulled herself up, lit the lamp next to her bed, and picked up the book she left on the table before retiring. Half a page in, she heard a rumbling through the window she had left open to let in the cool night air. The rumbling grew louder, followed quickly by the commotion of people in the hall. Isabelle quickly pulled on her wrapper and opened the door to the hallway to see Ethan and Gabriel rushing down the hallway. She called out to Gabriel, but he must not have heard because he and Ethan soon disappeared from sight.

"Isabelle." Brenna came up behind Isabelle, calling her name in a panic.

"What's going on?"

"Ethan said the cattle are stampeding." Brenna fumbled with the ties of her robe but gave up and let the narrow strips of fabric fall.

"Is he certain? Is that the noise I hear?"

Brenna nodded. "Yes, he's certain. He told us to let no one leave the house. There's no way to tell how difficult it will be to get the cattle under control in the dark."

Isabelle leaned against the bannister that overlooked the lower hallway. "That sounds foolishly dangerous, Brenna."

"They know what they're doing, Isabelle. Trust that," Brenna said reassuringly, though she couldn't stop the rising worry knowing her husband was out there.

The men in the bunkhouse had been quickly moved into action by the sound of the cattle rumbling across the land. Ben and Colton saddled horses for Ethan and Gabriel and were ready when they arrived at the stable.

"What in the hell happened?" Ethan shouted to Ben over the noise from outside.

"No way to know yet."

Gabriel mounted Zeus alongside the others. He heard the cattle running over the pastures. They were somehow far too close to the house. Gabriel could only be grateful that the boys only brought down half the herd from the higher pastures. They were going to have a devil of a time getting these animals under control without the light of the moon.

"Gabe. You and some of the boys flank them, and the rest of us will try getting in front of them and turn them, but it might be too late for that." Ethan looked at the others in the stable, knowing the other men had already headed out to do their part. "Nobody play hero. If we have to let them run it out, we will." Ethan glanced back at the house. "I don't like this, Gabe."

"I asked Frank and Sam to stay behind," Gabriel said.

"You also suspect something's going on, don't you?" Ethan asked.

"We do think too much alike, brother." When his brother urged his stallion toward the stable doors, Gabriel reached over and stopped him. "Ethan, wait. You have a wife and son to consider. You take the flank."

"Not a chance, Gabriel."

"You've been big brother long enough. Consider what you'd lose."

Ethan slapped a gloved hand on Gabriel's shoulder. "Just remember it's only cattle."

Gabriel nodded and left the stable. Once outside, he, Ben, and Colton raced after the herd.

Isabelle waited and listened but heard nothing else unusual. She and Brenna joined Mabel in the kitchen when the ruckus first began. Frank came to the kitchen door to let the women know he and Sam would be just outside if they needed anything. Isabelle did wonder about the necessity. Surely they'd need every man to stop a stampeding herd, but she knew nothing of cattle except the obvious danger of facing them down. Mabel convinced both women to return to their rooms and try to get some sleep. They'd be no good to anyone if they fell over exhausted when the men returned. Both women argued, but Brenna's decision was made for her when she heard Jacob's faint squalling from upstairs. Isabelle soon gave up and returned to her room, checking on Andrew who remained asleep. Isabelle had always envied him the ability to sleep through almost anything.

About an hour later, Isabelle heard a faint creak in the hallway. After a moment, she heard nothing more and dismissed it as just a common noise from a large house. Ten minutes later, she heard a scream. Without thinking about her attire, Isabelle dropped the book she had once again attempted to read and rushed from the room, not bothering to grab a wrapper this time. Brenna was already running in her direction only partially dressed. Relief showed on Brenna's face when she saw her, but it lasted only a moment as they continued down the hall to where Andrew and Mabel slept.

She and Brenna didn't slow down until they reached Andrew's open bedroom door. Brenna heard Jacob crying from the nursery and hurried to take care of her son. Isabelle turned back to the doorway and a strangled gasp escaped her lips. On the thick rug lay a felled Mabel. Her eyes drifted to the broken glass beneath the window. Isabelle shouted for Brenna and rushed to Mabel's side just as Brenna returned to the bedroom holding Jacob.

"Good heavens, Mabel!" Brenna held her crying son close to her.

"Brenna, please check on Andrew!" Isabelle shouted, trying her best to staunch the blood flow from Mabel's forehead with the hem of her nightgown. She watched Brenna rush to the bed and pull back the covers, revealing an empty bed.

"No!"

Everyone needed to be calmed down at once,

and Brenna could only manage one at a time. She took care of her son first and put him back to bed, checking the windows and leaving the door open so she could hear him if he woke again. After seeing to her son, she went to the kitchen to gather some water from the pump and clean rags, all the while wondering what happened to Frank and Sam.

Brenna returned to the upstairs bedroom and helped a glassy-eyed Isabelle lift Mabel to the bed. It proved to be a difficult task, but after a few attempts they managed to get the older woman down on the edge of the bed. Isabelle successfully staunched the wound, and Brenna gently moved her aside so she could clean it. Without proper bandages, there wasn't much to try to prevent the gash from bleeding again, so Brenna folded one of the clean rags in half and placed it over Mabel's wound. She ripped enough fabric from the hem of her nightgown to secure the cloth in place. Isabelle went to stand by the window, obviously not noticing she stood on broken glass.

"Isabelle, please sit down. You'll cut up your feet." Brenna urged Isabelle to a chair. Still in shock, she allowed herself to be guided.

"Who could have possibly taken him, Brenna?" Isabelle's hands shook and Brenna took hold to steady them.

Brenna didn't respond.

Isabelle moved her eyes from the window to the other woman, but Brenna avoided looking at her directly. "Brenna?"

The breath Brenna released sounded uneasy and she said, "I don't know for certain, Isabelle."

"Why Andrew? There's no reason to take him."

"It's not Andrew he wants, but if he found out the boy was here, he might go to any lengths to get our attention." Brenna smoothed her hands over Isabelle's in an effort to calm them both down.

"Who is 'he,' Brenna? You know who did this?"

Brenna raised her moistened eyes and said, "I'm so sorry, Isabelle. I think it may be my grandfather."

Gabriel and Ethan sat atop their weary mounts gazing out over the herd. Gabriel held the reins of another horse, a body draped over the saddle. It had taken nearly an hour to get ahead of the animals, and in the dark, it took more time trying to turn them. A shot from Gabriel's gun finally got the lead cows turning to the right, and when they did, the milling began, and then it was only a matter of waiting until the cattle wearied from running in circles.

Carl's horse had caught a leg in a hole, and both horse and rider had fallen fatally to the ground, caught up under the pounding hooves of the herd. Ben reported seeing at least five cows dead, but they wouldn't know for certain until they came back in the daylight. The cattle managed to nearly reach the end of the Gallagher's border when Gabriel got the shot off. Guiding the animals back in the night proved to be nearly impossible, but even with the cold, the dead cattle would begin to smell, and pushing the herd past them would be difficult. They'd face greater danger if the wolves caught the scent of death and came looking for an easy meal.

Colton offered to take Carl back to the ranch, but Gabriel shook his head. They all suffered the weight of Carl's death, but Carl risked his life for Gallagher cattle and a Gallagher would see to him. The whole ordeal disgusted Gabriel. The loss of Carl sickened him even more because deep down he believed it wasn't an accident. Ethan agreed when Gabriel shared his suspicions about who might be behind the incident. They knew only one man depraved enough to risk so many lives.

The weary cattlemen and ranch hands guided the herd carefully through the night back to the ranch. Ethan put two men on night hawk duty, each pair in two-hour shifts until daylight. Ethan decided to take the first shift with Ben after he got a fresh mount from the stable. Gabriel planned to take the second shift with Colton. Ethan and Gabriel decided they'd head over to Hunter's spread at first light.

As they rode closer to the ranch, Ethan noticed lights still burned on both levels. He had hoped the women would've gone back to sleep, especially with Frank and Sam watching over things. He'd hold his wife and son for a few minutes, change clothes, saddle a fresh horse, and head back out to meet Ben to relieve the hands keeping an eye on the herd.

Those who rode up to the stable removed the saddles and bridles from their horses and brushed the animals down. Most of the men headed back to the bunkhouse for some much needed sleep while Ethan and Gabriel tended to Carl. They laid him out in the back room of the barn where the animals couldn't get to him. They'd have to drive him into Briarwood in the morning. The town didn't have an official undertaker, but "Doc Brody," a big Irishman who wielded thread and needle better than any woman in a sewing circle, tended to such things.

After covering and securing Carl's body, Ethan and Gabriel both took a moment before closing up the small room and placing the wooden bar securely in the door. Even with the cooler temperatures, they wouldn't be able to leave Carl laid out for long. Solemnly, they left the barn and walked back to the main house.

"You sure you don't want me to take first watch with Ben?" The stiffness slowly left Gabriel's body

"Not a chance, Gabe. You earned first sleep. Two hours will pass quickly enough."

Gabriel halted and shot his arm out in front of Ethan to stop him from walking up the steps to the front door.

"What is it, Gabe?"

Gabriel shook his head slightly as if trying to figure out what tugged at him.

"Where's Frank and Sam?"

Ethan looked to all visible points of the house and shrugged. "Probably just around back. Why don't we go in and find out? I have to get back to the herd."

Gabriel lowered his arm but still didn't move.

"Gabriel, what's going on?"

"I'm not sure." This time he walked up the steps, quickening his pace into the house.

"Isabelle!" he shouted once inside the door.

"Dammit, Gabe." Ethan put a hand up to the ear closest to Gabriel when he shouted out.

Both brothers lifted their gazes to the top of the stairs when Isabelle appeared. She stood for a moment on the landing and then raced down the stairs. Gabriel watched her moment of hesitation. Worry urged him to go to her and uncertainty kept him grounded. He didn't hesitate, though, when she reached the bottom of the stairs. He opened his arms to her.

The tears Isabelle thought gone now found new paths to streak down her skin. She buried her face in Gabriel's shoulder, allowing herself a moment of feeling safe and of blocking out everything horrible that happened. Reality would not, however, be pushed aside, and she raised her eyes to meet Gabriel's.

"He's gone, Gabriel."

Gabriel stepped back enough to study Isabelle—the moist, puffy eyes and trembling lips. *She's been at it awhile.* He didn't have to ask who was gone because only one person could affect her this way.

"What happened to Andrew?"

"They've taken him and hurt Mabel. Brenna is with her now."

"What?" Gabriel's whole body tensed. "When?"

No longer passively standing aside in the conversation, Ethan stepped forward. "Brenna?"

Isabelle shook her head and said, "She's fine. So is Jacob. They're upstairs."

Ethan didn't wait for her to finish. He took the stairs two at a time and called for Brenna when he reached the top.

Alone now with Isabelle, Gabriel pulled her back into his arms. "Shh now, we'll get him back."

Isabelle tried but failed to stop the tears from coming, and she turned into Gabriel's arms.

"I can't lose him, Gabriel, I can't."

"You won't. I promise." He continued to rub her back gently, doing his best to ease the fear and tenseness from her body. His every nerve wanted to race back out to his horse, but the logical side—the side that had tended to keep him and Ethan out of too much trouble as young boys—rose to the surface. "I need to know what happened."

"Brenna. She knows more than I."

Gabriel pulled away again slightly, though kept his hands on her arms. "What does Brenna know about it?"

"Something about her grandfather."

Isabelle watched as Gabriel's jaw tensed and his deep-blue eyes darkened.

"Is she right, Gabriel?"

Gabriel didn't answer her question—he couldn't. Every suspicion he and his brother had about tonight made sense. Without saying a word, Gabriel took the same quick path Ethan had up the stairs, barely registering Isabelle's softer footfalls following close behind.

Gabriel followed the quiet voices to the end of the hall, to the room where Andrew had slept. He looked around the room, his gaze settling on the three people at the bed, and walked over, bracing an arm against the bedpost. Brenna held Mabel's head up as the older woman drank water from a short glass. A crude, white bandage wrapped around the top of her head was a shocking contrast to her darker skin.

"You all right, old girl?"

Mabel nodded only slightly but looked past Gabriel. "I'm so sorry, Miss Isabelle. I came in here when I heard noise from next door. I thought your brother needed something. The man took him right there out that window. The other hit me. I couldn't stop them."

Gabriel and the others turned their heads when Mabel spoke. Isabelle stood at the doorway. Her tears dried up, leaving behind red streaks in the whites of her eyes. Gabriel's eyes followed her movements toward the bed, and he was pleased when she stood near him, though he didn't reach out to her.

Isabelle did her best to reassure the woman. "It's not your fault, Mabel."

"I need you to rest right now," Ethan told her.

The old housekeeper nodded again and closed her eyes against the pain.

Ethan looked up at his brother, said nothing, and left the room. Brenna excused herself and followed him into the hall. Ethan led her into their room, warning her to stay with Isabelle and Jacob and not to leave for any reason. Ethan pulled her against him and kissed her fiercely, grateful that she was still here with him and safe. He let go of her, quickly changed his clothes, and left the house.

Isabelle found herself once again alone with Gabriel, and she wondered about his sudden stiffness toward her. She then realized Gabriel had planned to come upstairs to speak with Brenna about her grandfather.

"You need to speak with Brenna. Please, Gabriel. I need to know what happened to Andrew."

Gabriel continued watching the injured housekeeper, relief pouring through him that she'd been spared worse. Anger coursed through him that Hunter had gone to such lengths.

Isabelle's fear vibrated through the air around them.

Gabriel turned to her and lightly gripped her shoulders. "Brenna will tell Ethan what we need to know," he replied softly, keeping his voice even. "I have to go now. I promise you, I'm going to get Andrew back. I want you to stay here with Brenna and Mabel. Don't look at me like that; you can't go. I can't think about keeping Andrew safe and worrying about you at the same time."

After a brief hesitation, she nodded.

Brenna came into the room again and took in the grim expressions. She walked over to Isabelle, draped an arm around her waist, and guided her from the bedroom.

Panic welled up inside of Isabelle. *If anything happened to him* . . . "Gabriel?"

"Don't." He put a finger to her lips. Not caring that his sister-in-law stood by, he lowered his lips to Isabelle's for a brief touch. "I'll bring him back," he whispered softly, then left the room.

10

According to what Brenna told Ethan, the men took Andrew not long after they had raced after the herd, giving Hunter's men plenty of time to make it back to the Double Bar. The distance between Hawk's Peak and the Double Bar was short, but Gabriel imagined a struggling boy might have made for a rough ride. He knew Andrew wouldn't be going without a fight. Gabriel also knew they wouldn't be wasting time—Hunter's men must have known they'd be found out.

Gabriel and the others beat themselves up over their stupidity. Considering how many guns slept under the roof, they never imagined someone to be foolish enough to take a child from inside the house. What bothered Gabriel even more was how the kidnappers got past Frank and Sam.

Gabriel quickly caught up with Ethan and three of the other men in the stable. The bunkhouse was once again cleared, and they told the men left behind to stay at the house and post themselves so they'd see anyone coming from any direction. The men would rotate with the night hawks to ensure that no one remained with the herd too long. Though winter was not yet upon them, the night air could grow too cold for a man. They were stretched thin, and Gabriel hoped they'd all manage to make it through this night without exhaustion causing an accident.

Ethan said, "I don't believe anyone will be coming back to the ranch tonight, but I'm not willing to take any chances."

"The men will keep an eye on things and hopefully find out what happened to Frank and Sam."

"Are you thinking—?"

"You know what I'm thinking," Gabriel said,

"because you're thinking the same thing."

"I wish to hell I wasn't."

"Frank and Sam wouldn't have just left and so help me, if Hunter's men killed them, he'll pay for that, too."

Staring down at the lighted windows of Hunter's main house, Gabriel sat atop his horse next to his brother and the other men. The cold wind lifted the edges of his dark brown hair, and he focused on the ranch.

"Gabe, we have to plan this out. Hunter is going to have men everywhere, and we won't be able to get to Andrew without getting him and everyone else killed."

"What exactly do you have in mind?" Gabriel asked, his thoughts on the young boy and not on planning.

"We give the old man what he wants."

"You mean us."

"Yes. It's almost as though he's daring us to come after him."

Gabriel contemplated his brother and knew he'd give his beating heart just as quickly as

Gabriel would for Andrew. He hoped they could resolve this without making that decision. "Heaven help us if we're wrong. Let's go."

The men urged their mounts forward onto Double Bar land and within minutes came upon the main house. A procession of semi-washed men stood with guns around the yard, all pointed at the riders.

"Didn't think you'd come, Gallagher."

"Which one of us?" Gabriel asked. He glanced over at the man who spoke, not immediately recognizing him. Apparently Ethan did because he addressed him gruffly.

"Either of you," the man answered.

"We're not here for you, Thatcher, at least not yet. Where is he?" Ethan asked.

Thatcher stepped forward. "He's expectin' you."

Gabriel inched his mount forward. "He meant the boy."

Thatcher looked from one brother to the other. "The boy ain't hurt, and he'll stay that way. Boss just wants to talk."

Gabriel glanced over at Ethan for a moment, and his brother nodded as though a silent understanding passed between them.

"Well, we have a few things to say to him," said Ethan, his voice smooth. "Where's Hunter?"

Confused by their behavior, Thatcher scratched the side of his balding head. "All right, but you'll have to leave them guns."

Gabriel pulled his gun and the others quickly followed, all mindful of the pistols and rifles trained on them but apparently not worried. "Tell you what. Why don't we just use the bullets now and save you the trouble of having to disarm us?"

Thatcher knew that the younger Gallagher moved fast with a gun—too fast. "You know he'll kill the boy if you don't do what he says."

Ethan moved alongside his brother and spoke softly, hoping his words wouldn't carry. "Gabriel, I don't believe Andrew's here. Something tells me this has all been a diversion. Hunter may be crazy, but he's not stupid. We want Hunter, but . . ."

Gabriel nodded slowly. "Andrew first." Never taking his eyes off the men on the ground, he addressed Thatcher. "Give you one more chance to tell us where he's keeping the boy."

Thatcher appeared to consider their demands when another man stepped forward, sneering at the Gallaghers. Ethan and Gabriel recognized Tanner James and knew he was just as stupid as his brother Bradford had been, but even more reckless.

"We heard all about you Gallaghers. You ain't got what it takes to kill a man," Tanner sneered. "And we've got you outnumbered." Tanner shouted to the other men on the ground, all guns ready. "Let's show them high and mighty cusses how real men fight!" Tanner raised his gun but the click of Gabriel's chamber proved to be Tanner's undoing. The kid fell to the ground, writhing in agony. "You shot me!" he screamed up at Gabriel. "You stupid cuss, you shot me!"

Thatcher reached the boy and set his rifle on the ground. "Shut your mouth, kid. He could've killed ya."

"One more time, Thatcher. Where's the boy?" Ethan asked. The air vibrated with energy from every cowboy wanting to take the next shot.

"He's not here!" Thatcher finally shouted back.

"Where?"

"I don't know," Thatcher said. When Gabriel shifted his gun just a little lower, Thatcher nearly screamed. "I swear, I don't know. He just told us to keep ya here and kill ya if we got the chance."

"We're riding out of here, Thatcher. Tell them to put down the guns and walk away."

Thatcher yelled out to the men to drop their weapons. None did. Another shot rang out from someone in the Gallagher group, putting a hole through one of the men's hands. The injured man dropped the pistol and followed it to the ground, clutching his injured limb to his body.

Thatcher yelled at them again. "Drop them guns before ya get yerselves killed!"

Each man finally dropped their weapon.

Ethan and Gabriel motioned for their men to head out, and they followed close behind as the wind picked up Tanner's moans.

They closed the distance back to the border between the lands in short time. "Blast Ethan, how in the hell did we miss them?"

Ethan shook his head. "I don't know. I still want to know how they managed to get Andrew out of the ranch. Did anyone happen to see Frank or Sam?"

Colton shook his head. "They weren't with the others when we all gathered."

"Jackson, take Tom Jr. back to the ranch and see if you can find them. The rest of us will look for Andrew, and then we'll worry about the how." Ethan saw how Gabriel struggled.

As Jackson and Tom Jr. left, Ben dismounted and studied the ground about fifteen feet north of where they had stopped on the crest.

"What do you have, Ben?" Ethan dismounted and joined the man on the ground.

"Riders. Two of them rode north of here. Their tracks on the original trail were covered by the others headed to the ranch. It appears they weren't traveling that fast through here. Probably how we missed seeing these before. We followed the riders leaving the trail we could see, not the one we couldn't." Ben continued to study the tracks. Gabriel and the others joined them.

"How many?" Gabriel asked.

"I count only the two riders. One horse is carrying a heavier load. I'd say that one has the boy with him."

Ethan spared his brother a glance, but Gabriel gazed north into the darkness. Ethan knew his brother wouldn't be willing to wait until morning. Since they didn't expect Hunter to try kidnapping a second time, they hadn't been prepared. They let their guard down just enough for Hunter's men to get through. None of them would rest until the boy was safely with his sister, home at Hawk's Peak.

"Ben, you head back to the Peak and let the others know what's happened. Grab two more men and tell the others they aren't to leave the main house or the women for anything. You'll be able to pick up our trail."

Ben nodded but cautioned, "Ethan, it's black as pitch out here, and the night is only getting colder. We'll need supplies and that's going to take some time."

Gabriel nodded, but said, "You're right, Ben, but bring only what you can carry on the horses. They can't have ridden far, especially in the dark. They probably picked up speed once they were out of sight of the ranch, but it shouldn't take long to find them."

Ben nodded, turned his horse, and sped back to the ranch. Ethan watched him disappear into the darkness, knowing that in some ways this differed from when Brenna had been taken. Her captors had been predictable, and she'd been smart enough to get away unharmed. No matter how bright Andrew was, he wouldn't be able to help them or himself. This time Hunter didn't seem to be taking any chances, and Ethan swore for the sake of his brother that they'd get the boy back, no matter the cost.

"Gabriel," Ethan said quietly. "Keep your head, brother. You'll need it."

"Oh, I'm keeping it, but you can bet just as sure as the sun rises over those mountains, that one way or another, Hunter will die by the hands of a Gallagher."

Ethan looked solemnly at his brother but let the remark go. "Let's bring Andrew home and deal with Hunter when the boy's safe." Ethan turned his attention to the other two men. "Pete, Colton, when we reach them, we're going to need you to give us a distraction. Just don't get yourselves dead doing it."

For the first time that night, someone found his smile. Colton grinned and said, "Don't you worry about that, Ethan. I've got something in mind." He patted his saddlebags.

Ethan didn't ask.

Gabriel glanced down at the tracks, then ahead into the darkness and up at the sky. He knew this land just as well as any Gallagher. He just hoped that on this starless night, instinct would guide him through the blackness.

11

Gabriel knew they were fumbling through the woods. The trail led them away from the open pastures into the dense trees of the forests northeast of their land. The land belonged to no one and therefore was rarely traveled except by those wishing to avoid all things civilized. The moon decided to make an appearance, but not much of the light shone through the heavy pines. If he remembered correctly, they weren't too far from a break in the forest. Gabriel hoped Hunter's men proved less capable than the old man and stopped somewhere up ahead. The mountains ahead were treacherous enough to navigate in daylight. They'd have to stop somewhere, but the tracks kept getting more and more difficult to find.

Gabriel and the others spread out, each making their own path through the trees, hoping to find a sign of the tracks. The last one they found had been nearly twenty minutes ago. Gabriel was about to suggest that they had veered off course when a soft whistle came through the trees. The only one to his left was Colton. Gabriel turned his horse and reached him first. Colton hunched down close to the ground and pressed against the earth with his fingers.

"Found them?" Gabriel asked from his saddle.

"It's them for certain. I figure not too far ahead now. They slowed down a bit through here."

"But they still couldn't go far tonight. I can't figure out what their plan is by bringing us out this way."

Ethan and Jake rode up in time to hear Gabriel's comment. Ethan glanced down to where Colton examined the ground. "I don't think they planned on us tonight, Gabe. They probably figured we'd wait until first light after wrangling that stampede."

"Still doesn't make sense. Hunter could have stayed out of the territory. There has to be something he wants desperately enough to risk a bullet."

"Let's find out, shall we?" Ethan urged his stallion forward through the trees.

"Isabelle, please sit and eat something." Brenna watched as her new sister in-law paced from one end of the dining room to the other. An hour ago, they'd been in the study, and before that, Isabelle had paced the length of the deck before the cold forced her inside. She didn't know Isabelle well, but she understood her quiet desperation. Brenna remembered being on the other end of this situation once before and knew better than anyone what dangers lurked in this wilderness, especially in the clutches of Nathan Hunter's men. She about gave up on Isabelle when the other woman stopped abruptly, as though to catch a sound she may have missed.

After a moment, she began pacing again.

"Isabelle, please. You'll only grow weak if you don't take care of yourself. Andrew will need you strong when he returns.

"And you're so certain he will?"

"Of course." Brenna saw Isabelle's worry.

"How do we know? He's so young, Brenna. He can't fend for himself out there."

"Listen to me please. Andrew will be found, and he will come back to you."

"How do you know?"

"Because once, not so very long ago, those men saved my life, and they will save Andrew."

Isabelle continued to pace, swiftly wiping a tear that fell unbidden onto her cheek. "Brenna?"

"Yes?"

"What could your grandfather possibly want with my brother? What good does taking a young boy do for him?"

"All of my energies have gone into trying to answer that question. Nathan Hunter may be my grandfather by blood, but he is not my family, and I do not have the answers you seek." Brenna stood and walked across the room to where Isabelle watched out the window. "No one expected him to return and truth be told, taking Andrew makes no sense to me either."

"What happened between you and your grandfather?" Isabelle asked.

"It's a story going back long before I came here. My grandfather waged a war on the Gallaghers long ago."

"Gabriel told me some of what he'd done, but why did it begin?"

"Feuding and wars," Brenna said. "These reasons are ancient and no good ever comes of them, but happen they do."

"I don't understand. What does this have to do with what's happening now?"

"Nathan Hunter holds great hatred for the Gallaghers, and from what I've learned, he has hated them since he first lost on a land bid," Brenna said. "He's an evil man, and there is no understanding why he continues to do any of this."

"Then why do it?" Anger slowly replaced Isabelle's worry. "You know more about this man, about what is going on around here than I do. What is he to gain when he must have known that Gabriel and the others would go after him?"

"I wish I possessed those answers, truly I do." Brenna's voice softened and her eyes moved to gaze out the window into the blackness.

Isabelle couldn't see whatever drew the other woman's attention. "Brenna?" What is it?"

"I didn't think . . ."

"Think what? Brenna, please."

"There might be a reason why he'd take Andrew. He'd have to take that risk in order to get what he wants most." Brenna stopped again in mid-thought just as Mabel walked into the room.

"Lordy child, are you all right?" Mabel asked after seeing Brenna's stricken face.

Brenna frowned at Mabel.

"What's wrong? What does your grandfather want most?" asked Isabelle.

"He'll want to make a trade, and he knows we'd do anything to get the boy back safely." Brenna sat down, her face becoming pale.

"Trade what?" Isabelle knelt on the floor next to the chair, desperately shaking Brenna.

Brenna lifted her wide, bright eyes to her new sister and spoke as though it pained her. "He must still want my grandmother."

The small cabin appeared to be deserted, but the telltale stream of smoke coming from the narrow chimney pipe told another story. Gabriel didn't recall seeing the structure on previous rides through these woods, but he believed it was possible a trapper had built it at some point. From the looks of the place, someone abandoned it long ago, but hunters and trappers did make their way through this area when the weather allowed. It took longer to cut through the forests and mountains, but many of the mountain men preferred to avoid towns and the well-traveled paths wagons and more civilized people preferred.

They reached the clearing around the cabin just as the clouds shifted, making way for the moon to take over the night skies. Jake and Colton walked a wide path around the sides of the cabin while Gabriel and Ethan kept an eye on the front. It took only a few moments before Colton quietly made his way back to them.

"Where's Jake?" Ethan asked.

"Keeping an eye on the back," Colton said, crouching down and supporting an arm on one knee. He continued to scan the area. "There are three horses tied up around the back against the mountain. No lights back there either, but the horses are saddled and from what I can tell, they're the ones we've been trackin'."

"Gabriel, I have a feeling Hunter's not in there." Ethan surveyed the small cabin.

"Not likely, but sure as certain Andrew is, so we go in."

Ethan nodded and pulled his .45 Colt from the holster, a gun he rarely had to use on the ranch. He half stood as Gabriel checked the barrel of his Winchester and returned a nod to his brother. Colton lifted his saddlebags and draped them over one shoulder.

"What do you have in there, Colton?" Gabriel asked.

"A little something we confiscated off those illegal miners a spell ago."

A small part of Gabriel wanted to smile. He hoped they all found reason to smile again when this came to an end. Ethan moved slowly away from him, keeping behind the tree line and quietly made his way to the west side of the cabin.

Gabriel watched as Ethan disappeared into the night even as Colton made his way to the east of the cabin. Hoping they'd have every possible escape route covered, Gabriel stood and walked slowly toward the front of the cabin. He cautiously kept close enough to the tree line in the event he needed to quickly find cover. Gabriel imagined the rifle was more weapon than necessary, but he felt more comfortable with the long gun than with a revolver, though the smaller gun was certainly good backup. He wasn't a gunfighter, just a cowboy, but he'd be whatever he needed to be in order to get Andrew out alive.

Gabriel caught the barest hint of movement from inside the walls of the cabin. A light glow now faded in and out through the windows. Someone must have added more logs to the fire.

Trusting his brother and their men, Gabriel cocked the rifle and yelled out, "You're surrounded! Let the boy go!"

Gabriel caught a glimpse of Ethan pressed up against the side of the cabin and then slowly moving inward to cover anyone coming out the front door. He kept his eyes focused on the front, waiting, hoping that someone would step out.

"You have one chance to let him go!" This time Gabriel heard movement, but he didn't take that as a good sign.

A moment later someone from inside yelled back, "Don't know what you're talkin' 'bout, mister! We got no boy in here."

"Don't be fools. There are more guns out here

than in there." Gabriel would have shot in the door if there wasn't a chance of hitting Andrew. The thought of it alone made him sick. "We happen you have the boy in there," Gabriel said. "Hunter isn't here to stop you from doing the right thing and letting him go."

"Shit, Hank, that must be one of them Gallaghers."

Gabriel heard this and knew they'd found their men. He caught Ethan's attention and saw that his brother heard it, too. Colton now rounded the front of the cabin from the opposite side from where Ethan waited. With any luck, they'd manage to flush the men out. He watched as Colton pulled something out of his saddlebag, struck a match, and lit whatever he held. Gabriel saw black smoke beginning to float upward and hoped Colton knew what he was doing. He watched as Colton moved back into the shadows, trusting that whatever he did wouldn't harm the boy.

This time another man yelled out from the cabin. "Mister, we ain't coming out there. You'll just kill us!"

"Not if you let the boy go."

Seconds passed before Gabriel heard the scrape of the locking plank against the door. He hoped the men wouldn't do anything stupid. Gabriel didn't relish the idea of a gunfight, not with the risk that Andrew would be caught in the middle. The door creaked open and few inches, though it wasn't a man that appeared but the barrel of a gun.

Gabriel ducked back behind the closest tree even as the first shot whizzed past him. He swore as the air around him stirred. Ethan and Colton had a better advantage, but Gabriel knew they avoided firing until they knew who stood where for fear of hitting Andrew.

Another shot fired, but this time Gabriel was ready and positioned the Winchester against him, stepping out from the tree and taking aim at the rifle barrel before someone pulled it inside. His aim proved true and the rifle dropped to the ground. Whoever stood at the door quickly shut it. Gabriel heard one of the men shouting.

Shots sounded from the back of the cabin, and he watched as Colton rushed back to aid Jake. The fools probably decided to try their luck at escaping. Gabriel only wished they'd come out his way. Smoke began to slowly wind its way up and over the cabin, black mixed with gray and white billows, but he heard no one coughing. Whatever Colton took off those miners was probably something the miners had stolen from a Chinese healer who dealt in potions. He watched as the smoke continued to seep through the crevices of the cabin and imagined the men couldn't see much of anything in there. When he thought they'd have to storm the cabin after all, someone from inside must have decided their lives weren't worth whatever Hunter paid them.

"Is that you out there, Gallagher?"

Gabriel finally heard someone coughing and prayed it wasn't Andrew.

"It is." Gabriel shouted back.

"We got the boy and we're comin' out! You shoot us and we kill 'im!"

"Let the boy go and you'll live."

The door slowly opened and two guns were tossed out onto the ground. Gabriel stepped out from behind cover and watched as Ethan did the same, both keeping aim on the men coming out. First one, followed by another, but Andrew didn't appear.

They stood close enough now to hear whatever Gabriel said. "Where's the boy?"

"You can't kill us now. We was only doing our job."

Ethan closed the distance and aimed low, shooting a bullet into the dirt beside the man who spoke.

"Wait! You said you wouldn't shoot."

"My brother said you wouldn't die if you let the boy go," Ethan said. "I don't see the boy."

"He's in there," one of them said as they pointed back to the cabin. "He ain't hurt. Another one of us is there with 'im, and he ain't gonna hurt the boy if you put down them guns and not kill us like you said."

"Or we could kill you now and retrieve the boy ourselves." Gabriel aimed higher this time.

"I'm not a man who kills humans if I can help it, but I'd feel no sorrow in putting lead into both of you right now."

"Just shut up, Hank." The smaller of the two finally spoke up and yelled back toward the cabin. "You better bring the boy out now, Billy. They's gonna shoot us if you don't."

Another man finally stepped through the door, using Andrew as a shield. Both wore a light black film on their faces. He held the barrel of a pistol to the boy's head. This one appeared to be more seasoned than the other two, and Gabriel didn't like the hard set of his face. He ran his gaze over Andrew, looking for any injury. Other than a few scuffs, he appeared unharmed. He looked frightened, though, and Gabriel wasn't sure he wanted to let these men go.

"I ain't letting this boy go until you drop them guns, Gallagher."

"I don't see that you have much of a choice," Ethan said from where he stood. Colton came around from the other side at that moment, gun at the ready.

"Jake has one of the fools tied up out back." Colton surveyed the activity and said, "That's the last of them."

"There are more men than horses," Ethan remarked.

"That's what Jake and I thought," Colton said.

"Doesn't matter," said Gabriel. "Let the boy go and you have a chance to live," Gabriel said to the man holding Andrew.

The man called Billy looked from one cowboy to the next and back to Gabriel. "I don't believe you. You got killing in your eyes, Gallagher."

"You have one last chance." Gabriel raised his gun and aimed high. If he pulled the trigger now, Billy would take the shot in the head.

Billy threw down his gun and shoved Andrew away, knocking the boy forward into the dirt. Gabriel's gun barrel was still aimed at Billy. *It wouldn't take much to end this.* Andrew stood, and Colton motioned for him to come to him. Gabriel barely took it all in as he focused on the man in front of him.

Ethan walked toward his brother, keeping an eye on one man, knowing Colton covered the other. He closed the distance and said Gabriel's name. His brother seemed to be thinking about whether or not he was going to listen.

"Gabriel," Ethan said again. "You don't want to do this."

"I'm not so sure about that."

This time Ethan placed a hand on his brother's arm. "You kill him, you become him. You're better than that."

Gabriel took another moment, and then as though he realized what he'd almost done, he handed his rifle to Ethan. As soon as his hands were free, Andrew ran to him and into his arms. Gabriel held the boy close, taking in the knowledge that he was real and safe.

"Colton, cover me." Colton took Ethan's gun and held both on the men as Ethan checked them for any other weapons. When he felt fairly certain they didn't have any, he took back his pistol and cautiously walked into the cabin to search for something to tie the men up with. The smoke Colton had released left a light, black film over everything inside, but the air was beginning to clear. Ethan finally found a few feet of rope. It would do until they got the ropes from their saddles.

After tying them up, Ethan watched the men as Colton went around back to help Jake with the fourth and bring the horses around. They'd have to double two men on a mount.

"You men are one horse short," Ethan said. "Where's the other?"

Hank spat in the dirt, and they said nothing.

"You can tell me, or I can tie you to a tree and leave you for the wolves."

The smallest one, who still hadn't said his name, answered this time. "My horse went lame and couldn't carry me no more. We let him go."

Ethan nodded and moved up alongside Colton. "What did you use in there?"

Colton shrugged and said, "Don't know exactly, but I'd seen a couple of Chinamen use it before when I worked the mining camps some years back. Spooked me but good the first time

I saw it. Thought I was a goner until I realized it wasn't killing me."

Ethan smiled at Colton and went to his brother, who stood looking down at Andrew's head, holding the boy against him. Ethan couldn't figure out what Hunter had accomplished this night. He didn't believe it was all just to keep them from getting any sleep. But seeing as how they'd been unable to find the old man, and they had Andrew back, his motives remained a mystery. Ethan knelt down next to Andrew. "How are you doing, Andrew?"

"I want Ibby."

"I don't blame you," Ethan said. "You'll see her again soon."

The boy nodded, still held close by Gabriel. "I didn't want to go hunting with the smelly man, but they said I had to go."

Confused by Andrew's words, Gabriel asked, "Did they say what they were hunting, Andrew?"

Andrew shook his head and buried his face back in Gabriel's coat. Ethan stood and shared a concerned look with his brother.

Gabriel knew how lucky they should all feel and how close they'd come to losing someone else. "Ethan," he said, watching Colton and Jake lead the horses toward them. "I have to get Andrew back."

Ethan nodded and spared his brother a glance now that the other two men watched Hunter's men. "Go Gabe, we've got this."

Gabriel paused a moment, looking at his brother. He gave an answering nod, lifted Andrew onto the back of Zeus, and nimbly mounted the horse, securing Andrew in his arms. He offered one last look to the men on the ground, then turned and guided Zeus into the night thinking only one thing: *Where was Hunter and how do we find him?*

12

Isabelle paced back and forth, her tall form casting shadows on the walls in the dimly lit room. She gave up on sleep hours ago, and let her mind wander to one absolute truth: If they'd never met Gabriel, if they'd never come to Hawk's Peak, her brother might be safe with her where he belonged.

Brenna had left the room an hour ago to tend to her son, and Isabelle's worry escalated with every passing hour. No matter how little Isabelle may have appreciated Brenna's calming presence at the time, and she needed that if she was to make it through this night.

Mabel also refused to retire for the evening, coming in every half hour asking if Isabelle needed something to eat or if she'd like to rest a spell while Mabel kept watch. Each time, Isabelle thanked Mabel but refused to leave her watch. Her sharp eyes never drifted far from an open window where they looked out into the darkness, hoping for any sign of life other than the animals. The first time she'd seen a man pass the window, she believed for a moment it might be Gabriel returning at last. It had only been one of the ranch men keeping watch out front. She vaguely remembered him telling her his name was Ben, that he'd be right out front, and if she needed anything, all she needed to do was call out.

Isabelle tended to error on the side of optimism considering all she'd been through, but she now lost her footing and positive things became difficult. Mabel had stepped into the room again when Isabelle heard shouting from outside. She nearly pressed herself against the cold panes of the window trying to distinguish shapes in the darkness. *Two riders.*

Isabelle rushed out the front to wait on the

porch, her golden hair unbound and falling in disarray over her shoulders. Brenna followed close behind and placed a comforting arm around Isabelle. Her tenseness mirrored Isabelle's. She, too, had someone she loved out there, but only two riders rode their horses into the yard. Isabelle heard Brenna gasp and watched as Brenna walked to the edge of the porch.

"Eliza!" Brenna hurried down the steps as the riders dismounted. Isabelle now saw that one was indeed a woman—tall, with dark hair.

"Brenna," Eliza said, hugging the smaller woman. "Please tell me they're back."

Brenna stepped back from her sister-in-law, puzzled. "No, they're not, but how did you know? And where have you been?"

"I'll explain about where I've been later. Decker here rode into town to wire the marshal. I came in on the evening stage and had planned to stay in town. When I saw Decker, he told me what had happened, so I rode back with him." Eliza swept her hat off her head, her long hair coming loose from two braids. Eliza handed her horse's reins to Decker who offered to brush and bed down the horses.

"What exactly did Decker tell you?" Brenna watched the ranch hand walk toward the barn.

"A boy was snatched, and my fool brothers went after him."

"I don't believe all the men know the details of what happened," Brenna said. "Come inside, and I'll tell you what I know."

When they moved closer to the front porch, Ben stepped forward and addressed Eliza. "It's good to have you back at the Peak."

"It's good to be back." Eliza took in the rifle at Ben's side and the other hand at the far end of the porch holding another. "What's going on here, Ben?"

"We're to watch over the house until your brothers' return, so that's what we're doing."

Eliza looked again from Ben to Brenna and then looked up to the porch and for the first time noticed the woman standing near the front door. She said to Brenna, "You'd better fill me in."

Eliza ushered everyone into the house and followed behind them into the study. She listened to Brenna's recounting, remaining silent as a slow-building anger filled her.

"Isabelle," Eliza said, taking Isabelle's hand in her own. "I wish we could have met under different circumstances, and I am so sorry that you and your brother have been drawn into this."

Isabelle studied the youngest of the Gallagher family. Her first impression was of a strong, capable woman who'd handle anything that came her way. She had the same stubborn jaw and the same deep-blue eyes as Gabriel, though hers seemed to bore into a person until you were willing to share every secret. Isabelle had to hold herself back from doing just that.

"Brenna said this might be about her grandmother."

Eliza raised her eyes to Brenna, and Isabelle saw something unspoken pass between them. "It's possible, but I think it's about more than that, Isabelle. We'll deal with the whys once your brother is back safely."

Isabelle shook her head. "I trust your brothers, truly I do, but they're ranchers. How can you be so confident they'll return unharmed?"

"Look at me, Isabelle, and listen carefully," Eliza said. "My brothers may just be ranchers, but I know what they're capable of and you have my word that they'll bring Andrew home." Eliza stood and abruptly walked over to the window. Brenna stood from her seat beside Isabelle and joined her.

"What do you see?" Brenna asked as her gaze cast over the horizon. The sky half shone with stars as the morning sun cast the faintest of light upon the land.

"Nothing yet, it's just that I thought . . ." Eliza's tired eyes lifted slightly with her half smile. "Gabriel's home."

Gabriel focused on the lights from the ranch guiding him home, though the help from the light wasn't necessary. The land upon which he guided his horse was as much a part of him as it had been his father's. The small boy he held securely in his arms brought back images of his father holding him in much the same way. He wanted to keep Isabelle and Andrew—forever if he could. Whatever Hunter really wanted, Gabriel knew the old man wouldn't stop until he got it. He'd already proven his daring by stealing the boy right out from under them. He promised himself there wasn't a risk of another snatching—they'd see to that, and Hunter must know that they wouldn't let their guard down for a moment until they settled this.

Gabriel pulled Andrew closer to him and urged Zeus forward. The animal knew the land as well as he did, and as they closed the distance to the ranch, Gabriel allowed the horse his head. When he rode closer, he made out the silhouettes of three figures by the front door— three women. *Could that mean . . .?*

"Eliza." Gabriel pulled Zeus to a halt, relieved to see his sister. Ben walked out to meet the horse, and Gabriel handed Andrew down to the ranch hand. He dismounted, rushed up to the porch, and embraced his sister.

"I should tan your hide."

"I missed you too, Gabe," Eliza said, enjoying the scent of Montana on her brother.

Gabriel stepped back and grinned down at his sister. "You have a lot of explaining to do."

"We'll get to that. Where's Ethan?"

Gabriel was about to answer but spared a glance to Isabelle, who now sat on one of the rocking chairs, holding her brother close. Soft tears glided down her pale cheeks. Gabriel walked over and knelt beside them.

"He's safe now, Isabelle. I promise he'll stay that way."

Isabelle nodded slightly, said nothing, and continued to hold Andrew. Gabriel frowned and wondered if something between them may have been damaged. He stood and faced Eliza.

"Ethan, Jake, and Colton are bringing back the men who did this. They should be along in a couple of hours."

"Hunter's men?" Eliza asked tightly.

Gabriel nodded. "Yes, Hunter's men. But by the time we arrived at the ranch, he was gone, or at least we think so." Gabriel scraped a hand over his stubbled jaw. "I don't know how he did it, Eliza. Hunter didn't have many places to go that I can think of.

"Are you certain he wasn't there?"

Gabriel paused for just a moment to think it over. "I'm not sure. His men didn't have reason to do any of this on their own. Hunter's after something, but I don't know what that is anymore."

"Well, I don't know about you, but I need some sleep," Eliza said. "If you're certain Ethan doesn't need help bringing those men in, I need to find my bed for a few hours." Eliza followed Gabriel's gaze to what occupied his attention. Isabelle still clutched her brother who'd fallen asleep in her arms. "We all need some rest."

Gabriel nodded in agreement. "I'll send Ben out to meet them. I saw Brenna out here with you, but why'd she go inside?"

"When she knew it was you and the boy, she

went to tend to her son. What a surprise he was."

"A new generation at the Peak," Gabriel said softly but didn't smile, his attention back on Andrew.

"Isabelle." Gabriel offered open arms. "Let me take him up. You both need some sleep."

Isabelle hesitated in releasing her brother but did so and allowed Gabriel to lift him away. She didn't miss the sadness in Gabriel's eyes, but she couldn't squelch her worry. She trusted Gabriel and believed the people at the ranch would keep her and Andrew safe, but the nagging thought that they might be safer elsewhere invaded her mind. Just days ago their lives changed, and they had a real chance for a new beginning. Now she didn't know what to do or how to feel.

Isabelle followed Gabriel up the stairs, barely making eye contact with anyone as they walked through the house. She already knew what must be done, and she pushed away the sudden pain enveloping her heart. Gabriel walked past Andrew's previous room directly to Isabelle's, grateful for his consideration. It's where she wanted her brother tonight.

Gabriel gently laid the boy down on the bed, pausing when Andrew stirred slightly.

"Gabriel?"

He sat on the edge of the bed, one arm on either side of Andrew.

"It's me."

"Did you get the bad men?"

Gabriel's jaw tightened, but for the boy, he forced a smile. "You don't have to worry about them again."

"I love you."

Gabriel leaned down and kissed his brow. "I love you, too." Andrew's eyes drifted close, and his chest rose and fell, strong and steady.

When Gabriel assured himself Andrew slept soundly, he stepped away and stood next to Isabelle who waited by the open door.

"Isabelle, I imagine there's a lot going through your head right now, but will you wait before making any decisions? Until we can talk?"

Isabelle let her gaze fall on her brother for a moment, relief filling her. His golden hair fell over his forehead, and he'd pulled his knees up toward his chest. She studied his breathing, ensuring herself he was really safe, before she gave her full attention to Gabriel. His eyes shared everything and yet gave nothing away, but she knew what he was asking of her.

"I'll wait."

Somehow Gabriel didn't feel as though he'd been given a reprieve. He ran his hand softly up and down her arm but let his hand drop after a moment. Giving one last glance to the sleeping boy curled up on the soft covers of the bed, he stepped out of the room and kept his back to the door as Isabelle closed it firmly behind him.

Gabriel had fallen asleep in one of the chairs in their father's old study. No matter how comfortable the chairs usually were, the furniture was not meant to be slept on. Gabriel stretched his tall form in an effort to ease the stiffness caused by the few hours in the chair. He wanted to be close at hand when Ethan and the boys returned with Hunter's men. He stepped over to the window, drawing open the drapes to let in the morning sun. Looking up at the sky, he saw it was taking Ethan longer to return than he thought it would.

Wiping the tired from his eyes, he took a quick drink of the now cold coffee he'd scrounged from the kitchen after he left Isabelle and Andrew. Now, he made his way to the kitchen where Mabel gave him her usual inspection. The woman should have been in bed, but with the bandage firmly in place on her head, there was no telling her what to do. After her inspection, she simply offered him some more coffee.

"Where's your brother?"

"He'll be back soon," Gabriel said, and when she looked at him with a disbelieving look, he added, "unharmed."

Gabriel's few and uncomfortable hours of sleep proved to be enough to keep his eyes open. The coffee slowly seeped into his system, waking him fully. Careful not to make too much noise walking through house, he left through the front door and reached the porch just as Ethan dismounted. Jake held the reins of the horses as Colton and Ben helped the men down from the saddles. Their tied hands prevented them from doing much on their own.

"You don't look good, Gabe."

Gabriel found his grin. "A sight better than you. They give you any trouble?"

Ethan looked back at the men with something like disgust. "Just the big one. Wouldn't get on the horse until someone beat a little sense into him."

"You do the beating?"

Ethan merely shrugged and asked, "Did Decker get word to the marshal? Is he coming?"

This time Gabriel actually smiled. "I know Decker came back, but he didn't bring the marshal."

"I figured it might take a little time. We'll just have to hitch the wagon and drag these boys into the jail ourselves." Ethan wondered about his brother's smile. After everything they just went through, he'd just as soon wipe it off his face, kiss his wife, and sleep for a week. "What's going on?"

"Eliza's home."

13

"She's what?"

"You're wearing the same look I did when I rode in last night."

"Did she say where she's been?" Ethan asked. "Did she say what in the hell she's been doing?"

Gabriel laughed. "She didn't say much, but I'd bet Zeus she has something to say."

Ethan removed his hat and wiped a sleeve across his forehead, looking across the way to the main house. "I imagine she's still sleeping."

"Imagine so. I know how worried we both were with her gone, but I believe she had her reasons for going. We both know that if Eliza felt she needed to do something, it's better to trust her."

"You mean because she's never wrong."

"Because she's never wrong."

"She's all in one piece, though?" Ethan looked again at Gabriel. "Nothing happened to her out there?"

"She looked well and sturdy as always."

"Good, then she's well enough for a beating."

Gabriel knew his brother wouldn't hurt any woman, so he smiled and said, "I'm sure she's expecting it."

Ethan nodded, as though something now distracted him.

The dismal situation they found themselves in and the events of what happened last night came rushing back to Gabriel, and he watched as his brother replaced his hat on his dark head of hair.

Ethan said, "Let's get these men inside the barn and make sure everyone who's not needed with the cattle will get some sleep."

Gabriel helped secure Hunter's men enough so they'd still be alive to face the marshal. In truth, Gabriel didn't care if the marshal strung them all up in the woods and let the animals tear up their carcasses. Carl was still laid out and covered, ready for the doctor. Knowing he'd never see Carl again or play another hand of poker with him, Gabriel closed the door and moved the men to another section of the barn, farther away from his friend.

"I'll keep an eye on things out here," Gabriel said after they'd made sure Hunter's men didn't have a way to get loose. "You go in and see that wife and baby of yours, and get a few hours of sleep."

Ethan nodded, his gaze touching over the door where Carl waited. "I'll go and check on the shift rotations for the cattle before I head inside."

"Ethan," Gabriel called out as his brother left the barn. "Thank you for what you did tonight for Andrew."

Ethan stood there staring at his brother for the briefest of moments. "It's what we do for family."

Gabriel watched his brother head over to the bunkhouse. He knew Ethan must be exhausted, much as Gabriel had felt after he rode back to the ranch with Andrew. He'd been elated to see Eliza, but he couldn't shake the image from his mind of Isabelle holding Andrew. She'd looked at him as though nothing in this world could tear the boy from her arms again. Gabriel remembered the brief uncertainty he'd seen in her eyes when he offered to carry Andrew upstairs. He didn't blame her, but he did want to find a way to fix it.

Ben walked into the barn a short time later and found Gabriel sitting on a square bale of hay, leaning up against an interior wall next to the door where Hunter's men were secured. He watched as Gabriel's eyes flew open the moment he stepped into the barn.

"Shouldn't you be in a bed somewhere, Ben?"

"Could ask you the same thing."

Ben walked over, adjusting his hat over his head of blond hair, and motioned toward the door. "They in there?"

Gabriel nodded. "They are. Hopefully not for long. Did Ethan find you?"

"He came by the bunkhouse," Ben said. "I got

enough sleep and thought to relieve Jackson over at the house. Ethan said you could use a hand in here."

Gabriel said nothing for a moment, exhaustion slowly overpowering his thoughts. "Has anyone seen Frank or Sam?"

Ben shook his head. "No one has found either of them," he said. "The house and outbuildings have all been searched. If something happened to them, then we're likely to find the bodies soon."

The thought of more of their men dead sickened Gabriel. He remembered what his brother said at the trappers' cabin: "You're better than that. You kill him, you become him." But they all knew in the end, killing might be their only option.

"Jackson came back in with the cattle report from the stampede," Ben said.

Gabriel looked at the ranch hand. "I heard— seventeen dead." Any destructive loss of cattle was senseless, but it didn't compare to the loss of life. Hunter may be calling the orders, but he wasn't the one carrying them out.

"Gabriel?" Ben stepped closer to Gabriel. "You all right?"

Gabriel nodded but said nothing. He shook the fog from his thoughts and stood up, walking from one end of the barn to the next. After a few passes, he stopped and said, "When we rode over to Hunter's spread, I saw a man standing back from the rest of them. He wore a gunslinger's rig, but he was the only one who didn't draw on us. I'd never seen him before."

"Could be Tyre Burton."

"You know him?"

Ben shook his head. "Just heard of him some years back down Wyoming way. He hadn't made much of a name for himself back then but that didn't stop him from working on it. I got myself out of there when the army and the Indians were making like they planned on going to war. Didn't hear much about him after that until last year when I heard he found his way into Montana Territory."

"How do you know it's him?"

"Only gunslinger I know of in these parts. Heard he was part Comanche with light blue eyes."

"That sounds like who I saw at the Double Bar."

Ben leaned up against the door and asked, "What has you thinking on him?"

"He didn't draw on us."

Ben didn't know what was going through Gabriel's head, so he waited patiently until his boss stopped his pacing again. He didn't have to wait long.

"He was the only one there who didn't draw on us. If Hunter went to the trouble of hiring a gunfighter, I'd bet the old man would want him close by."

"What are you getting at, Gabriel?"

Gabriel shook his head, disgusted with himself.

"Gabriel?"

"We were wrong, Ben," Gabriel said. "Hunter probably watched the whole thing from his window at the Double Bar. Dammit, we had him."

Ethan quickly found comfort in his wife's arms
and sleep took him almost immediately after he
lay down on their bed. After seeing that the
watches were covered for the herd and that the
rest of the men rested up, Ethan barely stayed
awake long enough to wash the dirt from his face
and arms before he stripped down and got into
bed. His wife joined him, and he found comfort
knowing she and their son were safe.

The dim blackness holding him prisoner
didn't want to release him, and Ethan was
content to let the darkness have him for as long
as it wanted. A vague awareness of light and
shadows crept over him, and a soft voice sang
softly. He finally forced his eyes to open, letting
in the offensive light. Ethan watched his wife
rocking slowly in the chair near the window,
nursing their son, singing Jacob's favorite tune.
Ethan had no idea what the words meant since
Brenna sang it in her Scottish language, but it
sounded pretty all the same.

Ethan moved his limbs just to be sure each one cooperated when he tried to get out of bed. It certainly wasn't the first time he'd gone all night without sleep or worked a full day on only a few hours, but it didn't mean he liked it.

"You're well, love?"

Ethan's eyes met Brenna's emerald-green ones, and he realized she'd stopped singing to Jacob and waited, studying him.

"I'll live."

Brenna smiled. "I can certainly promise you that."

"Is that so?" Ethan returned her smile.

"We're not about to let you go anytime soon, my love."

Ethan pulled aside the bed covers and stretched while he stood. He walked over to his wife and hunched down next to the chair, comfortable with his nakedness.

Brenna reached over with one hand and gently cupped her husband's face. "You are well?"

"I am, darling," he assured her. "I'll be better once we get those men to the marshal and Carl a proper burial."

Brenna lowered her hand and focused her attention back on Jacob. "You could bury him here."

"Carl may not have said much about it, but he was a religious man. I believe he'd want to be buried in the church cemetery."

Brenna nodded and continued to slowly rock as her son continued to nurse. "Gabriel came in a short time ago while I sat down in the kitchen." Brenna hesitated before adding, "He doesn't look well."

"He's feeling guilty."

Brenna lifted her head to look at her husband. "Whatever for? None of this is his fault."

"I know that, but I'm not so sure Isabelle is going to see it that way."

Brenna leaned over and kissed her husband, saying softly against his lips, "You still have much to learn of women."

Isabelle thought only briefly of ignoring the soft knock at the door, but she'd been trying to ignore the inevitable choice ever since Gabriel had asked her not to make any decisions until they spoke. But she'd already made her decision—she didn't want to leave. Andrew slept, but she still worried for his safety. Not only because he'd been taken and made a pawn in this feud with Brenna's grandfather, but also because her aunt may somehow find a way to take Andrew from her. She wanted to be strong enough to stay in Montana, to stay with Gabriel, but every bit of strength she still possessed was needed to protect her brother.

The knock came again at the door. This time Isabelle left her brother's bedside and quietly moved across the room. She wasn't surprised to find Gabriel standing on the other side of the door. She opened it only slightly and Gabriel looked over her head to the bed. Isabelle saw the obvious relief cross his face.

"Is it over?"

Gabriel studied Isabelle. What he'd nearly done at the cabin still clung to him. He'd never killed a man, but he knew he had it in him. He also knew that no matter which Gallagher came face to face with Hunter, the decision not to pull the trigger wouldn't be easy. Gabriel stepped forward. He could feel Isabelle's light and warmth and wanted nothing more than to hold onto that forever.

"It's over for now." Gabriel moved past her into the room, relieved when she offered no resistance to his entry. "I think it might be best if you went back to the cottage. I was wrong to keep you here, so close to the trouble. You can ride with us into town tomorrow."

Of all the things Isabelle thought Gabriel might say, that certainly wasn't one of them. Despite the fear and the worry of staying at the ranch, of staying with Gabriel, the thought of leaving him pained her far more.

"Is that what you want?"

"No."

"Then why send us away?"

Gabriel stepped forward, reaching for her, his strong hands on her arms. "To keep you safe," he said. "The danger, the risk, it's too close. We almost lost Andrew last night. This isn't your fight, and if I'd been thinking more clearly, I never would have asked you to come out to the ranch."

"I don't regret coming here, Gabriel. I may have been uncertain and afraid, but I was wrong to ever doubt you. You didn't create the circumstances that led us here." Tears slowly filled her gray eyes, but she continued. "I was angry at you and perhaps for a moment thought I couldn't trust you because of what happened to Andrew, but you weren't to blame."

"No, you were right," said Gabriel. "If you stayed in town, Hunter wouldn't have known about you, and Andrew would have been safe."

Isabelle wanted to laugh at both of them for they both seemed determined to accept blame. "Gabriel." She stepped closer, raising a hand to his rough cheek. "Our lives began again when we stepped off that stage, but it wasn't until I met you that I hoped for a future I once only dreamt about."

"You didn't dream for this."

"No, I didn't, and I'd be lying if I said I didn't still fear for Andrew's life. What's happening between your family and Brenna's grandfather is something I can't understand. From what Brenna has told me, the anger runs deep."

Gabriel covered her pale hand with his darker one. "The things he's done are unimaginable." He continued holding her hand, allowing their joined hands to fall between them. "I almost killed a man tonight. Partly because he'd taken Andrew, but I think it was mostly because I wanted it to be Hunter. I wanted this to end. You have to know that I have that in me."

Isabelle stepped into him and waited for his arms to come around her. She stood there for a moment, taking in his scent. She listened to the beating of his heart and the soft breathing of her brother coming from the bed on the other side of the room. Holding him close, she said softly, "Gabriel, there is darkness in each of us."

"I can't believe there's any in you."

She pulled away and looked up into his eyes. "There are things about my past, about my family that you should know.

"What about your family?" He pulled back enough to look at her.

"Not in here and not now."

"Isabelle—"

"Please," she begged. "I've only just come to realize that I want a tomorrow with you."

Gabriel's only thoughts the past two days had been for her and Andrew's safety and getting them away from the ranch—away from him— to protect them. Isabelle's words elated him.

"Are you certain? I don't know what's going to happen tomorrow, but I do know this isn't over yet. I know I failed you last time, but I swear I'll do everything in my power to protect you and Andrew.

"Gabriel—"

"No wait. I need you to be certain because I promise I won't be able to let you go once you say yes."

"I'm certain."

"Will you do something for me?"

Isabelle hesitated a moment because she didn't

like his tone or the look in his eyes. "What is it?"

"I want you to go back into town, stay at the cottage."

"I can't do that," she said, shaking her head. When she realized she'd raised her voice, she glanced over at the bed to be sure Andrew still slept.

Isabelle grabbed Gabriel's hand and urged him to follow her from the room, grateful when he said nothing and walked with her into the hall. She knew one of the ranch hands kept watch below her bedroom window. Everyone was on guard since Andrew's snatching, and Brenna predicted they would be until they finally settled the matter. She left the door ajar in case Andrew called out. It was light out now and she imagined the household would have been awake long ago if not for exhaustion. Isabelle walked quietly down the hall and into his open room. Once inside, she let go of his hand and waited for him to join her.

Gabriel stood just inside the bedroom, uncertain of the thoughts going through

Isabelle's mind. It was probably too much to hope that she thought of anything except keeping quiet so her brother could sleep. Uncertainty filled him as he looked at her. She fidgeted and appeared to be nervous. He closed the door as his eyes shifted to the window. Tired or not, the rest of the Gallaghers would be up and around before too long.

"About the cottage, Isabelle—"

"Why is it you believe we'd be safe there with no else around?"

"You and Andrew wouldn't be caught up in the middle of all this in town. Hunter has always been careful to keep his actions quiet from the people in Briarwood. You'd go back to teaching, and Andrew could be around other children."

"Is this what you call not letting me go?"

Gabriel hoped she saw how crazy she was making him. "I'm not letting you go, I guarantee you that. I don't know how long this is going to last, and I feel as though the worst is yet to come."

"You know the future now, is that it?"

He wasn't getting anywhere. "What if something else happened to Andrew or to you?"

"What if you're out there and something happens to you? There are no guarantees."

Gabriel couldn't help himself any longer. He walked to her and pulled her into his arms, enjoying the weight of her head on his shoulder. "I'm not happy about this, Isabelle."

Isabelle realized he teetered on the verge of letting her have her way in this. She didn't know why he'd give in, but she would take the advantage.

"I know, but can you see this from my point of view?"

Gabriel ran a hand over her hair, following the silky strands down her back and smiled. "What view is that?"

"When we first met you, I saw light and joy in your eyes. I can't begin to understand what it must be like to find any kind of peace with everything your family has been through, but I want to see that joy again."

Gabriel inched back from her and focused his

dark eyes on her lighter ones. He still worried for her safety, but he hadn't lied to her when he promised he'd do everything possible to keep her and Andrew safe.

Gabriel thought of no words to say. Darkness still filled him, but with her in his arms, finding his light again was possible. With only a touch, he lifted her face and lowered his lips to brush up against hers. Once, twice, until every emotion he held inside since he met her was released into that kiss. Pulling her close to his body and holding her tightly, he kissed her as he'd longed to from the moment he became her husband. He thrilled in the knowledge that she offered no resistance and responded to every stroke of his mouth and every caress as his hands moved freely up and down her body. Slowly he walked backward toward the bed, pulling her along with him, never releasing her from his arms.

Isabelle's body slowly burned as his lips found hers over and over again. The heat of his hands scorched through the cloth of her dress and imagined what it would feel like to have no barrier between them. She wanted it to never end, to be his wife in truth and to know that she'd always be his and he'd always be hers. Isabelle knew exactly where this was leading, and she hated knowing it must stop. With deep regret and a strength she barely mustered, she broke their embrace and pulled away.

"Isabelle?" Gabriel took a moment to control his breathing, but said nothing else and waited for her to explain.

Isabelle's heart raced and her breaths came just as rapidly as his. Her body ached and her skin tingled, longing again for his touch. It would be far worse to know him completely and then have him turn away after she told him her secret.

"It seems we need to have that talk."

"You said not here and not right now."

"I didn't plan on this happening, Gabriel."

Calmer now, Gabriel pulled Isabelle back into his arms. "What kind of man do you think I am? I would never force you."

Isabelle hugged him close to her, tears finding

their way down her cheeks, unbidden and unwanted, the pain of having to tell him everything only made worse by his comfort.

"Not all men are so kind."

"What do you mean?"

Isabelle wanted to say the words aloud but found it difficult.

"Isabelle?" Gabriel said her name and waited for her to face him. "What's wrong?" He asked the question but the sadness he saw in the depths of her eyes told him the truth without her speaking it. Gabriel never believed it possible to hate anyone as much as Hunter, but he knew without any doubt that he could kill the man who had made Isabelle shed these tears.

"Who was it?"

14

"Oh no, Gabriel, I know what you're thinking and it's not entirely true."

"Isabelle."

"What took place caused hurt and bruises, but it could have been far worse." She walked to the bed and lowered herself to the edge. "Please sit down, and I'll tell you what happened."

"You don't have to do this." Gabriel moved to sit next to her. In an effort to comfort her and reassure her that no matter what happened, he'd never walk away from her, Gabriel took her shaky hand into his.

"Yes, I do." Isabelle allowed him to hold her, and welcomed his support. She needed to feel his strength and hope for a short time that everything about her past might be forgotten, and she could have the chance at a real future.

"Three years ago, a young man from a prominent and wealthy family in New Orleans sought my father's permission to court me. He was a pleasant man, and I enjoyed his company on the occasions we saw one another. I didn't have any special feelings for him, but it seemed important to my father. He had business dealings with the young man's father."

"What was his name?"

Isabelle glanced up at Gabriel. "That isn't important." He continued to hold her gaze, and Isabelle found the connection equally unsettling and comforting. "His name was Justin. Justin Desrochers." She waited for him to say something, but he merely nodded. Isabelle took that as a sign to continue.

"After we had spent enough time together— innocent outings mostly—Justin asked my father for permission to take me for a carriage ride and picnic in the park. The park was public and frequented by many in our neighborhood, so my father made no objection." Isabelle paused for a moment. She had never wanted to relive this, and she never imagined she would be telling another man about it. Isabelle took comfort in knowing he still sat beside her.

"Justin drove us to the park, and we ate our lunch. It was such a lovely afternoon with the trees in full blossom, so he suggested we take the longer route home. I was foolish enough to agree. I was having a wonderful time and enjoyed being out of doors. When he drove the carriage toward the road that led into the surrounding countryside, I suggested we return. He simply grabbed me and drove out of town." Isabelle's hands shook, but Gabriel held them steady. "I knew many couples who enjoyed riding through the country, and I prayed that we'd come upon someone. Justin drove the horses farther away from town and pulled into the trees. He started to . . ." Isabelle didn't want to say it aloud.

"Please, stop." Gabriel didn't want to see her going through this pain. He remembered his ıster's anguish when her friend had been raped, and how it had affected all of them.

"I need to say it. I need to say it for me." Isabelle realized how true that was. She wanted to be honest with Gabriel about everything, most especially if they chose to remain together. But this retelling was more for her. That realization gave her the strength to continue.

Taking a deep breath, Isabelle said, "He began to kiss me, but I didn't like it and I wanted only to get out of the carriage. He held me down and pulled at my clothes. I struggled, but he was so much stronger than I. Too much time had passed before I heard another carriage approaching on the road. I suppose they thought we might be stranded, and they stopped. Thankfully, I knew the older couple, and they saw what was happening. Justin jumped from the carriage and ran into the trees. The couple helped me home, and I never saw Justin again."

"How far did he . . .?" Gabriel began. "I mean how . . . ?" His words trailed off, but Isabelle knew what he asked.

"Far enough for me to fear it ever happening again," she said and added, "but the couple saved me from far worse."

"What happened to Justin?"

"When the older couple, who happened to be friends of my parents, brought me home and explained what they'd seen, my father contacted the police. My father knew the superintendent of police, and they managed to keep the matter quiet. Justin's father had been supportive in trying to locate his son, but no one ever did. My father always believed that his father helped him to leave the country."

Isabelle sat there, waiting for Gabriel to say something. There was still more to tell, but she worried too much had already been said. He shifted and left the bed. For the briefest of moments, Isabelle's heart sank until he knelt in front of her and set his hands on her lap.

"If ever the opportunity presents itself in this lifetime, I promise you that the man who caused you so much pain will pay for what he did."

Isabelle expected many things but hearing

such a promise brought her relief. She needed to tell him the rest before it was too late.

"Gabriel, there's something else you need to know—about my parents."

Looking up into those beautiful, tear-filled eyes, Gabriel had no doubts. He'd known he wanted her and knew he cared for her, but he now knew that she represented his future and he'd do whatever it took to convince her he meant it.

"It doesn't matter. Not now." His hand circled the back of her neck, gently pulling her toward him. Gabriel sensed her brief hesitation and then her acceptance. He touched her lips lightly with his own—both warm, both willing. Pulling back from that welcoming softness was the hardest thing he'd ever done.

"Gabriel?"

"We do have a lot to talk about, but it will keep."

Gabriel stood and took her hand, helping her rise from the bed. Isabelle tried to understand the sudden change in him. Just a short time ago she had nearly given herself to him, nearly joined their lives forever without thinking of anything but the moment. Isabelle wasn't ready to let it go yet—she wanted to tell him everything and to build a home and life with him.

Before she could respond, a commotion out in the hallway drew their attention. Gabriel let her hand go, and though anxious to finish their discussion, she watched him walk to the door.

Gabriel opened the door to find Brenna there, holding Jacob. "Ethan went out to meet the marshal. He just arrived."

Gabriel nodded and turned back to Isabelle, leaving the door open. "I have to go now but I promise you'll be safe here."

"You're leaving?"

He walked over to her and leaned down to press his lips to hers. "I'll be back as soon as I can." He kissed her again. "Don't leave the house alone."

"We won't," she said softly, but he'd already rushed out the door.

Gabriel's thoughts remained on what Isabelle told him and how close he'd come to making their marriage real, their bond complete. If she hadn't stopped them, he may have done more damage and caused her even more pain. He needed to prove that he wanted permanence before committing her to their marriage.

He stepped onto the front porch to see Ethan and the marshal speaking. The marshal dismounted, but the man with him remained on his horse. This man noticed Gabriel first and drew the other's attention.

Ethan turned and waited for his brother to join them, preferring they hear the marshal's news all at once.

"Ethan, Marshal." Gabriel stood next to his brother and nodded to the man on the horse.

"Gabriel, this is Marshal Pickett and Deputy Lewis," Ethan said, taking care of the introductions.

Gabriel nodded at both men, though the deputy looked slightly familiar. "We have a bundle of problems and a few men for you,

Marshal."

"Ethan said as much," Marshal Pickett said. "Can't say I like you boys doing my job, but I can appreciate what you went through, and I'm sorry about your man."

Gabriel didn't need a reminder of the friend who lay out in the wagon ready to go to town. They had to move the wagon from the barn to the one of the larger sheds to keep the horses from panicking over the smell of death. "We're heading into Briarwood soon to get Carl to the doc, but we need to know what's going to be done about Hunter."

"Well now, boys, that's where I've got some news for you," the marshal said, though to Gabriel he sounded uneasy. "Some of Hunter's boys caused a ruckus over at the saloon last night and ended up in my jail. I heard the whole of it when I rode into town this morning and got the message left by your man."

Gabriel hoped there was a point to whatever the marshal was trying to say.

"Are they still in jail?" Ethan asked.

"They are and that's where they'll stay. You see, they got to bothering one of the serving girls over there and roughed her up a bit before old Loren heard the screaming."

Gabriel glanced up at the deputy who appeared to be in no hurry to get anywhere, then back to the marshal. "Is that the news?"

"Not exactly." The marshal appeared to be unaffected by Gabriel's impatience. "They wanted to make a deal with me. Said if I let them go, they'd tell me all about how their boss snatched a little boy."

Ethan sensed Gabriel tensing up next to him and spoke before his brother. "They told you Hunter took the boy?"

"They won't confirm which boy, and I'm not letting them go."

"That won't be necessary," Gabriel said. "We already know it was Hunter."

"And I reckon' we can get started on the whole telling of it," the marshal said. "Deputy Lewis is here to help take the men back to the jail in Briarwood."

"Appreciate that, Marshal," said Ethan. "Like Gabriel said, we'll be heading in ourselves to make arrangements for Carl." Ethan shared a glance with his brother before adding, "We'll be going after Hunter. We'd prefer you ride with us to make it legal, but we won't be waiting any longer."

Gabriel half expected the marshal to warn them from doing anything on their own. He'd never met Marshal Pickett, not since he took over the position some months after Marshal Wallis had been killed in the bungled bank robbery.

No one had been able to prove that the men who attempted to rob the bank worked for Nathan Hunter, but many suspected they had. Marshal Wallis took down two of the men before the third got him. Where Wallis had been a man of action, the new marshal had a reputation for being slow to move against the guilty, although he was fair.

"I'll go along with you. This is my jurisdiction, and I don't like knowing that man is here anymore than you do," said the marshal. "Now, boys, do you have any evidence of Nathan Hunter's crimes?"

Gabriel found himself wondering how this man became appointed to his position. "The witnesses to these crimes over the years should be sufficient evidence."

"Gabriel's right, Marshal," Ethan interjected. "We all know without a doubt that Hunter is responsible for these crimes and at least a dozen others. Marshal Wallis was ready to take Hunter in before the old man disappeared."

Gabriel noticed that Marshal Pickett didn't appreciate hearing about his predecessor.

"I didn't say I wouldn't arrest Hunter," said Marshal Pickett, "but some proof of his crimes would help."

"Like my brothers said, we won't wait."

Gabriel turned, along with the others, to face the front door of the house. Eliza had come outside quietly and had apparently heard enough of the conversation. Gabriel knew his sister, and right now he'd bet that she didn't trust either the marshal or his deputy. Turning back to the men, he said, "Marshal Pickett, Deputy Lewis, our sister Eliza."

Gabriel noticed the deputy sat up a bit taller in the saddle, though his eyes narrowed when Eliza walked down to join them.

"Marshal, it's time we head into town to see after Carl," Ethan said, realizing that something bothered his sister. He may not have seen her in nearly a year, but she stood next to him, wound up tighter than a wild mustang. He wanted to hug her, but first he had to get her alone and find out what she didn't like about these men. "If you'll give us half an hour, we'll be ready to ride, and we can help you back to town with Hunter's men."

Gabriel watched the marshal and his deputy carefully. He wasn't oblivious to Eliza's behavior either, knowing that she caught things about people that most folks missed.

The marshal took his time and finally nodded. "I reckon' that'll work. If you'll point us to the men, we'll get them ready."

Ethan nodded and called out to the ranch hand who was dismounting from his horse near the corral. "Henry!" They all waited a minute while Henry handed his horse off to the other cowboy who rode in with him and sauntered over to the group.

"Ethan?"

"Would you take these men over to the stable and get the stock wagon hitched?" Ethan asked and added, "Get Colton to give you a hand. We'll be riding into Briarwood and taking those men along with us."

Henry took a moment to study everyone in the group and then the brothers and sister. The three of them stood together like a wall that refused to be broken. "Sure thing," he said and motioned for the marshal and his man to follow.

When the men were out of earshot, Ethan turned Eliza toward him and pulled her into his arms. "I should tan your hide."

Eliza held him close, but thought better of this and lightly shoved her brother back. "You sound like Gabriel."

"Except Gabriel wouldn't have done it."

"And neither will you."

Ethan gently rubbed his hands over her arms. "What were you thinking, little sister, taking off on your own like that?"

"Get off my back, Ethan. Didn't you miss me?"

"Get back over here." Ethan pulled her into another hug. Ethan stepped back this time and spoke loudly enough so she knew just how worried he'd been. "Where the devil have you been?"

Eliza looked between her two favorite men in the world. "Let's just say I have some interesting news." She looked across the distance to the stable.

The direction of his sister's attention wasn't lost on Gabriel. "We'll get to your news, little sister. First, why don't you tell us what just happened?"

"Happened with what?"

"Eliza."

Eliza crossed her arms and stared across the

property to the barn. "You can't trust those men."

15

Gabriel rode alongside the wagon carrying Carl while Ben drove the team. Marshal Pickett and Deputy Lewis rode behind them with Hunter's three men tied up in the back of a supply wagon driven by Pete. Two ranch hands were all either Ethan or Gabriel felt comfortable taking away from the ranch. They still needed most of the men to round up the strays lost during the stampede. It took a lot of convincing on Gabriel's part to get Ethan to stay at the ranch. Neither was comfortable with the idea of both of them leaving, and though Ethan had wanted to ride into town for Carl's sake, they decided one of them should stay behind. Gabriel didn't think Ethan minded after they made the decision. He imagined Ethan would put the time to good use and attempt to get Eliza talking about what she'd been doing all this time.

The ride into Briarwood was usually a pleasant one for Gabriel, but this time he wanted it over with. He matched pace with the front wagon, riding alongside his dead friend who was wrapped up in a wool blanket and canvas. He'd been unable to look at the body after he helped place him in the wagon. Guilt weighed heavily on him. He decided that he needed to speak with Ethan about how to better protect the men working on the range. With the weather changing and everything happening with Hunter, keeping the men safe would be more difficult, especially since no one appeared to know where Hunter was hiding.

Gabriel didn't have a chance to find out everything Brenna knew, but he remained confident that Ethan had the information by now. Snow began to slowly fall in light flakes, and Gabriel hoped it would hold off until they reached town. It looked like they'd be bunking overnight in Briarwood. He leaned over to tell Ben about his decision to stay over when Marshal Pickett rode up alongside him. Gabriel looked back over his shoulder to make sure the men were still secure and turned his attention to the marshal.

"Marshal Pickett. Is everything all right?"

"It is," he replied. "I just thought we might talk a minute seeing as how we got a bit of a stretch with both these wagons slowing us down."

Gabriel thought it took the marshal far too long to make a point. "What's on your mind?"

"Well, now, these boys back there have been talking my ear off. They're saying you attacked them, and they just protected themselves."

Gabriel eyed the marshal narrowly. "I imagine they're saying all sorts of things, Marshal. Doesn't make any of it true."

"Oh, I believe what you and your brother told me back at the ranch, don't you worry none about that," Pickett said, "but you see, these boys also said something about their boss getting them out."

Gabriel pulled up slightly on the reins and turned fully to the marshal. He motioned Ben to continue on. "What are you getting at, Marshal?"

"Well, now, I'm thinkin' we might just have ourselves a bit of trouble when we get to town. We got a couple of Hunter's men in my jail and three more about to join him."

"And his men offered up this information?" asked Gabriel. "They told you that Hunter might try and break them out? How could they possibly know that?"

"I don't know there, son, but we'd better all be watching our backs. You especially. Whatever's going on between your family and Nathan Hunter, I don't want it to get out of hand."

Gabriel glanced ahead at the horses and wagons making their way across the rough land. It was land worth fighting for, but he asked himself if it was worth the lives they'd lost.

He looked back to Marshal Pickett. "It got out of hand too long ago to turn back."

Loosening the reins, Gabriel gave Zeus his head and galloped to catch up with the wagons, not looking back to see if Marshal Pickett followed behind him.

They arrived in Briarwood nearly an hour later than Gabriel planned. The snow slowed them down at one point when the wind picked up, blowing heavier flakes across the land, making the footing treacherous. Gabriel wasn't willing to risk one of the work horses stepping into a hole or breaking a wheel on a rock, so he made them stop long enough for the wind to calm down. Hunter's men did nothing except complain but had finally quieted down enough to huddle together. Ben held his wagon steady as Gabriel checked to make sure the canvas around Carl remained secure. Luckily when the wind subsided, so did the snow, and they were able to make the remainder of the trip with relative ease.

The streets were nearly deserted in Briarwood when the drove in. A few lamps lit up some of the houses, and the general store was open for business, but most of the noise and activity came from the saloon. Some of the townsfolk seemed to be getting an early start on their drinking. Most people avoided being out in the cold and snow if possible. Gabriel didn't like the idea of having to stay in the saloon's hotel and imagined if they did, there wouldn't be much sleeping that night. He didn't want them all to stay in the cottage, either. Perhaps he'd ask Mr. Baker if he'd be willing to rent a couple of rooms above the general store for the night.

They drove through town and the marshal, his deputy, and the other wagon headed to the jail while Gabriel and Ben drove to the edge of town where Brody kept his small clinic. Enough light remained in the sky that Gabriel hoped the doctor wasn't out at the café for supper yet.

Gabriel pulled Zeus to a stop in front of Doc Brody's place and said to Ben, "I'll go in and see if he's here. Why don't you pull around the back? Brody doesn't like the . . ." Gabriel had a difficult time saying *dead* in reference to his friend. "He'll want the wagon around back."

Ben nodded and maneuvered the team around the back of the building. Gabriel watched and then knocked on the front door. Only a few moments later, the door opened and the doctor stood there, wiping his hands on a white cloth. Gabriel stood tall and was a large man, but Brody was half again his size, educated back east, skilled with a scalpel, and as jolly a man as Gabriel had ever met. He watched the smile slowly fade from Brody's face. Gabriel imagined he must look worse than he thought.

"What brings you to my door, Gabriel?" Brody asked. "You and yours aren't hurt, I hope?"

"Not exactly," Gabriel replied. "I do have someone for you, though. Ben took the wagon around back."

"Well that's never something I like to hear. Let's go and have a look."

Brody pushed the door open wide and motioned Gabriel to follow him through the clinic. Gabriel knew that the doctor kept a set of rooms above the clinic as his living quarters and wondered at someone's ability to live above death.

Gabriel stepped out the back door with Brody.

"Who do we have here?" the doctor asked. He walked around to the back of the wagon and began to untie the rope holding the canvas down. Ben secured the team and helped Brody, but Gabriel could tell that it bothered the ranch hand, so he stepped forward and took over the task. Once they had Carl unwrapped enough so the doctor could take a look, Brody let out a low whistle.

"What happened to Carl?"

"Stampede," Gabriel said. He didn't offer any more information. Most people knew about the tension between the Gallaghers and Nathan Hunter, but few people in town knew the extent of the damage done by Hunter over the years. He'd just as soon keep it that way.

Brody shook his head and said, "Good man here. Played a nice hand of poker, he did." Brody covered Carl's face back up with the canvas. "I'll need a bit of help moving him inside. He's not a small lad."

Gabriel stepped forward to help Brody pull Carl from the back of the wagon. He wondered at Brody's ability to simply push ahead when a friend lay dead in his arms. Gabriel supposed the man had grown accustomed to death over the years. At least the doctor took care of such things in a room away from his clinic.

Once Carl was laid out on Brody's preparation table, Gabriel stepped back from the body.

"If you'll give me a minute, I'll get you the canvas and blanket."

Gabriel shook his head. "Burn them."

"Carl was a fine horseman," Brody said, making light conversation. "It's a wonder he got pulled under the cows."

Gabriel didn't respond. He didn't know how to respond without saying too much. Exhaustion slowly took over but didn't entirely consume the anger. He was tired of the fighting and the ugliness of death that Hunter threw at them. But he wanted justice for Carl, so he'd keep on fighting if necessary.

Gabriel didn't want to be in that room any longer but wanted to stay for Carl. Brody must have read his mind.

"I do prefer to work alone, Gabriel." Brody cast Gabriel a sympathetic glance. "I'll take care of the lad. I promise he's in good hands."

"He'd want a church burial," Gabriel said absently. "He felt strongly about such things."

"I'll fix him up proper, don't you fret over that."

Gabriel nodded, spared one last glance at his friend, and left the room out the back door. Ben waited in the wagon with his head bowed low but looked up at Gabriel when he called his name.

"I'm heading over to the church to speak with the reverend," he told Ben. "Why don't you head over to the general store, see if Mr. Baker will rent us a couple of his rooms for the night. I'll stop by and see how Pete's doing with the marshal, and we'll meet up with you at the café."

"We could make it back to the ranch tonight,

Gabe."

Gabriel knew that but wanted to be certain nothing went wrong with the men over at the jail. If what those men told Marshal Pickett was true about Hunter or some of his men breaking the others out, he knew they'd be needed in town. The last thing Gabriel wanted was to be caught up in another situation where he might lose more men, but it was a risk he unwillingly had to take.

"We'll stay over for the night and if all goes well at the jail, we'll head out at first light," Gabriel said. "The rest of the cattle have to be brought down from the high pasture, and we'll be needed for that."

"I'll see you at the café." Ben was about to drive the team away when he rested the reins on his knees. "You holler if there's any trouble at the jail." He snapped the reins on the team and headed toward the general store.

Gabriel watched the retreating wagon, then mounted his horse and rode back to the jail. He saw the other wagon out front but didn't see

Pete. Gabriel stopped his horse next to the wagon and dismounted, tying Zeus up to the hitching post in front of the modest building. Briarwood didn't have much need for a jail. Other than the occasional drunk or thief, Briarwood didn't see too much crime, which is also why they'd never bothered to appoint a sheriff.

Stepping through the front door of the jail, Gabriel took in his surroundings. He had entered the building only once before when he and Ethan had spoken with the marshal the previous year about Hunter. Pete wasn't in the front room, but the deputy stood there.

"Deputy Lewis, I'm looking for Pete, the man who drove the wagon in with you."

"He's gone out back."

"And Marshal Pickett?"

"He'll be along."

Gabriel's irritation escalated. Rather than speaking again to the deputy, he walked toward the back of the jail to the cells.

"Hey, you can't go back there!"

Gabriel ignored the deputy and walked through the inner door. Five men either lay or sat on the cots. The three they brought in plus the two Gabriel assumed were brought in by the marshal.

"You can't be back here." The deputy came up behind Gabriel with his right hand on the butt of his gun. Gabriel couldn't decide if the deputy would actually use it. He might have laughed if the dark look the deputy sent him didn't reveal how serious the man was.

"You can drop your hand from that weapon, Deputy," Gabriel said. "I'll just wait outside for my man."

"You do that, Gallagher."

Gabriel stepped around the deputy and noticed the man didn't remove his hand from the gun in his holster. He walked back to the front of the jail when Marshal Pickett walked in through the front door.

"Well, Gabriel, didn't expect to you see over here so soon," said the marshal. "Thought you'd be over at Doc Brody's."

"Already took care of that. I'm looking for Pete."

"Well, now, I do believe he left."

"The wagon's still out front, Marshal."

"So it is. I reckon he'll be here directly."

Gabriel was tired of the runaround they kept giving him. The deputy stepped into the front room and continued to cast dark looks Gabriel's way.

"I'm headed over to the café. If Pete comes back by, let him know. I'll be taking the wagon."

Gabriel didn't wait for a response. He left the jail and tied Zeus up to the back of the wagon. A few minutes later, he pulled up to the livery and made arrangements for the horses and wagon to be put up for the night. He saw that their other wagon was already there, and their horses were secured in the corral. Gabriel pulled his rifle and saddlebag off of Zeus and left the animal in the care of the blacksmith. As he passed the general store, Ben stepped out the front door.

"Mr. Baker has only one room to rent us for

the night, but there are cots."

Gabriel nodded. "Has Pete been by here?"

"Thought he was at the jail."

"So did I," Gabriel said. "I'll drop my gear off upstairs, and we can head over to the café."

Ten minutes later, Gabriel and Ben sat at the café, ordering supper. Gabriel preferred Mabel's cooking, and Isabelle's company. He was seriously reconsidering heading back to the ranch tonight.

Isabelle tucked Andrew into bed. She hadn't been comfortable leaving Andrew alone again in his own room, but he insisted he was all right.

"You're warm enough?"

Andrew nodded, his soft eyelashes skimming his cheeks as he tried to keep his eyes open. "Where's Gabriel?"

"He had to go with some men into town."

"The bad men won't hurt him, will they?"

Isabelle brushed a hand over Andrew's forehead. "No, they won't. You need to sleep now so that when Gabriel comes home, you can tell him all about the names you chose for the other horses."

Andrew turned over on his side. "Do I get to see my friends again?"

Isabelle covered him with another quilt and tucked it under his chin. "The ones from school?"

Andrew nodded, his words broken up by a long yawn. "I told Mason about the horses at the ranch. Maybe Gabriel will say Mason can visit."

She bent down to kiss her brother's cheek, grateful for his kind heart and sweet innocence. "I know he will, and I think Mason would like that. We'll talk more about it when Gabriel is home. Sleep now."

Andrew's breathing slowed, and he turned over onto his other side before burrowing beneath the quilts. In a few minutes, Isabelle rested easy knowing he slept in peace.

"Isabelle?"

The soft knock on the door brought Isabelle from her thoughts to the reality she currently found herself in. She moved from the bed to the door to see what it was that brought Brenna knocking at her room.

"Brenna, is anything wrong?"

"Thankfully, no," said Brenna. "I wanted to check on you both. Do you need anything?"

"Not tonight, thank you." Isabelle cringed at her own formal tone. She'd been unable to fully relax since Andrew's return or since Gabriel left. "I'm sorry, Brenna. I fear I'm not myself right now."

"That's understandable, though I do wish you would talk to me."

"I don't know what to say." Isabelle glanced over her shoulder to be sure Andrew still slept. He stirred slightly, so she stepped out into the hallway and quietly closed the door behind her.

"There are moments when none of this seems real."

"I know exactly how you feel."

"How is that?" Isabelle asked. "How could you possibly? You are where you should be. You have a husband, a son, a home. You don't have to wonder if you'll be here tomorrow or the next day."

Brenna found her first real smile in two days. The memories of the previous year flooded back to her and she said, "I wondered that exactly, barely more than a year ago."

"I don't understand. You and Ethan—"

"Are quite in love, yes, but it took us time and some unfortunate experiences for us to realize that." Brenna grabbed Isabelle's hand in a gesture of friendship and reassurance. "We almost lost one another because of our stubborn foolishness."

"I don't want to lose him, Brenna."

"Oh, Isabelle, you don't have to lose him."

"He married me to help save Andrew. I can't ask him to keep a vow not based on love."

"Did Gabriel tell you he wanted to end the marriage after you've solved your problem?" Brenna asked.

Isabelle paused a moment, remembering her time with Gabriel earlier and something he'd told her about there not being another woman.

"No, I do believe he wants to stay married."

"That's wonderful." Brenna noticed that Isabelle didn't share her excitement. "Is that not what you want?"

"A part of me does, yes. I just have to be sure it's for the right reasons. I have to know Gabriel wants to remain married for more than just a way to protect us."

"You've got my brother figured all wrong, Isabelle."

Eliza heard enough through her open bedroom door to know that it was time to step in. She couldn't sleep, and when she heard Isabelle and Brenna talking out in the hall, she shamelessly listened to their conversation. When it came to her family, she didn't follow rules.

"I think it's time we have a little talk, Isabelle." Eliza stepped into the hall. "Let's go down to the kitchen and fix some of that tea Brenna is so fond of." Eliza turned to Brenna and asked, "Ethan asleep?"

Brenna nodded and said, "He agreed after I promised him I'd wake him in a few hours. He only came up to our room a short time ago."

"That's because he was out helping some of the men with the cattle. Of course he wouldn't be as tired if he hadn't run me through the mud about taking off the way I did."

"Speaking of that, Eliza—"

"Not now, Brenna. One crisis at a time, and right now we have a wagon full." Eliza remembered sitting down with Brenna less than a year ago in an effort to help her better understand Ethan. Now she had a new sister-in-law in the same situation. "Let's go on down. I have a few things to say about your situation with Gabriel."

Pete finally showed up at the café just as Tilly served them their meals.

"Where in blazes have you been, Pete?" Gabriel asked.

"Telegraph office. Got some news."

Gabriel wondered how Pete even knew there'd been a telegram. If it was ranch business, the message wouldn't have been given to anyone but a Gallagher.

"What news?"

Pete waited until Tilly brought over another plate and set it down in front of him. "About Hunter."

Gabriel set his fork down. "What about Hunter? More to the point, who told you there was news of him waiting at the telegraph office?"

"Now that's the odd thing." Pete stopped to enjoy a healthy spoonful of the stew. "Deputy Lewis told me a telegram waited for us and said he'd keep an eye on the wagon while I headed over. I reckoned it might be important, so I went on over. Sure enough, it was news of Hunter." Pete pulled some papers from his coat pocket and handed them over to Gabriel. "There was also these two letters. Horace asked me to pass them along."

Gabriel absently took the letters and tucked them away in his own coat. Everything Pete told him left him uneasy.

"What exactly was the news?" Ben had nearly finished his meal.

"Said the sheriff down Bozeman way spotted

Hunter boarding a train," Pete said.

He'd nearly finished his meal, too. Gabriel found he couldn't eat anymore. He knew there was paper on Hunter issued by Marshal Wallis. He remembered watching the marshal post the papers himself. Most people had ignored the notice.

"Did the sheriff say why he didn't stop him from leaving?"

Pete shook his head. "That's all the telegram said."

Gabriel pushed his chair back, then sat up from the table and placed a couple of bills in between the plates. "Head back over to Loren's and grab our gear. I'll meet you at the livery. We're headed back tonight after all."

"Where are you going?" Ben asked.

"Back to the jail." Gabriel picked up his hat. "Something's not sitting right."

Gabriel left the two men, picked up his pace, and ran the conversation he'd had with Deputy Lewis and with Pete through his head. Gabriel's initial instincts about the deputy and Marshal

Pickett rose to his thoughts, and put him on edge. He didn't care for the marshal and he didn't trust Deputy Lewis—from the moment the deputy saw Eliza walk out on the porch to when he lied to Gabriel back at the jail.

The town had grown quiet as the sun began to set over the mountains. The temperature had dropped to near freezing and the only sounds Gabriel heard came from the saloon. The smart ones were all warmly tucked away at home by their fires.

Gabriel saw the jail and noticed the soft glow of lantern light through the windows. He paused when the ground rumbled beneath his boots, and he heard the unmistakable sound of horses. He turned around to see a small herd of horses stampeding through town and heading straight toward him. Gabriel quickly got out of the way, but he felt the heat of the animals as they raced passed him.

Some men from the saloon stepped outside to see what was happening.

Gabriel noticed Pete and Ben walking down

the exterior steps of the general store. "Watch out!" he shouted, though their focus was on the herd.

"What the—?" Gabriel saw, through the evening light, three riders among the stampeding horses. He knew the moment the riders saw him because they began firing. Gabriel ducked away behind the posts of the general store. He clenched in pain as a bullet grazed his shoulder. "Dammit!" Gabriel felt the blood seep down his arm.

"Ben! Pete!" He shouted out hoping they'd hear him over the din of pounding hooves, but he only heard gunfire. He aimed and fired back but couldn't tell if he hit the rider he aimed at. Shots continued coming from the other direction.

Gabriel watched as the front door of the jail opened and there stood the deputy with all five prisoners. *Son of a*—another shot splintered the wood behind him. He didn't know who shot this time. He heard shouts coming from somewhere close by but didn't pay much attention. Gabriel watched as the prisoners—Hunter's men—jumped on the back of horses two of the riders pulled along behind them. The stampeding horses were long gone now, and the riders were open to attack. "Lewis, you bastard!"

Gabriel braced his injured shoulder, raised, aimed, and shot at the closest rider. The rider jerked back slightly and hunched over as another rider took hold of the reins. They raced from town almost as quickly as they'd come.

Gabriel swore to no one but himself and looked back to where Hunter's men stood just moments before. Free. He pressed his hand against the graze on his shoulder in an attempt to stop the bleeding. He stepped down the general store steps as Ben and Pete raced over to him.

"Blazes, Gabe, what in the hell is going on?" Pete asked.

Gabriel just shook his head and let Ben tie a bandana around his upper arm to help staunch the bleeding. "Deputy Lewis letting the prisoners go is what's going on."

"We couldn't see much from over there," said Ben. "Have to wonder if the marshal is on Hunter's payroll, too."

"I don't think so." Gabriel walked toward the jail. The door stood open, and he saw the lantern burning low on the desk. People began to gather out front, and he left Pete and Ben to answer questions. He picked up the lantern with the hand of his good arm and quickly walked back through the door to the cells. Moving the lantern in front of him, the light settled on the body of the marshal, lying front down on the hard cell floor. Ben came into the room and Gabriel said over his shoulder to him, "Find the keys, Ben. Marshal's out cold."

Pete woke Brody and brought him over to the jail. It took some time, but he finally managed to rouse Marshal Pickett. Whatever Lewis used to hit the man, it left a long gash in the marshal's forehead that the doctor had to bandage up. Fortunately, the marshal would live.

"Marshal," Gabriel said, "we'll be heading

back to the ranch, but I'll tell you now that we'll be going after those men and Lewis."

Marshal Pickett looked up at Gabriel, though the movement suggested he was in great pain. "I won't be stopping you, Gallagher. Just do me a favor?" asked the marshal.

"What favor?"

"You get your hands on those men, you bring them back here. I don't want you killing them. We still have laws, and I'm still the territorial marshal."

Gabriel knew Marshal Pickett waited for some kind of agreement. Instead, he gave his thanks to the doctor, who had bandaged Gabriel's shoulder properly, said good-bye to the marshal, and left the jail with Ben.

Pete had left earlier to get the wagons and horses from the livery. Most of the town awoke with the ruckus, so the blacksmith was awake and helped Pete hitch the wagons. Gabriel didn't mistake the doubting looks that both Pete and Ben sent him.

"You sure you don't want to stay on in town

tonight, Gabe?" Ben asked.

"I'm sure. With those men now free and Hunter still out there, we'll need every man we have at the ranch." Gabriel had another reason to return tonight, but he didn't want to share that with his men. Gabriel remembered Hunter's gunfighter who refused to pull his gun. He wondered what Hunter had planned for Tyre Burton.

16

Gabriel tied Zeus up to the back of a wagon and rode up front with Ben. About halfway home, the snow began to fall again and by the time they saw the dim lights coming through the windows of the main house, the snow fell heavily, coating the ground with a thin layer of white.

They drove the wagons directly to the barn. Henry was closing the doors as they drove up, a lantern in one hand, rifle in the other.

"We weren't expecting you back 'til morning." Henry set the lantern down on a nearby crate and took the reins from Pete's team.

"We had good reason to return tonight," Gabriel said and with his good arm, carefully lowered himself to the ground.

"Dagnabbit, Gabe," said Henry. "What you do to yerself?"

"Got in the way of a bullet," Gabriel said and added, "I'll be fine." He untied Zeus and walked him over to the barn. Pete jumped down and reopened the barn doors. Gabriel walked Zeus to his stall and removed the saddle and tack as best he could. The others unhitched the wagons and brought the horses into the barn.

"Did Ethan tell you to keep all the horses inside tonight? I noticed we're a little full in here."

"He did," said Henry. "Didn't want no surprises or to go chasing horses in the corral in case we have to get to them right quick."

"Anything happen today?"

Henry shook his head. "It's been real quiet here. Ethan had all the men taking turns sleeping and watching the herd. Said we'd be up early to bring the rest of them down to the lower pasture. We've also been taking shifts looking for Frank and Sam."

Gabriel looked up at Henry. "Find anything yet?"

"Not a thing," Henry said. "Most of us are thinkin' we won't find anything, but we ain't giving up just yet. Jackson and Kevin are out checking the shacks along the fence line by the eastern pasture. Ain't nobody lived in them for years, so Ethan wanted them checked out."

"Those belong to Hunter," Gabriel said, looking at Henry. "Hunter's men would have no reason to keep them alive."

"That's what Ethan thought, but he told us to check everywhere, so we're checking everywhere."

Gabriel nodded but said nothing in reply. His brother did exactly what he would have done. He finished brushing down Zeus with his good arm, refusing help from Ben, and settled the horse into his stall with fresh oats and checked the water. "Three men down and a bad arm aren't going to keep me from doing what has to be done, Zeus. You know how it is, old boy." The horse responded by moving to his feed bucket.

The men stabled the other horses the best they could in the remaining space.

Gabriel waited until everyone left the barn and the doors were closed and secured before he headed back to the main house.

"You boys go on and take the lantern and get some sleep. It won't be an easy one tomorrow."

Ben looked as though he wanted to say something but must have thought better of it. He joined the other two men and headed for the bunkhouse.

The light coming from the lower window guided Gabriel to the house. The thick snowflakes coated the ground, but it appeared wet and Gabriel predicted it would melt. They needed just one more week to bring down the rest of the herd. After that, winter could give them whatever she wanted.

Gabriel, cold now from the wind that picked up while he'd been in the barn, reached the porch. Colton sat in one of the rocking chairs wearing a heavy coat with a Winchester laid across his lap.

"Expecting trouble, Colton?"

"Ethan has everyone in shifts watching over things. He just finished the last shift," Colton said. "What happened to the arm?"

Gabriel had always liked Colton. An observant man and skilled tracker, he proved useful in a tough situation. "A little trouble in town."

"Wondered why you're back early." Colton stood, still holding the rifle. "And Carl?"

"He's being taken care of. I made sure of it," Gabriel said. "Reverend's holding a service as soon as he can get some men to dig the hole. The ground is near frozen and will be tough to dig."

"I never was much for going to church," Colton said. "But I suppose I'll be making an exception for Carl."

"I suppose we all will."

Gabriel left Colton to his watch and entered the house. A lamp burned on the hall table, and Gabriel figured someone must still be awake.

He paused a moment at the sound of a creak from the wood floor and saw Ethan step around the corner, cup in hand.

"Not that I'm not glad to see you, but what happened, Gabe?"

"Trouble in town." Gabriel carefully shrugged out of his coat. "Hunter's men all escaped."

Ethan stepped forward, nearly spilling the coffee. "How in the hell did they manage that with both the marshal and deputy there?"

"Deputy Lewis set them free." Gabriel hung the coat on the peg near the entrance.

"What happened to your arm?" Ethan asked. Ethan stepped forward and looked at Gabriel's arm through narrowed eyes.

Gabriel glanced down at his arm and saw the dark stain on his shirt. He hadn't realized it was bleeding again. "Just a graze, don't worry about it. Doc Brody bandaged it up. I wouldn't let him take the time to put in stitches, so it's my own fault."

"Where was Marshal Pickett when all this happened?"

"Knocked out cold. We found him after they got away during the stampede."

"Stampede?"

Gabriel nodded. "Those boys went to a lot of trouble to get Hunter's men out. I just can't figure what the old man has planned or why he thinks he'll win this in the end."

Ethan didn't comment and instead said, "Come on back to the kitchen. You look like you need something hot to drink."

"What I need is a bed," Gabriel said, but followed Ethan back anyway. "No other trouble while we were gone?"

"It's been quiet, so I've put the men on shifts."

"I saw Colton out front."

"Not taking any chances." Ethan pulled a chair out for his brother. "We've got a real problem here. Hunter with a deputy on the payroll and don't forget that gunfighter."

"Tyre Burton." Gabriel sat down and accepted the cup from Ethan. "I haven't forgotten. There's only one reason to hire someone like that."

"I'd be lying if I said I wasn't worried."

"There's no place safer for the women and

children than here, Ethan."

Ethan nodded and took another swallow of his coffee. "We can't count on the law for this one."

"I've been realizing that. Any idea on what Hunter might want?"

"Brenna believes he wants Elizabeth."

"He has to know Elizabeth would never willingly go with him, and she'd only leave again if he managed to get to her."

"True, but if Hunter somehow managed to get his hands on someone she cares about, you can be certain he knows Elizabeth would do whatever he wanted."

"He has to be after Elizabeth's money."

"I agree, and it wouldn't take much pressure on someone innocent for her to just hand everything over," said Ethan. "Think you could get in touch with that private detective you hired?"

"I'll try, but last time I heard from him, he came up dry. I'd guess that's because Hunter had already come back here."

"That's not why we need him."

Gabriel realized where his brother's thoughts headed. "You want him to look into Hunter's finances?"

Ethan nodded. "Hunter's owned one of the biggest spreads in this territory for more than a decade, but when was the last time you saw his men running cattle?"

"The marshal said something about Hunter's man picking up mining supplies before he was arrested at the saloon."

"I thought the veins were all dried up here."

"There's a lot of land. Heck, even some of our own land hasn't been given more than a glance. I'll have one of the men ride into town tomorrow and send the telegram."

"We might have to make some unpleasant choices."

"You mean Tyre Burton."

"Hunter has his reasons for hiring the man," said Ethan.

"How will Brenna feel about us fetching her grandmother and bringing her back to the ranch until this over?"

"I'm certain Brenna will want that, but I doubt Elizabeth will come willingly. She's made a good, secret home for herself up there."

"And if you told her it was to keep Brenna or someone else from harm?"

"Using guilt won't be fair."

"It's not about fair anymore."

"I'll talk to Brenna," said Ethan, though Gabriel could tell he'd rather not. Something else. Brenna happened to mention that Isabelle's having a rough time of things."

"Can't blame her, and I haven't made things easier on her."

"You want to keep her?"

"Hasn't your wife taught you yet that you can't actually 'keep' a woman? She keeps you."

Ethan laughed. "According to Brenna, I still have a lot to learn." Ethan finished his coffee and met his brother's eyes. "So, do you want her to keep you?"

"Most of the time I have no doubts that I do."

"You wait too long to be certain, and you might risk losing the best thing that's ever happened to you. Someone had to bash my head a bit before I learned that lesson."

"You deserved it."

"I know."

"I don't know how you did it," Gabriel said, his eyes on the kitchen doorway. "You're still an ornery mule-headed cuss, and Brenna's an angel."

"I don't know, either. She's my very own miracle."

"Do you think she's changed you?"

"For the better."

Gabriel nodded and set his unfinished cup of coffee on the table. "I'm going upstairs."

"I believe Isabelle's still awake."

Gabriel didn't comment and instead walked toward the kitchen door He remembered the letters and went back to the entryway to pull them from his coat pocket. Returning to the kitchen, he handed the one for Brenna to Ethan. "This came for Brenna. Another one came for Isabelle."

Ethan stood up quickly and knocked the chair

over in the process. "You look at this? It's from Kentucky."

Gabriel shook his head. "Nearly forgot about it. Is it Tremaine?"

"I can't tell," Ethan said absently. "I have to get this up to Brenna."

"You'll let me know tomorrow?"

"I will." Ethan started to leave but turned around and said, "Don't be waiting too long to figure out what you want. Oh, and get that arm cleaned up."

Gabriel stood alone in the kitchen staring down at the other letter in his hand. The return address listed New Orleans. Gabriel hadn't forgotten about the aunt. He hoped for Isabelle's sake that the letter carried good news.

With the letter in his hand, Gabriel left the kitchen to find her. No matter what news the letter held, he'd stand by Isabelle's side. He belonged to her now and forever. Now all he had to do was convince her to keep him.

17

Gabriel turned down the lantern in the entryway until darkness bathed everything around him. His eyes passed over the open window and saw that the snow had stopped falling. Gabriel made his way up the stairs, and the dark hallway welcomed him. He hesitated a moment in indecision and then turned right toward the rooms at the opposite end of the hall. It astounded him that a woman should frighten him more than any stampeding herd or wild mustang.

He heard movement coming from the other side of the door, so he knocked softly. It took a few minutes before she answered his knock. The door opened only slightly, and Gabriel saw why.

Isabelle was dressed for bed and more than likely had taken the time to put on a robe. He wouldn't have minded her without it.

"Gabriel." She lowered her voice as she glanced around him to see down the hallway.

"No one else is here."

"We weren't expecting you until morning." Isabelle stepped aside to let him in the room.

Gabriel hesitated only a moment before he entered. Considering how he currently felt, he should have walked away, but he didn't want to stay away any longer.

"How's Andrew?" Gabriel watched Isabelle's face soften.

"He's going to be fine. He's a stronger child than I gave him credit for." Isabelle then caught sight of the dark stain on Gabriel's arm. "What happened?" She reached out to finger the fabric. Her fingers came away with splotches of dark red.

"Just a little trouble in town." Gabriel pulled the fabric away from his arm. "The doc patched it up, but we had a rough ride back."

Isabelle took his good arm, led him toward the bed, and told him to sit down. Bemused, Gabriel did what she said and watched as she gathered up her washbasin and a towel from the bureau.

"You'll need to remove your shirt so I can get to the wound." Gabriel continued to study Isabelle as she moved around the room gathering a few more items. He told himself he'd tell her about the letter after she'd finished doing whatever doctoring she was determined to perform on his arm. Gabriel removed his shirt, and it reminded him just how much a bullet graze stings.

Isabelle stopped as she turned to Gabriel after he removed his shirt. His solid torso was more than what she'd imagined. She now understood the strength she'd seen him expend. His body spoke of many years of hard work. It also stirred up a new set of feelings inside of her, feelings she did her best to set aside.

She carefully cut away the soiled bandage and tenderly pulled it from around Gabriel's arm. She looked closely and saw that while it wasn't a deep wound, it should have been stitched. She didn't have much experience with wounds, but she'd been present when her father suffered a bad riding accident. He had landed on a fence post. The resulting wound to his side hadn't been deep, but the doctor had stitched it to prevent continued bleeding.

"This should have been stitched."

"It's not that bad."

She paused with her cleaning of the wound to see if he meant that.

"I wasn't willing to wait for stitches."

"Well, your 'doc' didn't do you any favors by letting you leave with just a bandage."

"I don't have a lot of patience for people doctoring me," Gabriel said and thought to add, "until now." He smiled at her. "You do whatever you want with the wound. I'll stay still for you."

Isabelle went back to her ministrations and did her best to ignore the tug in her heart. If Gabriel wasn't saying something to make her smile, he was making her cry with joy for how he treated her brother or scaring the very heart from her body with how strongly he made her feel about him. If ever there was a man who she'd be willing to risk everything on, it would Gabriel Gallagher. She didn't want to be afraid, and she didn't want to allow her past to prevent her from having a future.

The wound really wasn't as bad as she originally thought. Once she cleared away the dried blood, she saw that it had stopped bleeding, and if Gabriel allowed himself to rest, the wound should close up well enough on its own. She cut two long strips from an old petticoat and used the cloth to rewrap his arm, making it tight enough to hopefully stop further bleeding.

Stepping away from Gabriel, she busied herself gathering the soiled towel and other items she'd used and returned everything to the bureau. She poured fresh water from the pitcher over each hand and watched as the clean water mixed with the bloody water in the bowl. So much these past days had happened to remind her that life is more precious than she ever realized. Losing her parents had been painful, but if she lost her brother or if that bullet that hit Gabriel had been more than just a graze to his arm, she would have lost everything precious to her.

Isabelle's thoughts distracted her from hearing Gabriel walk up behind her. His hands pressed down on her shoulders, and as he leaned toward her, his warm breath heated the skin on her neck. She reached up to take his hand in hers and leaned back into him. His heat radiated through her white cotton nightgown and robe. His other hand left her shoulder to encircle her waist, and she gave in when he pulled her against him completely. His breath moved lower until it caressed her neck, and his arm tightened around her. The words he whispered to her imprinted forever in her heart.

"Will you keep me, Isabelle?"

Isabelle hesitated. She didn't have the words, and she realized in that moment that words could never answer that question. She moved his arm from around her waist just enough to turn and face him. Without fear, without worry, Isabelle met his eyes, hoping he saw his answer, for breath and speech became difficult for her. He led and she followed.

What Gabriel saw in her eyes was more than he ever dreamed possible. If it took his last breath, he would give it to keep her safe. He'd give anything to keep her safe. Losing her now was no longer a choice he could risk making.

Gabriel took her hand in his and led her to the bed. He dimmed the lamp and stood in front of her, pulling her near enough to feel her warmth.

Gabriel sensed her acceptance, her willingness and gave in to everything he now knew he wanted.

Isabelle welcomed every touch, every caress and when she gave herself to him—to her husband—she lifted herself up and whispered to him, "I will keep you."

The silence of the evening enveloped the house. Isabelle vaguely recalled the moments before Gabriel entered her room, but in the stillness her thoughts focused only on the man beside her. He gave her a good deal to think about. She willingly bound herself to this man with her choice. She was wrong when she continued to think of Gabriel as a stranger. He ceased to be a stranger the moment she pledged herself to him. Now they were bound in body and soul. Isabelle smiled with contentment and knew if anyone looked at her now, they would believe her to be the happiest woman alive.

She certainly wasn't forgetting everything that brought them to this moment. Proof of the turmoil they've faced was evident in the stark-white bandage on Gabriel's arm. His heavy breathing drew her attention away from her troubling thoughts.

Allowing herself to smile, Isabelle carefully slid from beneath the covers. She would return to him this night, but she must check on Andrew. Isabelle walked to the other side of the bed to retrieve her robe and blushed, remembering Gabriel's tenderness in undressing her. She picked up the other clothes strewn on the floor and quietly put them up on the trunk with Gabriel's coat. Her eyes adjusted well enough to the dark, but the unmistakable feel of paper beneath a bare foot had her bending over to retrieve whatever fell.

Isabelle saw only that it was a letter and walked over to the window and held it up to let the moonlight wash over it. Seeing her name and a return address in New Orleans, Isabelle stepped toward the bed with the thought of waking Gabriel. Instead, she tucked the letter away in the pocket of her robe and quietly left the room.

Darkness also bathed the hallway except for slivers of moonlight coming through the windows. She stepped softly and quietly down the hall to the next bedroom and opened the door just a few inches to look inside without waking Andrew. Her brother's small form lay in the bed where she'd left him, and she took comfort in the sound of his soft breathing.

Isabelle left the door ajar and stepped back into the hall. She pulled the robe closer around her and considered returning to the bedroom and Gabriel but thought of the letter in her pocket. The house remained quiet, which likely meant that Ethan and Brenna were tucked away in their own room. Isabelle made her way down the stairs and entered the library. She hunted around for a match to light the lamp on the small table near the chair, grateful for the snatches of moonlight coming through the window. A shadow joining the soft light on the wall startled her until she realized it was only one of the men outside keeping watch. She appreciated the extent to which the family went to keep them all safe but regretted the necessity.

Once the lamp gave off enough light to read by, Isabelle pulled the letter out and hesitated only a moment in opening it. Halfway through reading the words on the fine linen paper, Isabelle wished she'd awakened Gabriel. Perhaps then she wouldn't feel as though the world was caving in on her without anyone to prevent it from crushing her.

With no thought to extinguishing the lamp, Isabelle rushed from the room and lifted the hems of her nightclothes to hurry up the stairs. She thought little of being quiet once she entered her bedroom. Gabriel still slept where she'd left him just a short time ago, though his body invaded the space she once occupied. Moving to the side of the bed where she once slept, Isabelle quietly said Gabriel's name. When he offered no response, she pushed at him lightly. *It shouldn't be this difficult to wake a man.* Not that she had much experience. This time she pushed at him harder and said his name until he moved and opened his eyes.

The stiffness from the bullet graze to his arm made turning over difficult, but in the back of his hazy mind, Gabriel was aware of his name being called. Once he recognized the voice and the urgency in it, the fog cleared. He opened his eyes and saw Isabelle standing next to the bed, her face paler than usual. He sat up, cursed the man who shot him, and took the weight off that arm.

"Isabelle, what happened?" Gabriel's first thought was that she regretted what they'd done.

Relief flowed through him and the sick feeling in his gut subsided when she sat on the edge of the bed and shoved a piece of paper in his hand.

"What is this?" he asked as his eyes perused the paper. He then realized what he held. "You found the letter."

"Read it. She's going to take Andrew away from me."

Gabriel reached out, took her hand in his, and read the letter.

October 25, 1883
Dear Miss Rousseau,

On behalf of your aunt, Mrs. Picard, we are writing to inform you of the impending arrival of one Mr. Daggert, an agent working on behalf of this office, and a Mrs. Wolds, a nurse employed on behalf of your aunt to care for your brother, Andrew Rousseau. Mr. Daggert and Mrs. Wolds will be arriving in Briarwood, Montana, within days after you receive this letter.

You may be assured that your brother will be in good care. Your aunt is exercising her right as the legal guardian of Andrew Rousseau and claims that the marriage to one Gabriel Gallagher is invalid and was entered into under false pretenses.

As Mrs. Picard is named as the legal guardian of Andrew Rousseau in the will of the late Julien Rousseau, she is demanding that he be turned over to her by way of Mr. Daggert and Mrs. Wolds.

With kindest regards,

Mr. Jameson Prince, Esq.

Gabriel read through the letter twice and could scarcely believe the audacity of the woman and her lawyer.

"Isabelle, listen to me, love. You've done all that was required in order to ensure that Andrew remains with you. Your father's will clearly states that upon your marriage, you become Andrew's legal guardian."

"Why, then, is she disputing that?" Isabelle asked. "You sent a copy of the marriage certificate."

"I did." Gabriel set the letter aside. "We'll take care of this together. I promise that you won't lose Andrew."

Together. That word helped to calm her racing heart, and when Gabriel pulled her into his arms, she went willingly. When her tears began to fall, Isabelle did nothing to stop them. When Gabriel held her close against his warm chest, she didn't pull away.

"They might be here any day now, Gabriel."

"I know, and when they arrive, we'll get this sorted out."

"You're so certain."

Gabriel rested his cheek against her hair and gazed into the shadows of the dark room. On a deep breath he said, "Out here in the frontier, there are rules, and generally if a person wants to make it, they have to follow those rules. Sometimes though, in order to survive, those rules have to be bent a little."

"You mean broken."

"No, I mean bent." Gabriel smiled. "You see, this is hard land, but it can be good to people if you figure out a way to live in it and live by its rules. Sometimes those rules don't follow those of people. This land is wild, and there are times we have to get a little wild, too."

This time Isabelle did pull away and looked at Gabriel, studying him. "What exactly are you saying? What rules will you break?"

"Out here we keep who and what's ours."

18

How final and dangerous those words sounded to Isabelle. She knew that Gabriel meant it. He had already proved the lengths to which he was willing to go to protect them..

"No matter the cost?"

"Isabelle, are you willing to risk losing Andrew?"

"Of course not."

"Please, trust me. These people—your aunt and her lawyer—have no legal standing to take Andrew away, no matter who they work for."

"And you're certain of this?"

"I am certain that your aunt is going to a lot of trouble to take on a young child. You said your father's will granted custody to your aunt only if you didn't marry, right?"

"That's correct."

"Well, you're married now, so according to that will, you are Andrew's legal guardian, not your aunt."

Isabelle nodded and picked the letter up off the bed. It had been crumbled from her laying on it. "I still don't understand it. My aunt was older than my father and from what I knew, she never wanted children."

"What else would come with Andrew should she get custody?"

"Nothing. My father's creditors took everything."

"There has to be something more to it . . ." Gabriel said, but his voice trailed off. He heard pounding, and it sounded like it came from downstairs.

A second later, Eliza opened Isabelle's bedroom door with a lantern in her hand.

"Should have looked in here first," she said, though she didn't smile. "Sounds like we might have trouble. Ethan is already down there." Eliza left the door open and walked away. Gabriel heard her footsteps on the stairway.

He left the bed and comfortable with his nakedness, walked to the other side before Isabelle spoke up.

"Your clothes are on the trunk."

Gabriel walked back to the end of the bed and began to dress. "It may be nothing, but I want you to stay here. Brenna is probably awake, too." He was dressed in less than five minutes and out the bedroom door in under six.

Andrew wouldn't wake for hours, so Isabelle dressed, doubting she'd be able to sleep anymore that night. Once she cleaned herself up a bit, she removed the sheets from the bed. There was no need to advertise what she and Gabriel had done. After she saw to that chore and not knowing where fresh linens might be kept, Isabelle went to check on Andrew, this time going to his bedside. He still slept calmly.

Closing the door only slightly this time, Isabelle left the room and went in search of

Brenna. She knocked softly on the room Brenna and Ethan shared.

"Come in," Brenna's soft voice said through the closed door. "Oh, Isabelle, please come in."

Isabelle stepped into the room and watched as Brenna laid her sleeping son in a large bassinette.

"Do you know what is happening?" Brenna asked. "Ethan rushed out of here so quickly."

"Eliza didn't sound pleased about it when she came to fetch Gabriel."

Brenna looked up at Isabelle. "You were with Gabriel?"

Isabelle's cheeks reddened, though she had no reason to be embarrassed. "Yes, I was."

Brenna nodded, and Isabelle couldn't tell in the dim light, but swore that the other woman smiled. "I wondered how long it might take you two."

"Excuse me?"

"Well, I shouldn't confess this, but Ethan and I made a little wager as to how long it would take Gabriel to make yours a real marriage."

Isabelle didn't know how to feel about that.

"In the midst of everything that has happened, you actually wagered on the outcome of my marriage to Gabriel?"

"Oh no, not on the outcome." Brenna did smile this time. "Just on how long it might take the two of you to see what the rest of us saw from the beginning."

"The rest of us?"

"Don't worry," Brenna said. "The little wager was only with Ethan. Eliza mentioned that you two have already spoken." Brenna left her son's side and motioned Isabelle from the room. "She likes you, and Eliza isn't an easy one to please."

"What do you mean?" Isabelle asked once they stood in the hall.

"I recall the first time I met Eliza. Those Gallagher-blue eyes of hers bore into me. It felt as though every secret I possessed surfaced for her to see."

"I recall feeling that way when I first met her. I almost wanted to tell her everything."

"You'll feel that way more than once," Brenna said. "Eliza just has this way about her. It's what took her from here while Ethan was off chasing me in Scotland, and what brought her home. For now let's go downstairs and wait for them to tell us what's happened."

"But Gabriel sounded adamant about us staying up here."

"I see I have a few things to teach you if you are to survive here, Isabelle."

"You mean this land?"

"No, I mean with these Gallaghers."

Outside the air was cold and the conversation heated. Gabriel's private investigator had ridden through the night to bring them news. Unfortunately, it was worse than any of them expected.

"How sure are you about this, Jeb?" Gabriel asked the man.

"I wouldn't have ridden out tonight if I wasn't sure," Jeb said. "I heard it from three of Nathan Hunter's men at the saloon."

"Could they have just been talking to talk?" Eliza asked.

Peters shook his head. "They were liquored up well and good, Miss Gallagher. I ain't sure they knew what they were sayin'."

"We know where they're going, Ethan," Gabriel said.

Ethan nodded. "Elizabeth. She's the only reason for Hunter to go up that way."

"But why now? We know that Hunter suspected Elizabeth may be up near Bright River because that's where they were headed with Brenna when she kidnapped. It wouldn't have taken him long to find her if he'd put in a real effort," Eliza said.

"Unless he's figured out a way to use Elizabeth to get what he wants."

"Our problem is that we believed he was after Elizabeth," said Gabriel, "when in fact, we don't know for certain. We keep thinking he's after the land or even after her money, but it doesn't make sense anymore."

"I agree," Eliza said calmly, "and I just might know what he wants."

"And how do you know that?" Ethan asked.

"Wait," Gabriel said and turned his attention to Jeb. "Are you up for heading back into town? We need a new marshal, and they need to know what's going on."

"I can do that, but it's going to take near to a week or two for a territorial marshal to get here, and that's after they appoint one. Maybe we can get them to send another one temporarily."

"Do whatever it takes," replied Gabriel. "Just get one here, and let him know what's going on."

"I'll take care of it," Jeb said. "But Gabriel, that isn't the only reason why I came out here, though I would've waited until morning."

Gabriel looked to his brother and sister before giving his attention back to Jeb Clancy. He knew what else Jeb was looking into for him, but he hadn't told Ethan or Eliza. "Go ahead." He knew that Jeb, for all of his outward simplicities, was sharper and deadlier than anyone might have guessed.

"I found Ramsey."

Gabriel heard Eliza's sharp intake of breath

but ignored it. "Did you find him in Kentucky?"

Jeb shook his head. "He was there, but I didn't have to go that far. Found him in Missouri. He bought a train ticket."

"To where?" Ethan asked.

"Here."

Eliza swore under her breath, but Gabriel still caught it. Eliza never swore. "Appreciate it, Jeb."

"Anytime," Jeb said and turned to his horse. He mounted up and without even a glance or word, he rode into the night toward Briarwood.

Eliza interrupted their thoughts and said, "It's not Elizabeth he wants or needs." She knew this conversation wouldn't end well. "Hunter does want money."

"Which takes us back to Elizabeth," said Gabriel.

"No, it doesn't." Eliza took a deep breath this time and hoped she was making the right choice. "It's Brenna and Ramsey. They're the ones with the money. It's their inheritance he's after, and Ramsey is certain that Hunter will do anything—"

"Ramsey is certain?" Ethan stepped forward and softly asked, "How do you know what Ramsey is certain of?"

"Listen, Ethan, Gabriel," Eliza began. "Please, just save the neck throttling for later and listen to me. Ever since Brenna arrived and Hunter found out she was here, he did everything possible to get his hands on her. It stopped until she came back again, right?"

"Just a minute, Eliza. None of this is Brenna's fault."

"I'm not saying it is." Eliza stomped her feet to get feeling back through her body. The cold began to break through her coat, reminding her that they stood outside at night in October arguing. "It's not Brenna's fault. It's not anyone's fault." Eliza stepped away for a minute and then turned back to her brothers. Neither looked pleased.

"Before you continue," Gabriel said slowly, "how much time did you spend with Ramsey, and did he know who you were?"

Eliza grew frustrated because they were

running out of time. "I met Ramsey the night before I came home." Eliza may have taken some satisfaction in the surprised looks her brothers wore if the situation had not been so serious. "Yes, he knows who I am, but I stayed with Nathan and Mallory Tremaine while I was in Kentucky. And before you ask, I didn't find out about them until I arrived there. I went on a hunch, and it paid off."

"So you decided to solve all our problems on your own and find Ramsey while you were at it?"

"Ethan, you went to Scotland, where you should have been, and Gabriel never would have left the ranch with you gone," said Eliza. "I was the only choice, and you know well enough, Gabriel, that if I'd told you before I left, you wouldn't have let me off the ranch."

Gabriel remained silent, which confirmed what she said was true.

"You've made your point," said Ethan. "Now back to Brenna and Ramsey before we freeze out here. I don't want Brenna hearing any of this just yet. By the way, she doesn't know anything about an inheritance. From what I know, she doesn't need it."

"I don't think either of them need the money, but it's there." Eliza pulled her coat closer together. "Ramsey has kept busy since he left Hunter all those years ago. He found out about Brenna and their parents' deaths."

"Why didn't he go to Brenna?" Gabriel asked. "She needed family."

"I don't know that, and he refused to tell me. I just know that he's been aware of his family for a long time now and that what Hunter wants, he can only get from Brenna and Ramsey."

"And he'll do anything or go through anyone to get them to do what he wants," Gabriel murmured.

Eliza nodded. "Yes. Even if that means taking Andrew, stampeding cattle, or any number of the other things he's done."

Ethan pulled an ungloved hand from his coat pocket, ran it over his face, and said, "What makes Ramsey so sure of all this, Eliza?"

"He wouldn't tell me that either."

"Does he plan on doing anything about it?" Gabriel asked. "Or is he leaving his sister to fight this for the both of them?"

"Your detective confirmed Ramsey was on his way here," Eliza said firmly. "I promise you, he'll be here."

"Well, until he arrives we still have problems here." Ethan nodded toward the house. "I have to go after Elizabeth, for Brenna."

"There is a chance Hunter hasn't found her yet," Gabriel said. "He may have gone to Bright River, but there's a lot of land around there. Even if he did find her, he can't have much time on us."

"I'll be the one to go, Ethan."

Ethan shook his head. "I have to do this, Gabe. Elizabeth is Brenna's family."

"Which makes her our family," Eliza said.

Ethan pulled his sister toward him and kissed the top of her head before gently setting her away again. "I'll take two of the men with me, and we'll head straight for Desperate Creek."

"If you leave tonight, you're likely to end up

with lame horses."

"We'll take it slow and easy, Gabe. We could wait until morning, but I'm not willing to risk it." Ethan stomped his feet. "I have to go and explain to Brenna what's happening, and then I'll head out."

"I'll get the horses saddled up for you."

Ethan nodded and watched as Gabriel headed for the bunkhouse. He stared up at the night sky, grateful to see the stars shining brightly overhead.

"If the snow could hold off for a while longer, they just might make it north and back again without being caught in a storm." Unable to mask his disappointment, Ethan turned to his sister. "When did you plan to tell us about Ramsey?"

Eliza hesitated. "I didn't know if there would be a right time."

"Did you know he planned to come here?"

Eliza shook her head, though Ethan still didn't look at her. "I hoped, but I didn't think it would be so soon."

Ethan gently tugged on a bit of her hair. She hadn't worn a hat when she came outside. "You'll freeze out here, and I need to speak with Brenna before I leave."

"This is all too much, Ethan. Somehow this has to end. Hunter obviously isn't doing all of this himself, but whoever he's hired seems to be one step ahead of us."

"I agree, and unfortunately I think Gabe and I met the man."

"When?"

"Hunter's ranch. You ever hear of a man called Tyre Burton?"

"Are you certain of all this, Ethan?" Feeling unsteady on her feet, Brenna lowered herself to sit on the trunk.

Ethan kneeled in front of his wife and held her hand. "Nothing is certain except that I have to go to Desperate Creek. Whether Hunter is there or not."

"Eliza has met Ramsey? She's certain it was him?" Her eyes glistened.

"It sounds like it might be him, but it has been a long time since Ramsey stepped foot in Montana. Until we know more about why he never came back after he knew about you, we need to be careful." Ethan stood but held a hand to his wife's face. "I have to leave now."

Brenna stood and unexpectedly pulled him close to her. His larger body enveloped hers, and she spoke into his chest, even as her arms wrapped around his back. "I need you to come back to us."

Ethan pulled back enough to lower his lips to hers and whispered against her mouth, "I promise you that I will always come back." He kissed her again and without another word, left the room.

Gabriel waited near the front door when Ethan came down the stairs. "You be careful out there, and I have to say that I still wish I was the one going."

Ethan nodded in the direction of the stairs. "We'll get through this. Just make sure you still have her when it's all done."

Gabriel looked at his brother curiously. "You doubt I will?"

"I almost lost Brenna forever because of my stubborn pride, but I didn't see it until she was gone. Don't make mistakes. Too much is happening right now for a proper courtship." Ethan turned toward the door but turned back. "The reason why the two of you married. Is there anything we can do?"

"There could be, but let's get through this first."

Ethan nodded and left the house. Gabriel listened to the sound of horses riding over hard-worked ground and hoped Ethan knew what he was doing. Ethan's words filled his thoughts, and his gaze traveled back to the staircase. The house needed to be secured, and he wanted to walk around the outbuildings. Gabriel still had the men taking shifts watching over the house and cattle, but they were stretched to every limit. Now with Ethan and two of the ranch hands gone, there weren't enough of them to safely keep watch. Gabriel told Colton he'd take the next three-hour watch and with regret, he glanced once more at the stairs and went outside.

Less than an hour later, Eliza found him and handed him a cup of coffee. Gabriel accepted and took a long swallow. "Thanks. I figured you'd be getting some sleep. We all need to get what we can, when we can."

"I'll head up soon," Eliza said. "I'll be taking the next cattle watch with Kevin."

Gabriel turned around quickly. "I don't want you out there right now."

Eliza shook her head and gave her brother a hard look. "We all do our part, and if these men are going to keep risking their lives, then every Gallagher better be willing to do the same."

"Damn, I missed you, Liza. What is it you wanted to talk about?"

"Ethan told me about Tyre Burton."

Gabriel's body stiffened. "You've heard of him?"

"No, but Ethan suspects he's the one carrying out Hunter's orders. Hunter would have to be paying a man like that a lot of money."

"How much money exactly is this inheritance of Ramsey and Brenna's?" Gabriel turned his attention fully to his sister. He knew the sounds of the night well enough to focus on both.

"I don't know, but from what I read between the lines of Ramsey's vague details, it's a large fortune."

"And it's from her parents?" Gabriel asked. "I find it hard to believe that they didn't tell her about it somehow or that it would have been left out of the will."

"Well, when Ramsey gets here, hopefully he'll have answers for Brenna," Eliza said. "But about Tyre Burton . . ."

"I imagine he's capable of anything, and if it is him that has been causing all these recent problems, that could explain why it's been so difficult to catch up with the old man." Gabriel finished his coffee and set the mug on the porch railing. Eliza automatically picked it up.

"With sunrise coming later now, Ethan isn't going to have an easy ride up north," Eliza said. "I'm worried about him. I worry every time either of you leave the ranch when it concerns Nathan Hunter."

"You mean concern like what I must have felt when you just up and left for Kentucky?"

Eliza hunched into herself slightly. "Point taken."

They stood in tense silence for a few minutes. The night air remained still and promised snow, though neither of them said as much. Eliza knew that the only way for all of this to end would mean the end of Hunter. But she didn't want her brothers pulling the trigger. If they crossed that line, they may not come back from it. Ethan had a wife and son. Gabriel was now married and had a new brother to think of. Eliza had no one else but her brothers; no one else to miss her, and no one else counting on her. She could cross that line. Eliza turned her eyes back to her brother and found him looking at her.

"What's going on in that mysterious head of yours?"

"Too much thinking," Eliza said. "Listen, I don't think I can sleep and there's only one hour left before I head out to the cattle. I'll keep an eye out and you go talk with Isabelle."

"Not going to happen."

"Gabe, I'm capable of keeping watch for an hour."

"Oh, I know you're capable of many things, but it's still not going to happen." Gabriel hoped that'd be the end of it. At times their Gallagher pride became a nuisance. "A little sleep is better than none. Who knows what the morning will bring."

"One of these days, Gabriel Gallagher, you and Ethan are going to realize that you can't tell me what I can and cannot do."

"Sweet sister, no one can tell you what to do. We try, but we know you'll do whatever you want to in the end."

Eliza smiled up at her brother. "Well, so long as you know it."

Gabriel watched as she walked back into the house. He pulled the collar of his coat up to cover his neck and walked the length of the porch. His thoughts drifted toward the room upstairs where right now he hoped Isabelle slept. Andrew would be tucked away and unaware of the worry the adults experienced.

Though his father did leave them all with the stubbornness to face any challenge, Gabriel was grateful he wasn't around to see all that happened over the years, This land was theirs by right, law, and blood. Gabriel thought of what might happen to the land for generations to come, and his thoughts returned to Isabelle and to Andrew. He wanted Andrew to have the choice of being a Gallagher and to having a piece of this legacy.

When Ben relieved Gabriel, he knew there wasn't much sense in trying to sleep. With Ethan off the ranch and his brother's words still fresh in his mind, Gabriel cleaned up using the washbasin in the kitchen. He glanced at his reflection in the small mirror above the basin and scrubbed a hand over his tired face. None of them would be able to keep up this pace without sleep for much longer. He'd prefer to remain awake until Kevin and Jackson returned with news on what they might have found at the line shacks.

Gabriel bypassed putting on the kettle for more coffee and made his way upstairs. He walked down the hall toward Isabelle's room but saw no light beneath the door. He knocked gently but only silence met him. It wouldn't be fair to wake her, no matter how much he wanted to talk with her. Gabriel went to the next room over and opened it to more darkness. He walked over to the bed and relaxed a moment, seeing that Andrew was safe, but not asleep.

Andrew sat by the window and stared out at the snowy landscape.

"Andrew?"

The young boy turned. "The stars are out."

Gabriel walked across the room, sat on the bench beneath the window, and pulled Andrew into his arms. "Did you see the stars in New Orleans?"

"Not too much."

Gabriel reached for the top quilt off the bed and covered Andrew. "Sometimes, the stars are so bright, they light up the whole sky, and you don't need a lantern to see your way."

Andrew leaned forward and pressed his face to the cold glass. "The whole sky?" He twisted his head so he could see more.

Gabriel chuckled. "Well, at least the sky above us." Gabriel tucked the blanket under Andrew's bare feet. "Why aren't you asleep?"

"I was thinking."

"About what?"

"Ibby said you went with some men to town, but you then got hurt and she said you wouldn't."

"That's not her fault. Sometimes grown-ups get hurt, and we can't do anything about it." Gabriel shifted Andrew so he faced him. "But see, I'm just fine. Nothing will ever keep me from coming back home to you."

"Really?"

"Really."

Andrew wrapped his short arms around Gabriel's neck, and Gabriel carried him back to the bed.

"Gabriel?"

"Yes?"

"Can I show my friend the horses?"

Gabriel sat on the edge of the bed, smiling at Andrew's losing battle with sleep. "Which friend?"

"Mason. He goes to school."

One more regret. Isabelle and Andrew had both been thrust from their new lives before they even had a chance to settle in.

"Tell you what. As soon as we can, we'll see if Mason can come out, and I'll take you both riding."

"Mean it?"

"I mean it. Now, get back under those covers. A rancher has to get as much sleep as he can."

"Do I get to be a rancher?"

Gabriel smiled. "Is that what you want?"

Andrew's head bobbed, and he slipped his arms under the blankets. "Like you and Ethan."

"Then you best start with a good night's sleep."

Andrew nodded and rolled over. Within

seconds, he quieted. Gabriel left the room and walked down the hall in the opposite direction, passing Eliza's room along the way. Her door stood ajar, but the room was dark. Since he was checking on everyone else, he may as well check on her. Thankfully, Eliza slept. Gabriel smiled; she was still fully clothed. He continued on to his room where a soft glow from beneath the door gave him pause.

Gabriel quietly opened the door and stepped into his bedroom. Someone had lit a lamp and it burned low next to the bed. Lying near the edge, curled up in his blankets, Isabelle quietly slept. Gabriel closed the door softly, careful not to wake his new wife. Gabriel stepped over to the large chair in the corner and sat to remove his boots. His clothes soon followed and he walked over to the bed, slipped beneath the covers, and pulled Isabelle toward him. She had undressed down to her white camisole but still wore her skirt. Her golden hair lay loose around her shoulders and across the pillow. She stirred next to him. They would get through this, and he swore that somehow, they'd do it together.

Isabelle soon became aware of a warm and comforting presence beside her, and she moved toward the warmth.

"Hello." She smiled at him. Isabelle didn't stop to wonder how perfectly normal it felt to be in bed with Gabriel. The troubles and worries that plagued her since arriving in Montana would still be there when the sun came up, but for this moment in time, he belonged to her.

"Hello yourself." Gabriel ran a hand lightly up and down her bare arm.

"I imagine you weren't expecting to find me here." Isabelle ran her eyes up and down his body, though it was presently half-covered with quilts.

"Actually, I knocked at your bedroom door first because I needed to talk, but finding you here gave me other ideas." Gabriel saw the worry cross over her face.

"Talk about what? Is everyone all right? Andrew." Isabelle moved as though to leave the bed, but Gabriel held her down with a light touch.

"Wait, Andrew's fine. He's sleeping." Seeing his hopes for that "something else" fade away, Gabriel said, "Hang on a minute." He grumbled and got out of bed. He walked over and picked his pants up from where he had tossed them and slipped into the wool. Once semi-clothed, Gabriel returned to the bed, this time lying over the covers. Isabelle didn't appear to regret what they both were missing out on. Perhaps that was for the best.

"Please, tell me what's happened." Isabelle looked around and realized it was too dark to see the clock across the room. "How long have I been up here?"

"Not long enough," he said. "You needed the sleep."

"I should check on Andrew." Isabelle once more moved to leave the bed, but Gabriel gently pulled her back.

"Andrew's fine." She relaxed a little more, and he smiled in an effort to ease her concern. "We do need to talk."

"I'm listening." She sat up, but remained close to Gabriel.

"Ethan has left to go bring back Elizabeth, Brenna's grandmother. We have reason to believe that Hunter may try to use her to get what he wants."

"And what is that?"

"Brenna and her brother Ramsey." Gabriel proceeded to tell her about hiring Jeb and then Jeb showing up tonight. He even told her everything Eliza told him. When he finished speaking, he waited for Isabelle to say something, but she sat there unmoving for a while before responding.

"So Andrew's kidnapping was just us being in the wrong place at the wrong time?"

"I take full responsibility for that." Gabriel moved closer to her and took her hand in his. "I didn't think of the consequences and that's my fault, no one else is to blame."

"Gabriel—"

"I promise you that nothing else will happen to you or Andrew, and I won't let anyone take him away."

Isabelle lifted her fingers to his lips in an effort to quiet him. "I don't blame you for anything that has happened. Perhaps at first I did because I was angry and terrified, but none of it is your fault." She lowered her hand back down to her lap. "And it's not just up to you to see that Andrew stays with us."

Gabriel liked hearing her say "us." He studied her closely. "You seem different somehow."

"I feel different."

"You're happy with your choice to stay?"

"You foolish man." She leaned into him. "I told you I was keeping you, and I meant it." Isabelle enjoyed the feel of his arms wrapping around her and moving her to his lap.

"I won't be letting you go." Gabriel held her closer to him. "Not now, not ever."

"I'm counting on it." She closed her eyes, knowing they both spoke the truth.

"There is something I need to do right now, though," Gabriel said.

Isabelle worried over the seriousness in his

tone. "Is everything all right?"

"I need to head out to meet Jackson and Kevin," Gabriel said in a way of answering. "I'm not going to be able to rest well until I know what happened to Frank and Sam."

"But your shoulder—"

"It's well enough to ride."

Isabelle didn't feel as confident about that as Gabriel. "You'll be careful?"

"That's a promise."

Jackson and Kevin waited behind a grouping of pine trees with their horses. They watched the two men leave the largest of the line shacks and ride back toward the Double Bar.

"Don't rightly know what them boys would be doing at that old shack. Hunter don't use those no more," said Jackson.

"I haven't seen activity around this part of his land in months," Kevin agreed.

"You think maybe they kept them two alive after all?" Jackson asked as he continued to watch the shack in case any more of Hunter's men were nearby.

"Only one way to find out," Kevin said. "Come on."

"Wait!" Jackson said in a harsh whisper. "I hear somethin'."

"What?" Kevin listened and said, "A rider. I hear it too."

Keeping behind the trees, the men waited until the rider came close enough for them to recognize the horse.

"Gabriel?" Kevin said as loudly as he dared.

The rider turned slightly and moved the horse in their direction until the moon shone on his features.

"You scared the tar out of me, Gabriel," Jackson said. "Thought you mighta been one of Hunter's men."

"I saw them head for the Double Bar, too."

"That arm there is going to start bleeding again," Kevin said, indicating Gabriel's wound.

"I'll deal with it later if it does. Right now, let's go and see what brought those men out in the middle of the night."

The men urged their horses forward at a walk until they were certain no one else was nearby, and then they pushed the horses into a gallop. They quickly reached the line shack and waited a few minutes before dismounting.

Gabriel's feet hit the ground first. "Kevin, you come with me. Jackson, stay with the horses and whistle if you see anyone coming."

"Will do," Jackson said.

Kevin got down and followed Gabriel to the door of the shack. Gabriel stepped forward and listened for any sound of movement coming from the other side. He rapped quickly against the door and continued to wait. Something thumped from the other side. Gabriel pulled a pistol from his belt and waited for Kevin to signal that he was ready. He pressed down on the latch handle of the door and slowly pushed it in. It took a moment for his eyes to adjust to the darkness of the shack. "Son of a—"

Gabriel tucked the pistol back in his belt and rushed to the corner of the shack. He saw Frank's eyes soften as the man realized it was

Gabriel. Gabriel fumbled a bit but managed to untie the knotted leather strip holding a rag in place against Frank's mouth. He heard Kevin in the other corner but didn't pay attention to what he was doing.

"You gave us a scare, Frank." Gabriel cut the ties around Frank's hands. Hunter's men had tied him up to an iron bar bolted into the wall.

It took Frank a moment to respond, and his voice sounded hoarse when he spoke. Gabriel yelled out to Jackson to bring in a canteen. "I sure am glad to see you, Gabriel."

"I didn't know if we'd find you two alive," Gabriel confessed.

"You might not have after another day out here." Frank's eyes darted to the door when Jackson stepped inside. He licked his lips when he spotted the canteen in Jackson's hand.

"Well damn sakes, Frank." Jackson only stared at his friend as he walked forward and handed the canteen to Frank. "Where's Sam?" Jackson asked, but then turned when Kevin spoke.

"He's here, but he's not looking too good.

He's unconscious and bleeding bad from a cut on his leg."

Gabriel finished cutting through the ties binding Frank's feet and moved over to the other corner where Kevin was hunched over Sam. He said over his shoulder, "Jackson, help Frank outside, and we'll bring Sam."

"He's not breathing so good, either," Kevin said softly.

"We'll stop the bleeding best we can and get him back to the ranch. Mabel might be able to do something for him, and we'll send for Doc Brody."

Gabriel removed the cloth from around his neck and tied it around Sam's leg to stop the bleeding. "I'll need your help lifting him, Kevin. My arm won't hold his weight right now."

Kevin lifted up Sam on one side while Gabriel used his good arm and shoulder to lift the other side. Together they half-carried Sam outside into the fresh night air. Jackson stepped over and took Gabriel's place and together with Kevin, they managed to lift Sam onto the back of

Kevin's horse.

"We'll need to double up back to the ranch," Gabriel said. "Kevin, can you hold onto Sam?"

"Don't you worry, Gabe, I've got him." Kevin climbed up behind Sam who had been braced over the saddle horn. Kevin pulled Sam against his chest so that the man sat as upright as possible and secured an arm around his waist.

"You keep him on that horse, and we'll take it slow and easy back to the ranch." Gabriel mounted his own horse, a bit unsteady.

Frank managed to get up on Jackson's horse by himself, sitting behind Jackson. Once Gabriel felt certain they'd all manage to make it back to the ranch, he urged his horse forward. He ignored the pain shooting up through his shoulder and the wetness seeping down his arm.

Ethan smelled the snow before it began its descent. The weather had been on their side during the harrowing two-day ride north, but they needed to get back before that changed. He saw Elizabeth's house from where he and the men waited. Darkness bathed the house which either meant Elizabeth was inside and safe, or Hunter's men already came and took her with them.

"I'm going around to the house," Ethan said to Jake and Tom. "If I don't come out before Elizabeth, you be sure and get her home."

"We're not leaving you in there," Jake said.

"Hopefully you won't have to. If we're lucky, Hunter's boys never made it. Either way, we're taking Elizabeth back to the ranch."

The cold air remained still except for the light fluttering of quiet snowflakes. Ethan hoped that meant he'd find Elizabeth tucked away safely in bed.

He moved slowly toward the front of the house and walked quietly up to the front door. Obviously Elizabeth didn't worry about intruders—the door was unlocked but still intact. He made his way through the house and up the stairs. Only one door stood closed in the short hallway, so Ethan walked to it quietly and turned the knob. Darkness shrouded the room, and it took a moment for his eyes to adjust. A soft breeze fluttered the curtains covering the windows. Ethan walked to the bed and let out the breath he'd been holding—Elizabeth was safe. He turned away to go and look out the window, wanting to signal to Jake and Tom. Before he managed to push the curtains aside, he sensed a movement behind him and heard a shrieking scream.

"You get out of my room! You get out right now!"

"Elizabeth!" Ethan shouted above her screaming. "It's Ethan Gallagher."

"Ethan?" He saw her shuffling about but couldn't make out her features. Ethan took a step toward the bed.

"Yes, ma'am." Ethan stepped close enough for her to see him clearly.

"Well, sakes alive, Ethan," Elizabeth said in between attempts to catch her breath. "What in heaven's name are you doing in my bedroom?"

Jake and Tom chose that moment to burst into the room, and Elizabeth let out another scream. At least this time the sound didn't have Ethan covering his ears.

"What on earth is going on here?"

Elizabeth sat quietly as Ethan explained what happened and why they had come. Jake and Pete apologized over and over for barging in the way they had, but Elizabeth shrugged them off. Her interest lay in her new family.

"I have a great-grandson," Elizabeth said in awe.

"You do, ma'am." Ethan smiled. "And you can spend as much time with him as you'd like when we get back to the ranch."

"I do want to see him Ethan—Brenna too— but I can't just leave. There's no one else here right now."

"That might explain why no one else has come in," Ethan said. "But why leave you alone out here?"

"Let it alone," Elizabeth said with a wave of her hand. "They go into Bright River a few times a year for supplies. I'm expecting them back tomorrow."

"We'll be halfway back to the ranch tomorrow."

"If I'm not here, they'll worry. I can't do that to them."

Ethan knew he was in for a rough trip home. "We'll leave them a note, Elizabeth, but you're leaving with us. If I come back without you, Brenna will have my hide. With everything going on right now at the ranch, she'd feel a whole lot better if everyone stayed together."

"Making me feel guilty is not fair, Ethan Gallagher, and you know it," Elizabeth scolded.

"That may be, but we were led to believe that you were in danger. Now that I know you're safe, it makes me worry more about what could be happening at the ranch. Now I can't keep Brenna and our son safe if I'm worrying about you up here."

Elizabeth gave her full attention to Ethan and huffed a little. "Well, that does it. If you boys will leave, I'll get myself ready."

"Can you ride?" Ethan asked.

"Son, I'll be cold and dead in my grave before

I can't ride a horse."

19

Gabriel's shoulder ached, but he knew it was nothing compared to what Sam and Frank must be feeling. He kept glancing back to make sure Sam was okay on Kevin's horse, but no matter how he looked at it, Sam wasn't having an easy ride. Once back at the ranch, Gabriel shouted out a signal and watched as the men at the ranch came into sight.

Colton rushed up to Zeus and held the horse while Gabriel dismounted. His eyes, though, were on the other men.

"Where'd you find them?" Colton watched as the other men helped get Frank and Sam off the horses.

"One of Hunter's line shacks"

"Any idea how they're still alive?"

Gabriel shook his head. "No, but I plan to find out."

Four days later, as night descended, Hawk's Peak finally came into sight. The ride back to the ranch took longer than Ethan planned, but Elizabeth's endurance and gumption impressed him.

Ethan saw Gabriel sitting out on the front porch, and worry hit him when he noticed Gabriel holding his arm up against his body. Once the riders reached the hitching post, Ethan dismounted and walked up the steps to his brother.

"What happened, Gabe?"

"We found Frank and Sam."

Ethan leaned back slightly and tilted his head, his eyes wide with surprise. "Alive?"

"Alive," Gabriel confirmed. "Mabel fixed Frank up, but he'll need time to mend. Sam was unconscious when we found him, but he finally woke up and Mabel's been fussing over him ever since."

"Has she been taking care of that shoulder?"

"Just needs fresh bandages occasionally." Gabriel looked around Ethan and smiled. "Looks like your trip was successful."

Ethan nodded. "It certainly was." He watched as one of the men helped Elizabeth down from her horse. He spoke quickly before the others came onto the porch. "Did either of them say what happened? And how in the hell did they manage to stay alive?"

Gabriel spoke just as softly. "They took a good beating, the both of them. Frank said they were beaten for information."

"About what?"

"Mostly about Brenna. Frank said they kept asking if anyone else had come to the ranch to see her." Gabriel watched as the others walked toward the porch, and he pulled Ethan to the side. "Frank described the man who did the beating. It sounded like Tyre Burton."

Ethan stiffened. "Is Brenna in danger?"

Gabriel shook his head. "Frank didn't seem to

think so."

"And they're going to be okay?"

"They both will, Ethan. Sam even refused a doctor, but they'll both need some time to heal up."

Ethan was stopped from saying anything else as Elizabeth walked up on the porch.

She looked at Gabriel. "You look just awful, Gabriel. Now where's that grandson of mine?"

The reunion between Brenna and her grandmother brought tears to both women's eyes. Mabel gave a big hoot and holler when she saw Elizabeth.

The introduction to Isabelle and Andrew had been equally joyful for Elizabeth.

"Are you Brenna's grandma?" Andrew asked.

"Well, child, I certainly am."

"I don't have a grandma."

"Well, it looks as though you have a pretty good start on that, young man." Elizabeth pulled Andrew into a gentle hug and turned her attention to Isabelle. "It's comforting to know the women in the household now outnumber the men."

"Now, hold on there," Ethan said. "You're forgetting about Jacob." He smiled as Brenna returned to the room with Jacob in her arms.

"Now there's the best reason for coming back I've ever had." Elizabeth looked to Brenna. "You are too, my dear, but it warms my heart to see how things have turned out for you and Ethan."

"Pleased I am too, Grandmother." Brenna draped an arm around her husband.

"Are you going to give this family one of these, Gabriel?" Elizabeth asked and turned her attention away from Jacob long enough to look at Gabriel.

Gabriel looked at Isabelle and smiled when her faced infused with color. She looked so becoming with a blush. "I'll get to work on that, ma'am."

Jacob fussed in Elizabeth's arms, and Brenna stepped forward to take him. "A hungry one he is," she said. "We won't be but a few moments."

"Take your time, dear."

"That's right, Brenna," Mabel chimed in. "I'll get Elizabeth settled in. I imagine she'll be with us a spell."

"Enough of that, Mabel, I'm not a guest here," Elizabeth said. "Family pitches in, so let's get supper started."

"Do you truly want children, Gabriel?"

Isabelle pulled the heavy wool shawl closer together as she moved next to Gabriel. He stood on the porch looking out over the land like a man who knew exactly where he belonged—she envied him that.

Gabriel wore his heavy sheepskin coat unbuttoned and when he noticed Isabelle shiver, he pulled her into him and closed the coat around her sides and lowered his head close to hers, taking in her fresh scent. He didn't answer her question directly.

"Do you want children?"

Isabelle leaned back against Gabriel and her heart lurched at the possibilities his question presented. If recent events taught her anything, she learned that nothing was certain and each moment mattered.

"I do, Gabriel," she said quietly. "I really do."

Pulling her tighter against his body, he whispered against her ear, "So do I. As long as they look like you."

Gabriel stared up at the ceiling above his bed and thought over his conversation with Isabelle, where they more or less committed to one another, and turned his body toward hers as she curled her form into his. They weren't out of danger yet. Nathan Hunter must be found before any of them could feel safe or before he could keep his promise of never letting her go. Gabriel and Ethan agreed that Hunter must have found a way to stay underground while giving orders to his men. Gabriel didn't understand why any of Hunter's men would follow the old man's orders, but it was certain that Hunter didn't plan to surface anytime soon. Ethan suggested they find a way to bring Hunter out into the open once and for all, but none of them could figure out what would lure him out. Elizabeth would be safe and as much as Gabriel had hoped Hunter had been with her, he was grateful she'd been spared that confrontation. He sent word to Jeb to find out what happened. The conversation he overhead must have been a way to mislead them, but to what end?

Gabriel glanced over at the window though he saw nothing outside. The sun rose long after the household this time of year, and it was time Gabriel got up, though he hated leaving Isabelle's side. He'd bet Mabel was up gathering her eggs. The family insisted she ask one of the men to take care of that for her, but she would hear nothing of it. Mabel proved time and again to be the most stubborn of them all. Even so, Gabriel thought it was probably early enough that he could beat Mabel to the egg gathering and figured he'd grab some jerky from the storehouse on the way back.

With one last look at Isabelle, Gabriel reluctantly left the bed. He moved around the room as quietly as possible and with boots in hand, left the room. In the hallway, he slipped his boots on and made his way downstairs and into the kitchen. Mabel wasn't there, but someone had put the kettle on and something smelled like it might be burning. A quick glance in the oven showed him that Mabel's delicious bread was baking perfectly. Gabriel was amazed at how little sleep the woman survived on. Resigned to enjoy a cup of coffee before heading out to the cattle, Gabriel poured himself a cup and made his way through the house to the front porch. He barely made it through the kitchen doorway when he heard the front door slam open and hit the wall. A moment later Colton stood in front of him, breathing hard.

"The barn's on fire!" Colton shouted and ran out as quickly as he'd come in. Gabriel ran into the front hall and shouted up to Ethan, knowing he'd hear him. Not bothering with a coat or hat, Gabriel ran out through the door that Colton left open and raced across the distance between house and barn. He came up short to take in the scene.

The men scrambled with buckets, some still coming out of the bunkhouse. He saw that the animals had all been pulled from the barn, and some were still running away. The men who'd been on watch obviously saw the fire first and attempted to fight the growing surge with water from the troughs. Gabriel rushed in to join the fray, but he saw through the open doors of the barn and watched as the flames engulfed the store of winter hay.

"Colton!" He ran over to the ranch hand. "Where did it start?"

"I don't know!" The sounds of burning timber and shouting men overpowered one voice. "I think the south side, but I can't be sure," he said when Gabriel came closer.

Panic welled up inside of Gabriel. Mabel hadn't been in the house, but the kettle was on. "Have you seen Mabel?"

Ben and Jake both heard and dropped their buckets. There was no saving the barn at this point.

Ben ran toward Gabriel. "We haven't seen her.

What's going on?"

The chicken house stood behind the barn. Gabriel ignored the shouts of his men and ran toward the fire. He came up short at the back of the barn. Where the chicken house had once been, flames danced in its place to join with the flames consuming the barn. He heard shouting behind him but blocked the noise and rushed toward what was left of the opening. He saw nothing but fire around him and dirt below. His foot hit something solid and ignoring the smoke, Gabriel opened his eyes against the stinging pain and lowered himself enough to feel Mabel's still form on the ground. Boards from the raised beds held her down and scorched her clothes. Gabriel shoved the burning boards aside and with every bit of strength he could draw, lifted Mabel into his arms and struggled back through the smoke and into the morning air.

Ethan heard the shouts and left Brenna's side to look out the bedroom window. The sight of flames greeted him, and he shouted to Brenna before grabbing his clothes and nearly tore the door off its hinges to get out. He stopped long enough in the hall to slip on his pants and boots and pulled his shirt on as he ran, though he didn't take the time to button it. Eliza came up behind him wearing the wool pants she sometimes wore on the ranch.

"Where's Gabriel?" she asked as they both rushed down the stairs.

"Outside!" Ethan yelled back to her and ran faster. Eliza nearly tripped over him at the bottom of the stairs, but she righted herself and they ran for the door.

Once outside, Ethan heard the roof of the barn crashing before he saw it. Some of the men stood a safe distance from the flames, buckets still in hand. But he didn't see his brother. One of the men shouted at him, and the others ran toward the back of the barn. Ethan's heart raced faster than his legs as he followed the men around the fire, knowing Eliza followed right behind him. Sparks flew from every direction, and Ethan ignored the pain of the tiny burns on his clothes and skin. The men stopped and Ethan halted, his body shaking and his mind frozen in disbelief.

"No!" Eliza screamed and grabbed Ethan's arm and clutched it to her body. On the cold ground in front of them, out of striking distance from the fire, Gabriel cradled a burned body. Eliza let go of Ethan, rushed to Gabriel, and slid on the ground in front of her brother. Ethan took a step forward and then another as he watched Eliza crying over the woman who had been a mother when theirs left the earth. Ethan ignored the other men and knelt down next to Eliza. He ran a hand over the face smeared with soot until his hand met scorched skin.

Mabel's eyes fluttered open and stared at her children. Gabriel lowered his face close to hers and brushed back what was left of her hair.

"I'm so sorry, Mabel." Gabriel pulled her closer.

"Don't be sorry, child. I get to see your ma again." Her smoke-stained whisper barely cut through the noise before her body went limp in his arms.

Gabriel raised his eyes to look at his brother, and he saw tears falling down Ethan's face. Together they grieved as flames melted the falling snow. Ethan struggled to pull Eliza away, so with care, he lifted her off the ground, and brought her to Ben who guided her away.

Gabriel ignored the pain in his shoulder and helped Ethan lift Mabel's body. Together they carried her around the fallen timbers that continued to burn. Brenna and Isabelle stood near the house, holding onto each other. Elizabeth had remained inside with the children. When they were only a few hundred feet from the house, Brenna raced over to them.

"No, please, no!" Brenna reached out to Mabel, but Eliza grabbed her hand and pulled her away as the men walked past, carrying her body.

Isabelle watched, unmoving, and cried. She hadn't known Mabel well, but she'd come to love her. Her eyes met Gabriel's as he came closer. She looked over at Ethan and both brothers' faces conveyed their deep pain and unmistakable anger. Their eyes, wet and stricken with grief, focused on Mabel as they gently lowered her body.

Brenna lifted a tear-streaked face to Isabelle. "Would you check on Jacob? I can't . . ." She choked out before fresh tears filled her eyes. Isabelle's eyes met Gabriel's once again, but he said nothing. Not trusting herself to speak, Isabelle wiped away her own tears and nodded to Brenna before disappearing into the house.

Gabriel watched Isabelle leave and turned his attention to Eliza and Brenna, who both leaned over Mabel. He looked at all of the men who had gathered around them, but no one spoke. The looks on their faces told him they already knew Mabel was gone.

"Like hell I am, Ethan." Gabriel shoved away from his brother, but he didn't get far before Ethan pulled him back. His brother was one of the few men large enough to physically stop Gabriel.

"You'll get yourself killed, and where would that leave your family? You want to kill the bastard and believe me, I do, too, but stop long enough to think. If we don't keep our heads together, we'll lose everything and everyone." Ethan looked at the dark stain on his brother's arm. "And your damn shoulder is bleeding again."

Gabriel ignored the blood and shoved at his brother again, but this time Ethan only stepped away. He hunched over and braced his scraped hands on his filthy pants. Gabriel took a few deep breaths, then stood and looked hard at his brother. "This can't happen again."

Ethan stepped closer to his brother and placed a worn hand on Gabriel's good shoulder. "I know that, and we won't let it."

"He keeps slipping away!" yelled Gabriel in frustration. "And now he's burrowed away in some hole like a gopher. How can one man keep eluding us like this?"

"That's a question I'll be sure to ask once we find him. Now get that shoulder taken care of."

Gabriel looked at the streams of smoke billowing up from the debris and rubble of the barn. One side remained erect, but it would have to be torn down for them to rebuild. "The question is, will we find him before we lose anyone else?"

The cold ground made it difficult to dig the hole. The ranch hands volunteered, but Ethan and Gabriel insisted on doing it themselves. It took more than an hour for them to dig through the stiff earth. Gabriel stopped only once to have his shoulder re-bandaged, but he would not let someone else take his place. The sun deigned to shine in the two days since the barn had been torched and Mabel murdered. They'd debated briefly as to whether or not Mabel should be buried in the church cemetery, but Ethan, Gabriel, and Eliza all agreed that she would have wanted to be buried at the ranch. Mabel would have liked knowing she could watch over them, so they placed her grave next to their parents' grave markers.

White flakes began to coat the pile of soil as the mourners gathered around the grave. Tom Jr. drove the reverend from town to the ranch to say a few words over Mabel. Brenna and Elizabeth held onto one another while Eliza held Ethan's hand on one side and Gabriel's on the other.

Isabelle offered to stay with the children. The cold temperatures would be too much for little Jacob to handle. She may be a part of the family now, but she didn't have the same history with Mabel as the others did. Brenna didn't either, but she needed to be there for her grandmother, who had always considered Mabel a friend.

She watched from the upstairs bedroom window where Jacob lay on the rug next to Andrew, who took delight in watching the baby make faces. Andrew moved to stand beside her and slipped his hand into hers.

"Why was there a fire, Ibby?"

"Sometimes bad things happen, but we don't always know why."

Andrew pressed up against the window. "Is

that why you cried?"

Isabelle kneeled on the floor and turned her brother. "I cried because I was sad, but being here with you makes it better."

Andrew leaned over and whispered, "Is Mabel coming back?"

Isabelle stood, and her eyes scanned the debris left from the barn and across the snow-covered grass to the small Gallagher family cemetery. Three graves now filled that piece of earth, and Isabelle shuddered to think of what each of those deaths meant to the three siblings holding hands at the head of the freshly dug earth. If staying with Gabriel meant she must learn to fight for this land as he did, she was determined to find a way. Isabelle closed her eyes against the rush of tears. When she opened them again, she stared into a mirror image of her own eyes. "No, darling, she's not."

Gabriel held onto Eliza and stared at Mabel's body as four of the men lowered her beneath the edge of the earth. Her body shrouded in white had been placed inside the wooden box Tom Jr. brought back with him from Briarwood. Gabriel's eyes remained focused on the box as he thought about not being able to save her. He didn't blame himself for her death, but Mabel had taken her final breath in his arms.

"Gabriel?" Eliza said his name and tugged on his hand until he turned to her. "It's time."

"We need to talk." He stared at his sister. "You and me and Ethan—we need to talk."

Eliza nodded. "I know. We will."

She pulled again on his hand, but he shrugged her off. "I need to watch this. We all do." The "this" referred to the men filling the hole that would forever be Mabel's grave. Wisely, neither Ethan nor Eliza argued with him and stood their ground as the men filled the hole and covered the coffin with earth. A temporary marker was placed at the head of the grave. Tom Jr. had placed an order for a proper headstone while in town.

As Gabriel watched the last of the dirt cover the grave, he nodded to the men and silently asked to be left alone with his siblings. Brenna embraced her husband and whispered something to him. She gently guided Elizabeth back to the house. Alone now with his brother and sister, Gabriel turned to them.

"I've been giving everything that has happened a lot of thought."

"We all have," Ethan said.

"And has the name Tyre Burton come to mind in any of that thinking?" Gabriel's stiff tone reflected the tautness of his body. Gabriel clutched the edge of a chair, his body like an explosive charge and all that remained was for someone to light the fuse.

"The thought has crossed my mind."

"You aren't planning on going after him, Gabriel," Eliza said. It hadn't been a question.

Gabriel was going to disappoint her. "That's exactly what I plan on doing."

"You won't be doing it alone."

"Both of you are damn fools!" Eliza cried. "We just buried another one of our own. How many more are we going to put in this ground?"

Gabriel turned to his sister and cradled her face in his two large hands. "You know we have to do this."

Eliza shook her head fiercely but said just as softly, "I know." She hugged her brother tightly, taking in his warmth. Ethan's hand settled on her back and knew that when the end of this fight came, she would be right there with them. Stepping back, she looked up at Gabriel.

"This isn't going to end well," she said. "Are you going to wait for the new marshal?"

Gabriel looked over Eliza's head at his brother. Ethan nodded as though he knew Gabriel's thoughts. "Three days, Eliza," he said. "But not a day longer."

20

Gabriel quietly closed the bedroom door behind him and leaned back against it with his hand still on the handle. He closed his eyes for a moment, but flashes of the fire shot through his mind so he opened them and let out a deep breath.

Night descended more than two hours ago. Gabriel stopped into Andrew's room first to check on the boy. There hadn't been much of a chance to spend time with him, and Gabriel regretted that. Andrew's innocence soothed Gabriel like a balm over a wound. Gabriel needed to reach out and touch that innocence to remind him why he did any of this and to perhaps help erase the darkness that slowly invaded Gabriel's heart.

He didn't have to search for Isabelle after leaving Andrew's side. He knew she'd be in his bedroom, and he took great comfort knowing she waited for him. Now that he stood within a few feet of where she lay, the darkness shrouding his soul eased a bit more. He shed his clothes and cleaned himself the best he could at the small basin. When he was reasonably certain he wasn't able to wash away what couldn't be seen, he walked over to the bed where Isabelle lay, fully clothed and sleeping.

Gabriel lay down next to her and shivers ran through his body when she turned into him. Her eyes opened and looked up into his.

"I didn't want to sleep without you here. I should have been out there with you today."

Gabriel smoothed a large work-roughened hand over the back of her neck, down her shoulders, and up again to cup her face. "You were there." He brought her hand to his chest. "Right here with me every moment."

Isabelle took solace from the rush of his heart

and her own heart sped up to beat in time with his. "I see the pain in your eyes. I feel it as though it were my own," she said in a whisper. "I know it's not over, but I cannot stand by, unable to help."

Gabriel lifted her hand to his mouth and kissed the tips of her long, smooth fingers. "Tomorrow will bring with it what it brings, and we'll finish this with Hunter, one way or another."

"And for tonight? Will you find peace for one night or will you allow the hatred to consume you?" Isabelle watched Gabriel's deep-blue eyes as they grew darker and deeper, like the darkness of midnight sweeping through those haunted eyes. She saw everything in those eyes, and when his passion overshadowed every other emotion, she leaned into him.

Gabriel pulled her closer and slowly began to unbutton her dress, never taking his gaze away from hers. "There is only one thing I want to consume tonight," he said in a heavy whisper and removed the rest of her clothing. He took his time, piece by piece, until all that remained between them were the sparks that would ignite the fire within him.

As Isabelle slowly opened her eyes, she couldn't tell if a new day had arrived. Her eyes focused on the window and after a moment, she saw a faint light surrounding the stars as the earth prepared to welcome the sun. Gabriel's large form stretched the length of the bed, and his chest rose with each deep breath. She thought back to a few hours before when he'd come to her in need of a way to release everything he kept inside. He needed something to consume, so the hate wouldn't consume him, and Isabelle willingly gave herself over to every passion, good and bad. He'd shown her such tenderness until every muscle in his body tensed beneath her wandering fingers. He would have kept that inside, unwilling to hurt her. She wouldn't allow it and gave everything in her heart and soul to him until he snapped and gave everything back.

Isabelle watched him now and rested a hand

on the small scar that had begun to form where the bullet had met flesh. She traced it with the tip of her finger and when her eyes rose to look at his face, he met her gaze.

"How long have you been awake?"

Gabriel rolled over and pulled her closer. "Long enough for your touch to affect every inch of my body, but not long enough to forget what's happened."

Isabelle knew that nothing would ever make Gabriel forget, but someday perhaps he'd learn to move forward. It was their only chance for happiness together.

"You're going after him, aren't you?" Her hand moved slowly up and down his chest as his roamed her arms. He didn't answer.

"Gabriel?"

"Yes, we're going after him."

"Without the law?"

Gabriel kissed the top of her head and tucked it under his chin. He closed his eyes and breathed in the sweet scent of her. If Andrew's innocence was a balm for his wounds, then

Isabelle was the light in his soul that even now kept him from teetering over the edge.

The darkness wanted him, but she refused to let him go.

"We'll wait a couple of days for the marshal."

"And if he doesn't come?"

Gabriel knew she deserved to know the risks. "Then we'll go and do everything we can to find Hunter," Gabriel said. "But first we have to find the man responsible for Mabel."

"You know who it is?" Isabelle's heart worried for him, and she clutched at him.

Gabriel nodded. "We know."

"Will you do something for me?"

He worried about what she might ask because he would do anything for her—anything she asked.

"Yes, Isabelle," he whispered and kissed the top of her head again. "Anything."

"Come back to me," she said softly against his body. "Just make sure that no matter what you have to do or when you have to do it, just come back to me."

Moisture filled his eyes before he could prevent it. A salty drop escaped and fell down his sun-soaked skin. He pulled Isabelle as close to his body as nature allowed. "Always Isabelle," he choked out. "Always."

Gabriel slowly eased out of bed, careful not to disturb Isabelle. She had fallen back to sleep in his arms, and he never wanted to leave her side again. Knowing she'd be there and knowing that she'd never leave, gave him the strength he needed most to do what must be done. With regret, Gabriel dressed and quietly left the room.

He made his way down the stairs and hurried his steps to the kitchen when he detected the unmistakable scent of coffee and fresh bread. When he stepped into the kitchen, he didn't find Mabel bustling around in an apron. Elizabeth stood over the stove, adding more water to the coffee pot. Pain coursed through Gabriel's body, but he lifted his tired mouth into a smile and walked to the stove.

"Good morning, ma'am."

Elizabeth stepped back and let out a light laugh. "Goodness, Gabriel. I'm so used to living alone that you startled me."

"Understandable, ma'am," he said and nodded to the oven. "Whatever you have in there smells wonderful."

"Just a loaf of bread, and call me Elizabeth. Ma'am makes me feel as old as I am."

This time Gabriel did smile at her. "Elizabeth." He took the offered cup of hot coffee from her, but rather than sit, he leaned against the edge of the table. "I don't know if you've spoken with Ethan and Brenna yet, and this isn't really my business, but I believe I speak for all of us when I say I'm glad you're here, and I hope you stay."

Elizabeth stopped fussing with the stove to give her attention to Gabriel.

"I'm not going anywhere, young man. The only family I have left is right here." She choked up and wiped away the tear that fell down her cheek.

"Glad to hear it." Ethan stood in the doorway.

Gabriel looked over at his brother and wondered if he looked as sorry and near to death as Ethan. "How's Brenna doing?"

"She's up with Jacob right now." Ethan stepped into the kitchen. "How's Isabelle?"

Gabriel looked down at the half-filled cup of coffee he held and watched as the last bit of steam rose and disappeared. "She's a survivor."

"She'll need to be." Eliza entered the kitchen from the back stairs. "We'll all need to be for what's coming."

Ethan shifted uncomfortably. "Gabe and I talked last—"

Eliza held up a hand. "Don't say it." She turned her full attention to both brothers. "You've pulled the big-brother card too many times to count now. And you, Gabriel, have used guilt and responsibility to keep me out of harm's way. I love you both for all of it, but none of it's going to work this time." Eliza accepted a cup of coffee from Elizabeth who appeared to be hanging onto every word. "I don't have a death wish, so I promise not to do anything stupid, but

I have as much of a right to see this through as either of you."

Gabriel stood and set his cup on the table. His eyes met Ethan's and both seemed to once again be thinking along the same lines.

Ethan stepped up to Eliza and lifted her chin so he could look at her. "We won't keep you out of this, little sister," he said. "But if anything happens to you, I'll fix whatever is wrong first and then tan your hide for getting hurt." It sounded ludicrous, even to him, but Ethan didn't care.

Eliza smiled. "If ever there was a reason to keep breathing, that's the best I've ever heard."

Gabriel didn't smile because he still wanted to lock her up in the house. He hoped to convince her to stay behind with the others but knew she was right. She had as much right to go after Hunter as they did, but that didn't mean she needed to join them when they went looking for Tyre Burton.

"I need a favor." Gabriel stepped toward her.

"Don't ask me to stay behind."

"I'm not asking you to stay behind when we chase down Hunter, but I am going to ask you to stay with the others when we go after Burton."

"Gabriel—"

"Please do this for me. When we leave this ranch, we're leaving behind every last hope in those rooms upstairs. There has always been a Gallagher on this ranch, and it will always have a Gallagher. We made that promise to Pa a long time ago. We need you to stay here, at least for now."

"You don't believe you'll come back?" Eliza stared at Gabriel in complete disbelief. "So help me, Gabriel Gallagher—"

"We'll be back." He looked over his shoulder at Elizabeth who sat at the table crying. He turned back to Eliza. "We have a future to protect, and I, for one, don't plan on missing out on it."

"Tomorrow?" Ethan said.

Gabriel nodded. "Tomorrow. Hopefully the marshal will be here sooner than Jeb predicted and if he's not, at least we know what we'll be up against."

"We can't force the men to go," Ethan said. "They'll have to make that choice on their own. I won't ask another man to die for us or this ranch."

"You know they'll go." Eliza glanced over at Elizabeth, who stood and said something about checking on the children before she disappeared up the stairs. Eliza couldn't blame her. Family or not, it was all a lot for anyone to take in at once. She turned her attention back to her brothers.

"The men will go," Eliza said again. "They won't even hesitate."

Ethan nodded. "We'll just have to make sure they all make it through this."

Gabriel nodded, but what he meant to say was interrupted by a loud rap on the back door. It opened before any of them could walk to it. Ben stood in the doorway with a backdrop of snow falling in thick flakes to the ground.

"What's going on, Ben?" Gabriel stepped toward the other man.

"You've got company coming," Ben said. "Tom and Tom Jr. came back in from rounding up the last of the strays and said a wagon headed this way."

"Did they know who?"

Ben shook his head. "They didn't know the people. Said he saw an old man and an old woman with a driver. A fancy-type wagon, too."

"Thanks," Gabriel said.

Ben nodded and almost made it out the door when Ethan spoke up. "We'd like to have a word with the boys tonight. If you could let them know to meet up at the bunkhouse after dark, I'd appreciate it."

Ben nodded. "Is this about going after Nathan Hunter? Because if it is, the boys have talked and we've decided that we're all going with you."

Ethan and Gabriel looked at Eliza who only stared at Ben and nodded.

To Ben he said, "Thank you. That means a lot."

"You just tell us when and we'll be ready to ride." Ben went outside and closed the door behind him.

Ethan walked over to the stove and refilled his coffee cup. "Seems you were right again, Eliza."

"Sometimes I wish I weren't. You know that, don't you?"

Ethan nodded. "I know, but how about you keep on being right a bit longer? We may need it."

Gabriel left the kitchen and grabbed his heavy coat on the way outside to find out who would be foolish enough to make the ride from town to the ranch in this weather. Ethan and Eliza joined him just as the fancy buggy slowly meandered over the ever-hardening ground. A layer of white flakes broke up the brown of the ground beneath the wheels, leaving narrow tracks in the snow. Gabriel couldn't imagine how that contraption made it this far. He glanced up to the sky and frowned. Gabriel didn't like the idea of risking men in this weather because of foolish travelers.

He stepped to the edge of the porch as the buggy slowed to a stop near the hitching post.

Gabriel's gut twisted as he looked in at the passengers and recalled the last telegram Isabelle received.

"You're a long way from home, folks." Gabriel could almost feel Ethan and Eliza's gazes boring into his back.

"Sir, we are looking for a Miss Isabelle Rousseau." The older man spoke from the wagon before the driver assisted him down from the buggy. The woman remained inside.

"There isn't a Miss Rousseau here, but there is a Mrs. Isabelle Gallagher."

The man paused near the buggy and looked inside to the woman, who obviously decided that now might be a good time to step out. After helping the woman out of the buggy, the man stepped toward them and up the porch until both visitors stood beneath the protection of the overhang.

"Sir, I am Mr. Daggert and my companion is Mrs. Wolds. Miss Rousseau should be expecting us."

Gabriel leaned lazily against the porch railing,

but he felt anything but lazy. "I told you once before—it's Mrs. Gallagher now."

"Mr. Gallagher." Mr. Daggert took a brave step toward him, and he stood a full head shorter than Gabriel. "We are here under strict guidelines and the authority of Mrs. Picard to return to New Orleans with her nephew, Andrew Rousseau."

"You're wrong there again, Mr. Daggert. It's Andrew Gallagher."

"You don't have the authority, sir." Mrs. Wolds finally spoke.

"Ma'am, I do have the authority." Gabriel no longer leaned against the railing. "I am her husband and by all legal authority, Isabelle is the guardian of her brother and she's a Gallagher. Her aunt's claims were made moot the moment we married."

"Mrs. Picard does not recognize your marriage, Mr. Gallagher," said Mrs. Wolds.

"We have papers here, which clearly give us temporary custody of the boy in order to bring him back to his aunt," added Mr. Daggert.

Gabriel took another step forward and Ethan's hand grabbed his arm. He stopped his progress toward Mr. Daggert but stood close enough to the man to hopefully make his point. "You will not be removing anyone from this ranch, Mr. Daggert. Mrs. Picard can bring holy hell down on Hawk's Peak, and you still wouldn't get Andrew."

Mr. Daggert obviously didn't know how to respond. Gabriel watched the man's eyes dart from person to person, possibly in an attempt to gain cooperation from someone. When he realized he'd find no sympathy, he made one last attempt to state his case.

"Mr. Gallagher. I have legal papers here compelling you to turn Andrew Rousseau over to our care."

This time Eliza reached out and grabbed Gabriel's arm and stepped up alongside of him. "What's in this for you?" Eliza's question caught everyone off guard, but Gabriel turned abruptly from his sister to the older pair to see their evident surprise.

His eyes narrowed. "My sister asked you a question. What's in it for you?"

The man stuttered in an attempt at a speedy response. "We h-h-have been hired by Mrs. Picard to make this journey sir—n-nothing more."

Gabriel studied the pair closely and saw in their eyes that Eliza's question revealed she was close to the truth. "Answer the question."

"Take it easy, Gabriel." Ethan said quietly from behind his brother.

Mrs. Wolds clutched at the edges of her heavy shawl and tugged at her gloves. Neither man nor woman had dressed for the weather they had encountered.

"I want an answer."

Mrs. Wolds appeared to be the weaker of the two, and Gabriel directed his gaze on her until she panicked. "We've been promised a sum to bring the boy back with us. Mrs. Picard assured us that your marriage was not legal and that we were to bring the boy no matter what."

"Why?" All eyes turned toward the door. No

one heard it open or realized that Isabelle came outside. Their eyes followed her movements as she walked toward Gabriel and slipped an arm through his.

"I asked why?"

"Miss Rousseau, I presume?" asked Mr. Daggert on a sigh but didn't wait for a response. "It is good that you are here. We are here on behalf of your aunt—"

"I know why you're here. I want to know why my aunt sent you. What could she possibly want with my brother?"

"She did not make us privy to her reasons," Mrs. Wolds answered in a rush.

"I don't believe you."

"Well, I never—"

"Enough." Gabriel held onto Isabelle's hand. "Answer the question."

"The inheritance, sir!"

Isabelle tensed.

"What inheritance?" When they didn't answer, she spoke more forcefully. "What inheritance?"

"We saw the papers." Mrs. Wolds's eyes darted to Gabriel. "I'm sorry, Mrs. Gallagher. Your aunt promised a goodly sum of money and showed us the papers so we knew she spoke the truth about the size of the purse."

Gabriel looked down at Isabelle, but she shook her head. "There is no inheritance. The creditors took everything. My father's lawyer showed me no such papers."

"This wasn't from your father."

"Mrs. Wolds. That is enough."

Mrs. Wolds ignored her companion. "The inheritance came from your mother. The lawyer was there when your aunt spoke with us."

Isabelle shook her head. "That's not possible. I would have known."

"That's all I know, ma'am. I promise you." The older woman looked at each person on the porch and turned to her companion. "It is time for us to leave, Mr. Daggert."

Mr. Daggert also looked at each face, and Gabriel could see the man's defeat. "Very well." He took his companion's arm and helped her down the steps where the driver waited to help them into the buggy.

Mrs. Wolds stopped and looked back to meet Isabelle's gaze. "I am sorry. We were misinformed about your situation. We would not have otherwise traveled such a great distance."

Isabelle nodded at the woman but said nothing. She watched as the driver helped them into the buggy and then took his seat. She stepped to the railing and kept her eyes on the buggy as it disappeared into the snow.

Ethan shouted out to Colton who just stepped out of the stable with his horse. Colton mounted and rode over to the house.

"Everything all right?"

Ethan nodded and asked, "Would you grab Kevin and follow that buggy back into Briarwood?"

"Greenhorns?"

"The worst kind."

"They just don't know when to stay where they belong," Colton muttered. He rode back toward the barn and a few moments later, Isabelle watched as the two men also disappeared into the snow.

"What do you think they mean?"

Isabelle looked up at Gabriel. "I don't know. My father's lawyer said there was nothing left. If my mother had a fortune, I never knew about it."

"Would it matter if she did?"

Isabelle considered, her thoughts drifting to her brother, the orphans she taught in New Orleans, and young Mason Walker. "If there is an inheritance, I'd like to find out."

Gabriel kissed her brow and smoothed a hand over her cheek. "Then we will."

Isabelle circled her arms around his waist and stared after the men on horseback who followed the wagon. "Colton and Kevin will be all right, won't they? This weather is horrible."

Gabriel pulled her close to his body and smiled when his brother answered her question.

"Our darling Isabelle. It seems we have our work cut out with you but not to worry. We'll turn you into a Montanan yet." Ethan's laughter joined Eliza's. The sound carried over the air and brought Brenna and Elizabeth onto the porch.

"Faith, but it's frigid out here, Ethan." Brenna turned to Elizabeth. "While we've been tending the bairns, it seems we've been left out of the excitement."

With so much sadness blanketing the ranch, Gabriel's heart warmed to hear the laughter. Tomorrow would bring whatever it chose, but they'd do more than just survive the coming days. As long as they were together, they would endure.

21

"I'm proud of you, Isabelle," Gabriel whispered into her ear.

They sat together in the library with Eliza, Ethan, and Brenna. Ethan thought it best to have a family counsel, and now that their numbers had increased, he wanted everyone to know what was going to happen over the next few days.

"You will never have reason to feel otherwise, husband," Isabelle whispered back. She knew what this discussion would be about and knew the road ahead could be a difficult one, but she gave herself this moment with Gabriel.

"We've waited as long as we can for the marshal to show up." Ethan pointedly looked at

Eliza. "We gave him two extra days because of the snow and still no word."

"There hasn't been word from Jeb again, either," Gabriel added. "Not after he came out here to warn us about what he heard in town."

"Do you think he could have been setting us up?" Eliza asked. "Sending men up north left the ranch more vulnerable."

Gabriel immediately shook his head. "I don't believe that for a minute. I trust Jeb, so if it was a setup, they duped him, too."

"It doesn't matter now," Ethan said. "We have to take care of Tyre Burton before we can get to Hunter. My guess is that Tyre is playing watchdog."

"When do you plan to leave?" Eliza asked.

"Tomorrow. You remember what we talked about?" Ethan looked back and forth between his siblings.

"I remember, but I'll only stay behind this once."

"We'll take what we can get."

"That's settled." Ethan stood to move from

behind the desk. "Now, I'll go out and let the men know the plan—"

"Rider coming in!" someone shouted from outside.

"Too many new faces coming around these days." Ethan walked to the window, and Gabriel quickly moved away from Isabelle to join his brother. The snow had stopped, and now the cold air misted around the mountains in the distance. They could see far into the distance, and there was no mistaking the rider coming in at a run.

Only a crazy man chose to run a horse that fast over the frozen ground. *Damn fool idiot.* Gabriel followed Ethan from the library to meet the rider. Both men grabbed their winter gear and stepped outside. Eliza quickly joined them.

"Where are Brenna and Isabelle?"

"They're fine, Ethan. I asked them to stay inside." Eliza stepped up alongside her brothers as the rider closed the distance between him and the ranch.

Eliza now saw the lines of the horse and man

as he raced over frozen earth toward them. Something familiar stood out about the rider, and Eliza moved to the railing in an attempt to see more of him.

The rider came to an abrupt stop in front of the hitching post and lifted deep green eyes to the three on the porch. Gabriel heard his sister gasp and turned to her, but her focus was only for the man sitting atop a thoroughbred similar to Zeus.

"What's going on, Eliza? Do you know this man?" Gabriel looked back at the man.

Ethan hit the side of Gabriel's arm and walked to the edge of the porch. "Take a closer look."

Gabriel did and when the man stared back, seven years slipped away. "Ramsey?"

"Sorry I'm late, Gallagher," Ramsey said. "I had a devil of a time with the weather through Wyoming."

"What are you talking about?" Ethan glanced back and forth between Ramsey and his sister. Both continued to stare at each other. "We heard you'd be coming out this way, but as I live and breathe Ramsey, I didn't believe it."

"I'm here sooner than planned, but Jeb said you needed a marshal fast."

Eliza finally spoke up. "What does that have to do with—Oh my!"

Ramsey moved the edge of his heavy coat aside to reveal the small silver badge pinned to his wool vest.

"How is that possible? You didn't say—"

"There's a lot I didn't tell you, Eliza."

Ramsey dismounted and tied his horse to the post. He glanced around at the men approaching from two sides. "I'm glad to see you have numbers." He moved up to the porch.

"You're the marshal?" Gabriel asked, still disbelieving.

"When?" Eliza took a few steps toward Ramsey.

"Just after you left," he told her softly. "I figured it might come in handy, and someone owed me a favor."

Ethan stepped forward and slapped a hand on Ramsey's shoulder. "You have some explaining to do, Ramsey."

"I know that, Ethan, but there's something else I have to do first."

The front door slowly eased open and Brenna poked her head out. "Will our guest be joining us for breakfast?" she asked her husband. Ethan walked over to her, took her hand from the edge of the door, and pulled her outside. "It's as cold as the Highland hills out here, Ethan."

Ethan removed his coat and draped it over his wife's shoulders and leaned down. "There's someone you need to meet," he whispered against her ear.

Brenna's gaze moved to their guest. "Who might that be?" Brenna stepped back into her husband and gasped. "Faith, but it can't be!" Brenna stepped forward toward the image of her father as she remembered him from her days as a child. "Are you really here? Is it truly you?"

Ramsey stepped forward and turned all of his attention to the woman before him. He lifted his hands to her face, one on each side, and raised her tear-filled gaze to his own.

"It's really me, Brenna."

Thank you for reading
Gallagher's Hope

Don't miss *Gallagher's Choice*, the next book in the Montana Gallagher series.

Visit mkmcclintock.com/extras for more on the Gallagher family, Hawk's Peak, and Briarwood.

If you enjoyed this story, please consider sharing your thoughts with fellow readers by leaving an online review.

Never miss a new release!
www.mkmcclintock.com/subscribe

THE MONTANA GALLAGHERS

Three siblings. One legacy.
An unforgettable western romantic adventure
series.

Set in 1880s Briarwood, Montana Territory, The Montana Gallagher series is about a frontier family's legacy, healing old wounds, and fighting for the land they love. Joined by spouses, extended family, friends, and townspeople, the Gallaghers strive to fulfill the legacy their parents began and protect the next generation's birthright.

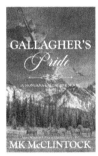

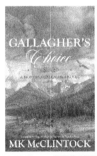

THE WOMEN OF CROOKED CREEK

Four courageous women, an untamed land, and the daring to embark on an unforgettable adventure.

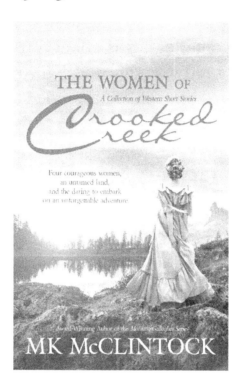

If you love stories of bravery and courage with unforgettable women and the men they love, you'll enjoy the *Women of Crooked Creek*.

Available in e-book, paperback, and large print.

WHITCOMB SPRINGS SERIES

Meet a delightful group of settlers whose stories and adventures celebrate the rich life of the American West.

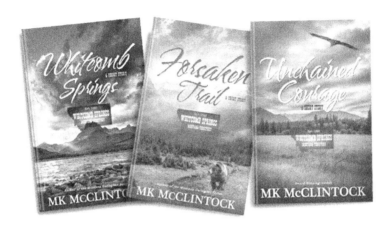

Set in post-Civil War Montana Territory, in the mountain valley town of Whitcomb Springs, is a community of strong men and women who have worked to overcome individual struggles faced during and after the war. Escape to Whitcomb Springs with tales of adventure, danger, romance, and hope in this special collection of short stories and novelettes. Each story is written to stand alone.

Available in e-book and paperback.

MEET THE AUTHOR

Award-winning author MK McClintock writes historical romantic fiction about chivalrous men and strong women who appreciate chivalry. Her stories of adventure, romance, and mystery sweep across the American West to the Victorian British Isles, with places and times between and beyond. With her heart deeply rooted in the past, she enjoys a quiet life in the northern Rocky Mountains.

MK invites you to join her on her writing journey at **www.mkmcclintock.com**, where you can read the blog, explore reader extras, and sign up to receive new release updates.

Made in the USA
Coppell, TX
08 February 2023

12398003R00260